ZAHARA'S GIFT

BOND OF A DRAGON

A J WALKER

To ARB, AWB, DW, and JW

ACKNOWLEDGMENTS

I want to thank all those who've helped me in creating the Bond of a Dragon series. This idea started when I was a young man and has grown into this magnificent story it is because of the help and inspiration of many people. Thanks to my parents, family and friends for their support and encouragement along the way.

Many of you might find it hard to believe that reading and writing didn't come naturally to me, as I am severely dyslexic. I wouldn't have developed the skills necessary to create these works without the support from my family. Thanks to Susan, the brilliant woman who spent long hours combing through my many mistake-ridden drafts. Your help has been instrumental in creating these stories. Thank you to my loving wife who's always inspired me to chase my dreams and desires no matter how ridiculous or far-fetched they may seem. And Thanks to you, the reader, for allowing me to express my creativity on these pages.

Special thanks to:

Susan Penner – copy and developmental editor

Mark Reid at authorpackages.com – cover design

Maggie Walker – Kartania Map, watercolor

Advanced Reader Team

KARTANIA
NORTHLAND
RIDGEBACK MTNS
HIGHBORN BAY
GRANDWOOD MTNS
WESTLAND
GRANDWOOD
MT SWIFTCURRENT
MT FARSIGHT
MT BLOODTOOTH
EVERLIGHT KINGDOM
NAGANO
SHARP STONE MTNS
FROZEN TIP MTNS
CEDAR BRIDGE
EASTLAND MTNS
EAST-LAND
ARGON
BROOKSIDE
THE RIVER LANDS
MT ORENA
ROLLO ISLANDS
BAREBACK PLAINS
MARAUDER'S SEA
GLACIAL MELT BAY
BLACK WATER BAY
AQUINA
N
W   E
S
BAREBACK PENINSULA
STARVE TO DEATH PLATEAU
ROUGH WATER BAY
HIGHSIDE PLAINS
PELAGIC OCEAN
HIGHLAND PEAKS
KINGSTON
SPLIT MTN
GOBLINS GROVE
YELLOW SANDS DESERT
RAMHORN
SOUTHLAND
CRESCENT ISLAND
KEWIAN ISLANDS
DRAKESHEAD

ONE

A STRANGER AND THE THEIF

Anders gripped the oars tightly, his muscles strained against the force generated by the storm. Freezing rain stung the side of his face as he rowed furiously through the rise and fall of angry ocean waves. The storm had come without warning, catching Anders and his younger cousin by surprise.

"Thomas!" Anders yelled against the gale force wind. Thomas clung tightly to the ribbing on the floor of the small fishing boat, fearing for his life. "The boat is taking on too much water! Grab the bucket and bail!" Anders saw his cousin lift his head briefly and search for the bailing bucket. "Now, Thomas, do it now or we'll sink!"

Thomas gathered his courage and let go of the floor he had clung to so desperately. He grabbed the bucket and vigorously shoveled water over the side of the swaying boat.

Squinting through the downpour, Anders could just see the rocky shoreline of Highborn Bay. The two were nearly back inside the safety of the bay's calmer waters. He was well aware that they had reached almost the exact spot where Anders had been eighteen years ago, when his family's ship had wrecked in a spring storm. The details of the tragedy were lost to Anders' memory because he'd only been one-year-old at the time, but he'd heard his uncle tell the story countless times since then.

He and his parents had sailed for nearly a week from Southland to Grandwood, a city nestled along the northern coast of Westland, where Anders' uncle Theodor and his newly pregnant wife were waiting to greet them. Anders' family was on track to dock in Grandwood's port when a storm suddenly forced the ship off course, missing the port and wrecking into the rocky spit of land that formed half of Highborn Bay. Theodor found infant Anders washed ashore among the ship's wreckage. The only survivor, he was left without parents, yet fortunately with his uncle and aunt to raise him.

The wind was unrelenting as they struggled to reach the bay. Thomas continued to shovel the salty water out of the small boat as wave after wave piled over the bow. Anders heaved the final strokes on the oars, skimming into calmer waters. It wasn't long before they were pulling the boat on shore. Thomas' younger sister, Kirsten, had watched as the two rowed themselves into the bay. She ran down the hill from the stone farmhouse through the rain, eager to help them despite becoming drenched in the downpour.

"Here," Anders said, handing her one of several baskets overflowing with salmon. "Take this up to the house."

Kirsten's blue eyes widened upon seeing the size of their days' catch. Taking the basket she staggered for a moment, allowing herself to adjust her feet under the surprising weight of the basket.

As she hauled the catch back up the hill, Anders called after her, "Kirsten, have Theodor come help us with the rest." Anders and Thomas filled their arms with waterlogged fishing gear and the remaining baskets of fish, struggling to carry them up the hill to the house.

When they reached the front porch, Anders dropped his load on the ground and heard Kirsten say from the open doorway, "Anders, I couldn't find him. I think he went out to do chores."

Looking at Thomas with a furrowed brow, Anders said, "In this weather? He'll probably need help. Thomas, finish bringing up the gear. I'll go help with the chores." Thomas nodded and headed back down to the boat.

"Don't be too long," Kirsten told them, stepping onto the wooden covered porch and drying her sandy-blonde hair with a towel. "Dinner is nearly ready."

Anders stepped out from under the protection of the porch and headed in the opposite direction away from the bay and toward the farm. He looked in the barn, the corral, and around the rest of the small homestead. Theodor was nowhere to be seen. Anders noticed most of the chores had already been completed. He decided to look behind the house, along the edge of the woods. Sometimes when the animals got out, they often wandered away from the farm into the trees. Though hard to tell in the rain, Anders thought he saw a set of footprints leading into the woods. He followed them. In places where the ground had not yet washed them away, Anders could make out just enough to see the outline of his uncle's boot tracks leading him farther away from the farm.

Anders thought about getting the others to help him search, but decided he would go a little farther before alarming them. His mind racing with possibilities as to why Theodor would be wandering into the woods, he continued following the tracks. Before long, the lone footprints angled sharply to the right. Anders saw they went up and over a small ridge.

If I can't see him from the top of this ridgeline, I'll go back for Kirsten and Thomas, he thought to himself.

Night was approaching fast and from the top Anders had a hard time seeing clearly down the backside of the ridge. He squinted into the darkness, hoping to glimpse any sign of his uncle. Out of the corner of his eye, he thought he saw something move. He watched as a figure walked out into a small clearing on the backside of the ridge below him. It was Theodor, Anders was sure because of his uncle's recognizable silver hair. He cupped his hands around his mouth to shout down to him, but held his breath when he saw someone join Theodor in the clearing. Anders couldn't make out who it was, this tall figure sporting dark clothes.

I have to get a closer look, he thought.

He looked around for a way to get closer without being seen. He knew his uncle would be furious with him if he learned Anders was spying on him, but something in his gut told him he needed to investigate what Theodor was doing out here.

To his left a cluster of short trees extended about half way down toward the clearing where Theodor and the strange figure stood talking. The dim evening light, combined with the trees' foliage, would be enough to provide cover.

He quickly ran to the thicket of trees. Water that had pooled on the leaves drenched him as he parted the branches. The sound of the rain falling covered the noise of his footsteps as he grew closer. Anders stayed low, crouching to keep from being seen.

He paused for a moment to see if he could hear what they were saying. Their voices were still too muffled to hear clearly, so he carefully crept forward to the edge of the small trees. Here, he was able to make out snippets of their conversation. Through a space between the branches, he could see they were arguing.

Dressed entirely in black, the tall man with Theodor wore a broad sword strapped to his belt. The stranger's face was weathered, creased and tanned from his travels. He displayed an air of ruggedness that Anders had only seen a handful of times on the faces of soldiers and mercenaries passing through Grandwood. Anders strained to hear what they might be arguing about.

"He's not ready," Theodor said sternly.

"You have to tell him," the stranger urged. "The time has come and he needs to know the truth."

"Are you sure there isn't more time?" Theodor asked the man in black. "How can you be sure he's the one they're searching for?"

"He may be your kin, but that doesn't change anything. He will have to face it, whether he's ready or not," the stranger replied in a commanding tone. "You have known as well as I that this day would come. Powerful forces are stirring in the east. The elves talk of orcs and kurr assembling by the masses. An evil that was once a great threat to the five nations of Kartania is clawing its way back into the world."

"So the rumors are true," Theodor noted soberly. "I thought those days of peril left when he did."

"You must have known he wouldn't stay in the shadows forever. He is coming back out from whatever rock he's been hiding under," the stranger said coldly.

Unconsciously leaning forward to hear more clearly, Anders put his weight against a small dead limb. Suddenly it snapped. He began to slide out from his hiding place, nearly exposing himself. Luckily, he grabbed hold of a low-hanging branch just in time; this one did not break.

Upon hearing the branch break, the man in black abruptly stopped talking and turned toward the hillside. He looked directly where Anders knelt in hiding. Anders didn't move, hoping the dim lighting and vegetation would conceal him.

"Did you hear that?" the man asked Theodor as he stared at the clump of trees.

Turning around to see what the man was staring at, Theodor answered, "I didn't hear anything."

"We are being watched," the man in black said shortly.

"Don't be ridiculous. No one knows we're here," Theodor said turning to face the man once again. The man, however, had disappeared leaving Theodor standing alone in the rain. He turned back and stared for a while at the slope, scanning for whatever it was the stranger had heard.

Anders' heart nearly beat out of his chest. It seemed so loud; he was surprised Theodor couldn't hear it. Theodor kept his gaze on the vegetation where Anders hid and even took a step toward him. A rabbit darted out from its hiding place just below where Anders crouched. It scurried across the open slope, through the rainfall, and down into its hole.

Theodor stopped his advancement and said to himself, "stupid rabbit." He left the clearing and headed back toward the house. Anders waited to make sure he was well out of sight before leaving his hiding place. Then he ran back through the woods as fast as he could.

While hurrying back toward the house, he thought to himself, *what did they mean an evil was crawling back into the land? Who was it Theodor needed to tell something to and why had he decided not to do it? Was the man talking about his cousin, Thomas? And who was it they were talking about hiding in the shadows?* The thoughts swirled in his head as ran.

Anders knew he had to beat Theodor back to the house. If he didn't get back before his uncle, Thomas and Kirsten would ask him questions. If they asked him the right questions, they were sure to uncover that he had not been helping Theodor with the chores. Anders didn't want to risk his uncle or cousins discovering his spying. The secret his uncle was keeping from them might damage their family's relationship, even more than the death of Thomas and Kirsten's mother had just three years ago; that was the last thing he wanted.

When Anders opened the door he saw Thomas tending the fire and Kirsten setting the dinner table, both unaware of Anders' newly discovered secret. Shaking off water like a wet dog, Anders closed the door behind him.

"Where's father?" Thomas asked noticing Theodor wasn't with him.

"He was just behind me. I'm sure he'll be in shortly," Anders answered, relieved to know he'd made it back before his uncle. He rushed to his room to dry off and change into dry clothes. In his room, Anders looked at his reflection in the small mirror on the wall next to his closet. He quickly practiced a straight-faced expression as he imagined how talking to his uncle would go. Throwing on a dry shirt and rubbing the water out of his thick brown hair, Anders practiced his unsurprised face one more time before returning to the dining room. Joining his cousins at the table, he smiled lightly at them, trying to avoid any suspicious looks from their piercing blue eyes.

Soon, Theodor was wiping his muddy boots on the floor mat and shedding his saturated outer layers. Hanging his coat to dry, placing his boots by the crackling fire, and taking a seat at the dinner table, he acted as if nothing was different from any other day.

Once they were all gathered at the table, he asked, "Tell me about your day. What happened?"

Thomas recounted the day's events as Kirsten and Anders began to hungrily inhale their sausage and potato dinner. He told his father how he and Anders had caught the most salmon they'd ever brought in while fishing. He also bragged that because of his heroism and ability to remain calm, he had saved them from almost sinking in the storm.

"Is that so?" Theodor said astonished, his thick eyebrows rising to expose the bright blue hue of his eyes.

"Nope," Anders said through a mouthful of sausage. "He was shaking like a baby. I nearly had to bail the water out myself *and* row us back to shore at the same time." He smiled at his cousin, who turned red in the face.

Thomas scowled at Anders' brotherly banter and stuck the tip of his tongue out through his pursed lips in his direction.

"I just tell it how it happened," Anders said, still smiling at his younger cousin. "We did catch quite a lot of fish out there today," he added to Thomas' credit. "Should be able to make some good money at the festival tomorrow."

Theodor congratulated them on their success and told Thomas he was sure his version of the story wasn't far from the truth.

After dinner, when the four of them turned in for the night, Anders lay in bed thinking about what Theodor was hiding from them. The conversation he'd overheard with the strange man kept replaying in his head. Anders lay awake late into the night thinking through all of the possible explanations for what he'd heard. He wondered if he should tell Kirsten or Thomas about it. He fell asleep not knowing what he would do with the sensitive information.

THE RISING sun beamed golden rays across Highborn Bay as it warmed thin patches of snow left behind from the heavy winter. The storm had passed during the night. Songbirds sang and spread their wings, flying through the clear blue skies. Anders awoke to floorboards squeaking under Kirsten and Thomas' feet. They shuffled over to the kitchen and began preparing the morning meal of eggs, sausage, bread and Anders' favorite tea loaded with caffeine called mate. Theodor always pronounced it wrong and Anders grew tired of correcting him, "It's mah-teh, not matee," he would say irritated.

He was still half asleep when he joined his cousins around the table. Unlike his uncle, who'd already been up for a half hour, Anders was not much of a morning person until he had his mate. Theodor walked in through the front door in his usual chipper mood. He had just finished the morning chores.

"Good morning," he said, rubbing the top of Kirsten's head, messing up her shoulder-length hair.

"Stop that!" she whined and ducked her head to the side, attempting to avoid her father's playful hand.

"How are we feeling this morning? Ready to go to the biannual Grandwood Festival?" Theodor asked, still chuckling at Kirsten's reaction.

"I'll let you know once I've finished my mah-teh," Anders replied emphasizing the syllables for his uncle. He held the mug tightly, his hands wrapped around its warmth.

"You'll want to be at the festival's market early if you are wanting to sell all of your salmon," Theodor said while pouring himself a hot cup of tea. He gently blew on it and said, "tasty stuff this matee." He glanced at Anders who shook his head and smiled. Kirsten, Thomas and Anders agreed with him about getting an early start but remained seated waiting for the caffeine to take effect.

Thomas was the first to leave the table. Anders watched him bring the horse and carriage around to the front door and load up their baskets of salmon. He wondered if he should talk with Theodor about the argument with the stranger he overheard the night before. But when he turned to look at his uncle, who was laughing at something Kirsten had said, he decided it was not the right time.

Anders took one last swig of his tea and said with a hint of sarcasm, "Well, what are you waiting for? Let's go to town; we need to be at the festival early if we are to sell all of our hard-earned salmon." Theodor smiled exposing his tea-stained teeth in acknowledgement of Anders' remark.

Anders jumped into the back of the wagon alongside Kirsten. Theodor and Thomas rode up front on the wagon's bench seat.

"And… we're off," Theodor said with reins in hand.

The crisp morning air washed over their fair-skinned faces as they trotted down the road to the City of Grandwood. The dirt road followed the edge of the forest as it wound through rolling foothills. The city was nestled neatly between the Pelagic Ocean and the Grandwood Mountains. After nearly a half-hour of riding, they crested a hill, able to see the sunlight glinting off the city's many rooftops and buildings.

It was the first time any of them had seen Grandwood since the arrival of the thousands of visitors for the biannual festival and Grandwood Games. At the far end of the city, Anders could see the masses of vendors' and visitors' tents that had sprung up over the last several days. The temporary gathering extended down the beach, nearly doubling the size of the coastal city.

"Anders, do you think you're ready for the competition?" Theodor asked. "It begins tomorrow."

"I'm nervous," he began. "I'm also confident I will finish this year. My goal is to complete the event, not to win. Although winning would be nice," he added smiling.

"The Grandwood Games is the most fierce and challenging competition of any in the five nations," Theodor spoke as if he was an announcer for the event. "This is the fiftieth year it's been held and nearly half the contestants don't complete it. Of course you know that because you were one of them last time," he chuckled lightly looking back at Anders. "You were lucky I knew the judges and they made an exception for you. After how it ended for you though, I would never advise anyone to compete while still under age. Just try to relax and enjoy the festivities while you can. There will be plenty of time to be nervous tomorrow," he said trying to buoy his nephew's confidence.

"I'll be betting on you, so you'd better do well this year," Kirsten chimed in. "And if you decide not to compete at the last minute, I will take your place. I may need to disguise myself so the judges think it's you, but I could pull it off," she said with great self-confidence.

"Kirsten, you think you're so funny, don't you! Too bad you must be eighteen to participate," Thomas said mocking her.

"In all seriousness," Anders said, "I know you could probably hold your own with the best of them, but you must not make the same mistake I did. You can cheer me on this time, and in two years we'll be able to compete alongside one another."

"Hey Thomas," Kirsten said, trying to shift the focus off herself, "It must drive you crazy not being able to compete next year when you turn eighteen. Too bad it's a biannual event, because all of the greatest contestants in history have done their best in their eighteenth year."

Thomas balled his fists together tightly in an attempt to hold back his anger. He knew what his sister was trying to do to him. "It'll be worth the wait," he said through a clenched jaw. "Then I can crush you at your first games."

"There must be a mutual level of respect for one another among all athletes," Theodor said, attempting to end the argument. "That includes the both of you."

Kirsten stuck her tongue out at her older brother behind his back while her father spoke.

"Real mature," Anders said in a low voice, giving her a loving shove with his forearm.

As they rode across town toward the festival's market, Anders enjoyed observing the many cultures represented at the event. People of all nationalities had come to Grandwood to participate in the trade and commerce. The market was beginning to fill with people when they found an open lot for their stand. Anders and Thomas used the wagon as their booth, displaying their fresh salmon in several wicker baskets. Kirsten and Theodor unhooked the horse and led her over to a nearby hitching post.

It wasn't long before the roar of the market was in full effect. The four of them had little trouble selling their fresh fish. They sold out within an hour.

Feeling the plump pouch of coins they'd just acquired, Theodor said, "Well done. This is more money than this family has had in months. I say we split up into groups and get supplies for the farm before we lose focus and become lost to all the festival has to offer." The three of them nodded their heads in agreement. "Anders, you and Thomas get supplies for the boat, while Kirsten and I get the rest. Sound like a plan?"

They set out into the vast market to gather what they needed. After Thomas and Anders had most of their supplies loaded into the wagon, Anders said to his cousin, "I'd better go find the registration tent for tomorrow's competition. I'll track you down afterward."

"Okay, sounds good to me," Thomas replied. "I'll let father and Kirsten know. I'll be trying exotic food and checking out all the new things people are selling this year."

"Have fun and don't get food poisoning," Anders said slapping Thomas on the back. He winced in pain because of the sunburn he'd suffered after spending the day fishing under the spring sun before the storm hit. He turned to tell Anders off, but his cousin had already disappeared into the crowd.

Anders pushed his way through the mass of people toward the registration tent. When he reached the beach and located the tent, he paused just outside the door. His nervousness came rushing back and his heart pounded fast. He took several deep breaths to calm himself down.

Exhaling, he reached out to open the tent door. Just as his hand wrapped around the handle, he was knocked violently off his feet. For a moment, he was lost. The world around him was a blur. He'd lost his bearings and found himself entangled with whoever had come barreling through the doorway in such a hurry. As he tumbled free from the stranger, he regained his composure. Rising to his feet, still confused about exactly what had just happened, Anders saw the man scramble to his feet and frantically try to escape. Two people from the registration tent rushed out after him.

"Thief! Stop that man! Stop that thief!" they yelled, hands raised pointing at the man who was now gaining speed along the crowded beach.

Anders quickly made sense of what was happening. Cursing under his breath, he took off at a dead sprint after the thief. As he raced through the crowd, he very quickly found himself gaining on the man. Running past tents and wagons, he saw a vendor with a row of hand-made tool handles. The fleeing thief turned sharply to the left and bowled through a group of people, knocking them out of his way. Anders quickly grabbed a shovel handle as he passed the vendor. He rounded the corner and saw he had a clear shot at the man. He hurled the hard piece of wood with a fierce side-handed throw. It spun twice through the air with great speed, colliding into the back of the man's head with a loud, CRACK! Instantly the man toppled to the ground like a sack of potatoes, dropping the large bags in his hands, spilling the contents. The people around him gasped when they saw the man fall, surprised to see such a violent end to the chase.

Anders rushed to the unconscious man. Beside him, the two bags of gold coins he'd stolen lay scattered on the ground. One of the people working at the registration tent had been just a few moments behind Anders throughout the chase. She quickly came to his side.

"Thank you so much!" Anders heard the girl say with a hint of an accent.

Anders lifted his head to see her walking swiftly toward him. Her brown eyes met his as her long amber hair ran down behind her shoulders. Her darker skin shone brilliantly in the light of the spring sun, captivating Anders. She was beautiful.

He opened his mouth, but no words came out. Anders managed something of a smile and rubbed the back of his sunburned neck. After what felt like much too long a silence, he finally squeaked out, "Yeah, don't mention it."

She chuckled at his inability to smoothly start a conversation. "That man took all of the proceeds for the games tomorrow. He snatched them from me when my back was turned. If he'd gotten away with it, I would be out of a job for sure," she said to Anders. "I bet you weren't expecting him to come barging through the door, were you?"

Anders, still smiling at her like an idiot, joked, "I sure wasn't. I'm just surprised he held on to those heavy bags when he ran me over." She smiled at him showing Anders the full beauty of her face and he felt himself instantly relax. "Well, I'm happy you won't be getting fired. Let me help you pick up this mess and take the bags back to the tent."

"That would be great! My name is Maija," she said, extending her hand toward him.

"Anders," he replied taking her hand and shaking it.

She seemed to be examining his face as they shook hands and said, "I like the color of your eyes."

Anders blushed, the redness rising up his neck and across his sunburned face. "Thanks. The brown in your eyes matches the color of your hair beautifully," Anders heard the words come out before he realized it might be rude to give a girl he didn't know such a tender compliment.

She smiled after seeing his facial expression change to humiliation, "Yours are lovely too. They're like the color of a storm rolling across the sea. What do they call it?"

"My uncle calls it gray-haze," he said bashfully.

"I haven't met anyone with gray eyes before," she said.

"I find that hard to believe," Anders said.

"Where I come from there aren't many people who have bright eyes," she said, gazing longingly into Anders' eyes.

"Where is that?" he asked.

"A small island off the coast of Southland," she said with a slightly accented Landish tone that differed faintly from other Westland and Southland speech. "They're called the Kewians," she smiled.

"It sounds like a lovely place," Anders said holding her gaze before awkwardly glancing down at his feet.

Together they gathered the scattered coins. Several of the town's watchmen had seen the chase and were quick to put the thief in chains. Anders and Maija carried the money back to the registration tent while the watchmen hauled the thief away.

"So, it would be safe to assume you were about to come in and register for the games when that man ran into you?" Maija asked Anders.

"Yeah, I didn't see that one coming," he replied. "He was moving pretty fast, too. He should've signed up for the event instead of trying to steal the money. Probably would've done pretty well," he joked.

"It looks like you got the best of him in the end, though," Maija said. "Good thing you got lucky with that shovel handle."

"Hang on," Anders said. "That wasn't just luck. I happen to be an excellent shovel handle thrower," he smiled at her.

Back at the tent Anders was thanked and congratulated by the others working alongside Maija. He glanced over at Maija, who was staring at him, but looked away embarrassed when he noticed. After shaking the hands of Maija's co-workers, Anders finally completed what he had come to do in the first place. He registered for the Grandwood Games. They told him to return in the morning to go over the rules before the competition began. He smiled brightly at Maija, who smiled back, before he left the registration tent.

After meeting up with his family, Anders told them what had happened.

"Anders, that's amazing," Kirsten said in admiration. "Maybe now you'll have an advantage in the judges' eyes."

"It certainly won't hurt," said Thomas in a hopeful voice.

"Good job, Anders. No matter what happens tomorrow, I'm proud of you," Theodor said as they climbed aboard the wagon to leave the Grandwood Festival.

He'd left out the part about meeting Maija, the beautiful Kewian girl who he now found himself thinking about.

The sun set over the horizon as the four of them rode up to their home above Highborn Bay. Anders and Thomas unloaded supplies from the wagon while Theodor went inside to start a fire. They warmed themselves by the fireplace as darkness fell, drinking warm tea and speculating how Anders would fare in the upcoming games. After placing several wagers among themselves, Anders wished everyone good night and went to sleep thinking about Maija's beautiful brown eyes and enchanting smile.

CHAPTER

TWO

THE GRANDWOOD GAMES

The morning of the Grandwood Games dawned with a clear blue sky. Anders had been training for this competition for almost a year. He'd taken a shot at it two years earlier when the judges had made an exception for him at the age of seventeen. The rules were clear; no one under eighteen could compete.

While not typically a rule breaker, Anders had wanted to compete so badly that he persuaded Uncle Theodor to lobby the judges with him for an exception. Reluctantly the judging committee made an exception for him. Theodor had served alongside several of the judges during The War of the Magicians and was able to talk them into bending the rules for Anders.

Unfortunately, after all of that effort, Anders failed to complete the last event of the competition, the mountain race. While he was running back down the side of the mountain, one of the other contestants pushed him off the trail and down into some jagged rocks. He fell out of control and broke his leg. On top of the pain, he was forced to show an incomplete time and forfeit the games as well as miss several months of work on their family farm. Theodor regretted helping Anders compete illegally and in the end paid a price for it. With his hardest and most valuable worker unable to help during the busiest part of the harvest, their family was hardly able to make ends meet.

Since recovering from his broken leg, Anders had been training hard for all four events in the competition. The events required performance of a special skill, a demonstration of strength, a test of knowledge, and finally, completion of the challenging mountain race. He wanted to make sure he would be prepared for anything the games could throw at him this time around.

Between working on the family farm and pulling in waterlogged fishing nets with his cousin, Anders had grown very strong for a nineteen-year-old. His work routine took care of his strength training. He spent the evening hours studying books his uncle kept in his private library. An avid reader and lover of knowledge, Theodor helped Anders sharpen his mind. For his specialty skill, Anders had been practicing knife and axe throwing. From an early age, he'd been a natural at throwing any object with remarkable accuracy, so it seemed like his best option. As for endurance training, Anders often spent any free time he had hiking far into the mountains behind their house. The winter months made it more difficult to hike great distances in the snow, but he did his best to fully prepare for the competition.

After eating smoked salmon and freshly baked bread for breakfast, Anders and his family traveled to the registration tent on the beach where the Grandwood Games were to begin. Upon arriving, Anders joined the long line of contestants outside the tent waiting for their information and placement in the games' different heats.

Anders stood in line behind a young man who must

have had his eighteenth birthday only a few days before. The young man seemed to be in especially high spirits and spoke loudly to anyone around him who would listen to his jokes, many of which were inappropriate for children's ears. Anders stood behind him and heard every word, often laughing at the comic relief he was supplying. He found the jokes amusing; they took his mind off the competition, settling his nerves. Anders introduced himself.

The dark-haired lad replied in kind, "Hello, Anders, my name is Max. Glad to meet you. Where're you from?"

Getting a good look at him face-to-face, Anders noticed Max had several inches on him in height. At around six feet tall, Max had a more slender frame than Anders' toned muscular body. Max's black hair was tied tightly into a bun near the top of his head.

"Grandwood. How about yourself?" Anders asked Max, curious of his origins.

"I come from the Riverlands of Westland. Just outside a town called Brookside. I came here with my younger brother, Bo, who's in the crowd somewhere," Max said in perfect Landish, humankind's most common language. Squinting as he looked over Anders, he scanned the gathering crowd for his brother. Not able to locate him, Max shrugged and continued, "We heard people talking about how difficult this competition was, and, well, I had to come try it. I love a good adventure, and it's not like me to turn down a tough challenge."

"You seem confident and in good spirits. I'm sure you'll do well. Best of luck to you," Anders said with a smile and Max returned the sentiment.

One by one contestants filed into the tent. Soon Anders heard someone inside shout, "Next." He entered, searching the room for the amber-haired girl he'd met the day before. She was standing near the back of the tent sorting through some parchment. He approached the table where a man sat scribbling into an open book.

"State your name, age, and where you're from," he said swiftly.

"Anders Valgner, nineteen, of Highborn Bay, Grandwood City."

The man raised his head when he heard Anders' name. He leaned back in his chair and looked to the far end of the tent where Maija stood with her head down, concentrating on her task.

"Hey Maija," the man shouted. "Is this the lad?" he asked, pointing his quill in Anders' direction.

Her head perked up. Upon seeing Anders, she smiled brightly and Anders weakened in the knees, "Yes, it sure is. Thanks to him we can offer prize money."

Anders blushed through his already fading sunburnt cheeks and shrugged bashfully.

The man was not among those who'd been in the tent the day before. Otherwise he would have thanked him yesterday. He rose from his chair and grasped Anders' hand, shaking it. "Well thank you kindly for getting that money back for us. It would've been a terrible loss if you hadn't chased that thief down." The man reached down and pulled a pouch out of a box next to his chair. "Here you are, take this." He handed Anders the pouch. Anders took it hearing the coins inside clink together. "A little reward for your generosity."

Surprised, Anders said, "Thank you," putting the pouch in his pocket and looking over at Maija who was smiling at him.

The man sat back down and grabbed a piece of charcoal and stuck it out toward Anders. "Take this and write your number on your left arm and right leg," he said. "Your number is forty-three. Then make your way down to the shoreline and the judges will explain what to do from there."

Anders did as he was told. As he left, Maija shouted, "Good luck, Anders!"

He smiled and waved to her as he left the tent. His family emerged from the crowd to wish him good luck. They met him near the group of men and women waiting for the judges to provide further instructions.

"It looks like you'll have some stiff competition this year," Theodor said eyeing the diverse group of contestants.

"Yeah," Anders agreed. "I can tell from the tribal tattoos that quite a few Rollo Island warriors are here."

The battle-tested warriors of the Rollo Islands were known to be very hard to beat in physical competition. Anders suspected one of them had shoved him off the trail during the last Grandwood Games because he'd heard a string of Native Rolloan words as he fell into the rocks.

"Just remember your training," Theodor said reassuringly. "Many of their warriors lack the ability to think for themselves and don't know how to perform when they aren't given orders. It could give you the advantage during a battle of wits."

"Thanks, I'll do my best," Anders replied.

Standing on a large rock at one end of the beach, a judge announced that he would be describing the rules shortly. Thomas, Kirsten, and Theodor all wished Anders good luck one last time as he joined his competitors for their meeting.

The judge stood tall on top of the boulder calling for them to gather around him and listen.

"This competition will involve four parts, each testing a different skillset. The first is a test of strength, which is made up of three challenges, with a maximum score of thirty points. Next will come a test of wits and problem solving, followed by a demonstration of a specialty skill chosen by the competitor, worth ten points each. The fourth and final event, the mountain race, will be timed. The faster your time, the more points you will receive.

"You will be judged individually on each of the four events. The contestant who has the highest overall score wins. If you fail to complete any of the four events, you will be disqualified, showing a 'no score.' The other four judges and I will determine the points awarded during each event. In the case of a tie for first place, we'll hold a sudden-death round, which will be explained if such an event occurs.

"You'll compete in six heats of ten. The last heat will only have eight, as there are fifty-eight of you competing today. Those are the rules. You'll be starting with the strength portion first, which is located here on the beach. The first heat will begin now. Contestants with the numbers one through ten written on their arms and legs follow me to the starting area," the judge said as he climbed down from the rock.

Anders was number forty-three, which meant he would have to wait and watch the first four heats compete before he would get his chance. He made his way over to a central location where he could see the first event clearly. The strength event included three parts; the first required lifting heavy stones. The five large rocks lined up for each contestant on one end of the beach varied in size and weight.

Contestants would have to pick them up, carry them across the sand and place them on their appropriate stands.

Anders watched as the contestants in the first heat carried the heavy stones and struggled to place them on the stands. The tallest of the stands was just above head height, so it behooved them to place the lightest of the five rocks on the highest stand, and the heaviest on the lowest.

Anders knew from his experience in the previous games that he couldn't place the largest stone on the lowest platform if he tried to do the others first. He had figured that trick out two years ago when he did the lighter stones first and was too tired to pick up the heaviest one. He watched many other people make that same mistake. Those who couldn't get all of the stones on the stands received lower scores.

The second and third parts of the strength event required distance-throwing. One of them tested to see how far individuals could toss a heavy log. Each would have to toss the log in such a way that the log made at least one flip end-over-end. The person who threw the log the farthest would earn the highest score. If the log failed to flip at least once, the thrower received an automatic minus two points. The second throwing challenge was a spear toss. The longest toss earned the most points.

Anders watched the four heats of contestants go before him. He knew that if he could put up all of the stones in the first challenge and make the log flip in the second, he would have a decent chance at placing in the top ten no matter how far he tossed the spear.

When his heat was called to compete, all ten of them stood in a line on the beach. Anders was placed next to Max, the lad he'd met earlier outside the registration tent. On his other side stood a tall, burly-looking Rollo warrior.

Anders recognized him as a second-time competitor from the last Grandwood Games, making him at least three years older than Anders. The warrior wore his clan's markings on his caramel-toned skin. He had a nest of dark hair curling down from his head. A large, full beard matched his unkempt hair and concealed much of the warrior's face. The Rollo Islander was intimidating, to say the least; Anders knew he had his work cut out for him if he wanted to beat the muscular man.

When the starting signal was given, Anders flew through the lifting portion. He started with the heaviest stone, which he could barely place on the lowest stand, then swiftly worked his way through the rest. At the log throw, Anders hoisted the heavy log up by its base. He held the log firmly against his shoulder, careful not to let it tip over. For a moment, it wobbled. Using the log's momentum, he leaned forward and began to run with it. After ten or twelve steps, Anders heaved the log up with all his might.

He watched as the top of the log rose up into the air, turning at a downward angle as it began to fall. The log spun one-hundred-and-eighty degrees in rotation before landing and sliding across the ground. He was able to gain enough speed before releasing it to see it fly through one full rotation. He was very happy with himself and knew then that he could relax a bit for the third part of the event.

When it was his turn, Anders picked up the spear, gripping it tightly. He raised it up behind his head and marched down the beach with increasing speed. Before reaching the throwing line marked in the sand, he planted his feet firmly and twisted his body, tossing the spear with everything he had. He watched as it flew through the air and bored head first into the beach.

A judge ran out and measured the distance. Anders

knew he'd done well, regardless of what the mark was. He threw his arms up in excitement and grinned as he saw his family cheering for him in the excited crowd.

As the sixth heat gathered to take its turn, Anders went to check the scoreboard the judges posted for each event. He was tied with about half of the people for second place, with a score of twenty-eight-and-a-half points. The Rollo warrior in Anders' heat took the lead with a score of twenty-nine-and-a-half.

In the test of knowledge that followed, each contestant would face the same problem and have to use his or her intellect to get through it. Contestants were not allowed to watch one another during this event, so nobody would have an unfair advantage on completing the challenge. It was designed to put their minds to the test and weeded out those who were only physically adept.

By the time it was Anders' turn, a quarter of the contestants had been unable to complete the event, forcing them to drop out of the games. As he walked up to the event's location, the large Rollo Islander nudged him aside, cursing him in broken Landish under his breath. Anders' instinct was to push the large man back, but he forced himself to avoid the conflict. In that moment, he realized the man was just trying to get in his head and throw him off his game. He didn't retaliate by engaging in a fight, but instead focused on beating him in this next event. If Anders could do that, he might be able to surpass the warrior's lead in the competition.

One by one the contestants were directed into their own private tents. The area around the tents had been walled off from the crowd, so they could concentrate without distractions. When Anders entered his assigned tent, he found a table in the center of the tent. Seated on the table was a large wooden tower about three feet tall. Anders instantly recognized the tower from a book of puzzles and riddles Theodor had in his library. The Lumbapi people of Southland created it, if he remembered correctly.

The puzzle was designed to hold a centerpiece hidden within the tower. The challenge was to extract it without making the tower fall over. The puzzle was especially challenging, he remembered reading, because you weren't allowed to completely remove any of the pieces. The pieces had to be arranged in a specific order to complete the task. Anders saw a piece of parchment next to the tower.

Picking it up, he read:

Before you sits the renowned Lumbapi Tower Puzzle. This impressive work holds a treasure within. Do the puzzle correctly and the treasure will reveal itself. Handle the puzzle incorrectly, and the tower will crumble. No piece of the tower is to be completely removed.

Good luck.

Anders began shifting the pieces of the tower around. Each one had to be moved a certain way to unlock the next layer inside. The tower puzzle in the book he read only had three layers and was much simpler than this one.

Struggling for nearly an hour and passing through six layers, Anders was about to give up, when he figured out how to place the last piece. He rotated it and locked it into its correct position. The center of the tower revealed itself. When it opened, he saw there was a tiny scroll hidden inside. He picked it up and read the small script:

For completing the puzzle you move on with a perfect score for this round. You are awarded ten points.

Anders took the scroll from the puzzle and left the tent

relieved that he had passed. He handed it to the judges who marked down his score with a perfect ten.

He walked over to the rest of the members in his heat who had also solved the puzzle. Max was among them talking with his brother, Bo, who joined him from the crowd.

"That was quite a challenge," Anders said as he approached them.

Max agreed, "We had one of those in our house growing up. We messed around with it a bit, but ours was not that complex."

"I've only ever read about them. Having that out of the way is a huge relief," Anders said, happy to be done with the second event.

Anders went to check the scoreboard. To Anders' surprise, the Rollo Island warrior had completed the puzzle as well. Anders had underestimated his intelligence. He was hoping to beat out the warrior, but since they both completed the challenge, the difference between their scores remained unchanged, so Anders went back to wait for the rest of the contestants to finish.

Nearly half of the men and women competing failed the puzzle and had to forfeit. Anders remained tied with quite a few people, including his new friend Max.

NOW CAME THE SKILLS EVENT. Each contestant had the option of choosing whatever skill he or she wished to perform to impress the judges. As Anders watched, his confidence grew that he could move ahead of some of the people with whom he was tied. During this event, other contestants were allowed to watch, so he sat in the crowd next to his family.

Many people chose to show off their skills as archers; others threw spears, none of which were that impressive. One person chose to dance. To Anders' surprise, the dancer was actually quite impressive. When it was Anders' turn, he grabbed his throwing knives and butterfly axes.

Anders had a routine that started with the knives, placing each one on three different targets, increasing the distance with each throw. Next, he would throw his axes. The first would hit the center of the target and the rest he stacked, sticking them into the handles of the previous axe. Then finally he would take three more knives and start from the farthest distance back. Running and spinning he would stick each knife into the handles of the first three knives he'd thrown.

Anders stood in front of his targets, throwing his first three knives into the middle of each one, taking steps backward between each throw. Now, holding his three axes and standing a bit farther away, he whipped the first axe through the air toward the fourth target. It landed directly in the center with the handle pointing straight out. The next two he tossed in quick succession. They hit the same mark splitting into the handle of the axe in front of it. Then as fast as anyone could see, he began throwing his last three knives. As though it was effortless, he stacked the three knives in the same fashion, one in each of the handles of the first three he had thrown. In a blur of spins and throws, Anders had completed the third event. All of his knives and axes stacked on top of each other, protruding in a straight line out from the center of each target.

The crowd erupted in cheers. Anders' display amazed

them. He faced them, took a bow, and returned to his family who stood together smiling proudly.

"That was brilliant!" Thomas exclaimed, giving Anders a slap on the back.

"I had no idea you were that accurate with your knives and axes," Theodor said, astonished.

He thanked them for their compliments, and together Anders and his family watched the remaining contestants' performances. Anders paid special attention to the large Rollo man who he saw as one of his main competitors. The brute's special skill was spear throwing for accuracy. While impressive, especially with the distance at which he could hit the targets, Anders was a bit underwhelmed by his performance. He thought his own accuracy was slightly superior, and if the judges saw it the way he did, Anders had a chance at closing the one-point gap between them.

Shortly after their heat had finished, new scores were posted on the board. Anders walked up beside Max and Bo to read the results. He shouted with excitement upon seeing his new score, "Yes!" He had gained another ten points, making his score forty-eight-and-a-half. Max and Bo congratulated him while the large warrior scowled at him, clearly frustrated. The Islander had fallen short in his performance. The judges awarded him nine points; he was now tied with Anders for the lead. Max scored nine-and-a-half-points, which had him tied for second place with two others, one of whom was the dancer. The rest of the competitors had fallen further behind in the rankings after the specialty skills portion of the competition.

The contestants were given a one-hour break before returning for the start of the mountain race. Anders took this time to sit alongside his family and quickly devour some of his uncle's famous 'gue' sandwiches before he had to be back. The 'gue' recipe was a Southland tradition where peanut butter was mixed with honey; not only tasty, the gue provided an excellent boost of energy. Together they marveled at the possibility that Anders had a good chance of winning the competition this year. He could hardly believe he had done so well.

When it was time for Anders to head back for the race, he heard someone call his name. Turning around, he saw Maija jogging toward him.

"Hey," she said, getting closer.

"Maija," Anders said, happy to see her.

"I wanted to wish you luck in the final event. You've been doing so well. I've been cheering for you from the crowd," she said blushing. "And..." she paused.

"And what?" Anders asked, curious about what she would say next.

"And this," she said. Maija leaned in close to him and kissed him on the lips. It was soft, gentle, and at the same time contained an intense passion he had never experienced before. He kissed her back, and for a moment he forgot about everything else around him. Pulling away she smiled as she looked into his eyes.

"I've been wanting to do that since yesterday," she said.

Anders stood there with a whimsical expression on his face. He couldn't find words to tell her how he felt.

"Good luck," she said and ran back into the crowd.

Anders could hardly believe what had just happened. His mind was no longer on the mountain race. It was on Maija. He stood there, adrenaline pumping through his body from having the unexpected and welcome kiss. Then he remembered he needed to be at the starting line soon.

It was late in the evening and the sun hung low in the sky. Anders stood tall next to the others who'd also made it to the final event of the Grandwood Games. Fifteen people were left, which meant there would be only one heat for this final event. He tried to focus on how he needed to set a steady pace so he could outlast the others as they ran up the mountain.

The judge at the starting line shouted in a loud voice so all could hear, "Runners, on your marks!" Each lowered into a running stance. "Get set!" Anders bent his knees and leaned forward. "Go!" the judge yelled.

Taking off quickly, they dashed across the beach to the trail that wound up the mountainside. Anders, Max, and the Rollo warrior were in the front of the pack. Max pulled ahead of them, setting the pace. They slowed as the slope increased, creating more strain on their bodies and building fatigue. The contestants fought, pushing and pulling each other as they climbed higher up the mountain. At times Anders and the warrior swapped places back and forth behind Max, who kept up his steady pace.

Exhausted, the three leading contestants fought their way up the mountain, putting more and more distance between them and the rest of the pack. Darkness surrounded them as they neared the top. Anders slowed and all three of them struggled to reach the peak. He forced himself to keep his burning legs moving.

He passed Max for the lead and was the first to reach the top of the mountain. Relieved to be at the top, he stopped and took a moment to catch his breath before making the descent. He looked down at the little dots of light scattered across the beach where people huddled around their warming fires.

Something in the distance caught his gaze. He strained to make sure he was really seeing what he thought it was. To his surprise, just off the coastline of Grandwood a fleet of ships sailed toward the shore. There were at least twenty of them altogether. Each one had black sails masking its approach at night. Instinctively, he knew what was about to happen. Just as the Rollo warrior and Max reached the top of the peak, their dark hair blending into the night sky, Anders heard the loud booming of the first round of cannon fire. Bright explosions followed, speckling the shoreline where the race had begun. Anders' heart sank and he sprinted back down the mountain, forgetting the games as the fear for his family's safety consumed him.

THREE

THE ATTACK

A nders' lungs burned as he ran back down the mountain. Many of the remaining contestants had already turned back after hearing the cannon fire, never reaching the mountaintop. Max and the Rollo Island warrior were close behind Anders. All three had made it to the top of the mountain when Anders saw the masked ships launch the attack. Now all of the competitive thoughts that had driven them up the mountain were lost.

Running, the three emerged near the edge of the forest. The expansive field where the race had started was unrecognizable, as cannon fire had torn the landscape apart. Explosions dotted the shoreline, leaving behind smoldering craters.

Anders squinted through the darkness. Among the blazing tents and wreckage, he could see the silhouettes of armor-clad men wielding swords and axes running across the beach. The laughter of people who had been enjoying the festival had turned to blood-curdling screams and cries for help.

The first to run out of the woods and into the field of

debris, Anders moved quickly across the field and slid behind an overturned wagon, timing his move to stay hidden from the attacking soldiers.

I have to find my family, he thought trying to stay focused.

Poking his head around the edge of the wagon, he peered over to where he'd last seen Thomas, Kirsten and Theodor, hoping he might spot at least one of them hiding amidst the rubble. Several bodies lay scattered on the ground near where his uncle and cousins had been cheering for him before the race.

Picking a moment when no soldiers could see him, he ran out from his hiding spot. Rushing over to the bodies, he began searching for his family. Despite the darkness, Anders could make out enough to tell that none of the bodies were his uncle or cousins. He felt some relief and hoped that they were still alive. His thoughts went to Maija and the brief moments they had together. He hoped she'd made it to a safe place before the soldiers made landfall.

Anders turned to run back to his hiding place behind the cart, but to his surprise three soldiers now stood between him and the cart.

They stared at each other for a split second before one of the soldiers pointed a crimson hand at him and shouted, "There's one, get him!"

Anders knew he was out-numbered and had no weapon. The soldiers rushed at him as he quickly searched the ground around him for something to defend himself with. The best he could do was a wooden table leg lying at his feet. He quickly picked it up. As soon as he gripped the sculpted piece of wood, the first soldier swung his sword at him. Anders blocked it, reacting out of instinct. Spotting a spear thrust from the second attacker, he spun to the right dodging it. As the soldier leaned forward following through with his stab, Anders smashed him with a backhanded swing of his table leg and he fell unmoving onto the ground. Unprepared to defend himself and lacking the reaction time to block the third soldier's sword descending rapidly toward his exposed neck, Anders feared his life would soon end.

Out of seemingly nowhere, Max tackled the soldier and disarmed the man. Together the two brought him to a swift end. The first soldier to attack Anders regained his poise, rushing toward him for a second assault. His sword in hand, the man raised it high above his head. Anders crouched, bringing the wooden table leg skyward to defend them. The Rollo warrior came from behind and grabbed the soldier by the arm, stopping him from bringing his blade down on Max and Anders. Turning around to see his attacker, the soldier was at the mercy of the large warrior. Still holding him by the sword arm, the warrior pulled a knife from his belt and thrust it deep into the soldier's chest letting his body fall lifeless to the ground.

Anders couldn't believe what had just happened. He was glad to be alive, while simultaneously horrified by the violence it took to do so. He walked up to the dark-haired island warrior who'd just saved his life, "I am in your debt. What's your name so I may thank you properly?" he asked.

In a thick Rolloan accent, the man said, "Red, clan leader and son of Chief Jorgen."

"Thank you, Red. You are a good man to have in a situation like this," Anders said as he extended his arm and shook the warrior's hand.

"That was down-right brutal," Max said, looking down at the destruction they had just caused.

"I'm in your debt as well, Max," Anders said thanking

him. "But first, I must find my family, then I'll be able to repay the debt I owe to you both."

Together they quickly gathered the weapons from the deceased soldiers. Max grabbed a sword and dagger, while Red picked up an axe he found on the ground. Anders grabbed a short-sword and a knife from one of the soldier's belts. Brandishing the found weapons, they could now properly defend themselves against the attackers. Though Anders was exhausted from the competition, the adrenaline coursing through his veins made him feel more alive than he'd felt all day.

"We should make a plan before more soldiers spot us," Red said, crouching behind a battered vendor's cart. He motioned for the others to get low and out of sight.

"If my family made it out of here before the fighting got too thick, they would have tried to make it back to the farm, just north of town. I'm sure they would have gone there first before fleeing," Anders said, joining the Rollo warrior with his back against the cart.

"Our ships are docked near the north shores of Grandwood. I'll help you to that point, but then I must leave you to search for my clan," Red said.

"I'd rather stay with you two than go it alone. I'll help you look for your family if you help me search for my brother," Max said, agreeing with their plan and Anders nodded.

"Anders, you lead the way since you know it better than we do," Red said speaking with the authority of an army commander.

"Right then," Anders said, and quickly gathered his courage before leading them into the chaos of Grandwood.

The three unlikely comrades struck out into the city sticking mostly to side streets to avoid the soldiers flooding all of the main roads. Anders led them through the shadows, staying close to walls and hiding in doorways of back alley shops as they progressed deeper into the heart of the city. They were roughly two-thirds of the way across town when they next encountered soldiers.

Anders could hear the footsteps as they came running down the side street where the three of them stood, trapped with nowhere to hide. The soldiers rounded the corner and, upon seeing the three of them, charged. Not knowing exactly what to do, Anders stood his ground and braced himself for the fight. He felt a rush of air swish by his side as Red sprinted past him headlong at the advancing soldiers. Anders and Max followed suit. Swords clashed; steel banging against steel echoed through the narrow alley. The three of them were locked in a heated fight to the death.

Anders swiftly dispatched two of the soldiers by delivering lethal strikes with his short-sword. Max took on another soldier while Red rampaged wildly with his axe, killing three of the four remaining soldiers. The last of the soldiers turned and tried to run, but Anders was quick to react. Drawing his knife, he took aim and threw it. Hitting his target, the blade sank deep into the back of the fleeing soldier, who fell motionless in the alley.

The fight was over almost as quickly as it started. Together they continued sneaking through the alleys to get across Grandwood. They had several more encounters with smaller groups of soldiers. With each fight they gained confidence they would make it to their destination.

Finally, they reached the north end of the city. Here they found more people armed and defending themselves from the enemy soldiers. With each group of friendlies they encountered, Anders asked if anyone had seen his uncle or two cousins while Red inquired about his clan's location and Max called out for his brother. Within several minutes of searching, Red learned his people were gathering near their ships.

"The Island warriors are planning to launch a counter-attack," one of the townspeople said to them.

After hearing this news, Red wished them luck and left Max and Anders to continue searching on their own. Anders saw someone he recognized from living in Grand-wood and asked if he'd seen his family recently.

"I saw your uncle not far from here," the young man said. "He was climbing up to a rooftop on one of the taller buildings down the street." The boy pointed them in the direction he'd last seen Theodor and they began looking for him on the tops of buildings. It didn't take long before they spotted Theodor's distinctive silver hair sticking up from atop a roof as he fired arrow after arrow at the soldiers below.

They rushed to the base of the building. Anders entered, followed quickly by his companion. Through the doorway, they found a spiral staircase leading to the rooftop. Theodor crouched behind a cistern of water. He had his bow in hand and a pile of arrows at his side. Theodor was surprised to see Anders as he moved across the rooftop quickly, trying to avoid being seen by the enemies below. When he reached his uncle, Anders threw his arms around Theodor in a tight embrace, glad to see him alive and well.

Theodor, relieved to see Anders as well, said, "I am so glad to see you! I feared the worst after the attack began. During the chaos, Thomas and Kirsten got separated from me for a while. I found them again fleeing across the city."

"Are they okay?" Anders asked, concerned for their safety.

"That was the last I saw of them. It wasn't safe to stay here so I told them to go back to the house, gather up some supplies, and hide in the woods until I returned," Theodor said.

Relieved to know that his family was okay, Anders brought his uncle up to speed on what had happened to him following the start of the mountain race. After briefly summing up his experience, Anders introduced Max. Shaking his hand, Theodor warmly thanked him for helping to keep Anders alive. When Theodor let go of Max's hand, the three of them simultaneously ducked and covered their heads in response to a loud explosion. After realizing they were unharmed, Anders uncovered his head to see that a cannonball had destroyed the building across the street. They looked over the roof's edge of to see the extent of the damage. Enemy soldiers emerged from the plume of dust that clouded the street below.

"Time to go," Theodor said sharply.

Anders led their retreat across the roof and back to the staircase that wound down to the ground level. Theodor strung his bow and released several well-aimed shots at the emerging soldiers in the street. In his final moments before turning to follow Max and Anders, he nocked another arrow while searching for his last target.

What he witnessed in that moment was a terrible sight that shook him to his core. From amidst the rubble in the street below, an enormous figure with grotesque features emerged. The beastly creature was covered in thick hair, dark as night, and sat atop a gigantic hound with red eyes and long sharp fangs dripping with crimson blood.

"Thargon," Theodor muttered under his breath.

He took aim, hoping to catch the beast off guard and let loose a shot. Just as the arrow was about to hit its mark, it came to a complete stop in mid-air and fell to the ground. Theodor didn't wait to see what the beast did next. He ran to join his nephew, only allowing Thargon to see the back of his head before disappearing into the building.

"Run!" Theodor exclaimed frantically as he flew down the stairs. They fled into the streets without hesitation and ran to the edge of town where they found several horses still tied to a hitching post. Together the three of them galloped up the road to their house in hopes of escaping the madness occurring in Grandwood.

When they arrived at the farm, Anders burst through the door shouting for Thomas and Kirsten. They were not in the house. Shortly after Theodor and Max joined him, Kirsten and Thomas came running from the forest behind the house.

"Anders! Father!" they exclaimed as they came in through the back door. They ran over and hugged them tightly.

"I thought I might never see you again," Kirsten said as she wiped tears of joy and relief from her cheeks.

"It'll take a lot more than a few angry soldiers to keep me from getting back to you," Anders replied.

"We were so worried about you and father," Kirsten said attempting to hold back her tears.

"Who is this?" Thomas asked, pointing to Anders' slender friend who stood in the doorway.

Anders introduced the two to Max and explained briefly the events that had occurred after the attack had begun. When he was finished, Theodor urged them to all go and take shelter in the woods near their house. He was worried the enemy would soon be at their doorstep.

"Stay hidden in the trees and don't come out for any reason," Theodor told them sternly.

"Aren't you coming with us?" Anders asked.

"Please don't leave us again," Kirsten pleaded with her father.

Theodor said calmly, "Go to the woods, stay hidden and wait for me to come find you. There is something I must to do before I can join you.

Anders and the others did as he asked and hid in the trees off to the side of the dirt road leading to their home. While they waited in the darkness, Anders heard the thundering footsteps of soldiers. They were coming up the dirt road toward them. He hoped Theodor had finished doing whatever it was he needed to do and was well out of the way of the approaching soldiers. Slowly and carefully, he crept to a place where he could see the road clearly. To his surprise, Anders could see Theodor standing alone in the middle of the road. The grunts and shouts of the soldiers advancing up the road grew louder.

What the hell is he doing? He's going to be killed, Anders thought to himself.

Theodor stood unmoving in the center of the road as if he was unaware of the danger approaching.

I need to get him out of there, Anders thought and took a step toward the road. As he did so, the soldiers came around the corner. Too late; the mass of soldiers was upon them. He stopped dead in his tracks, unable to safely get his uncle out of the way.

The soldiers rounded the corner and came to a halt when they saw Theodor standing alone in the road. They seemed surprised to see the old man standing there unarmed. From amidst the group Thargon rode up on his giant hound. The beast atop his ugly steed stopped several yards from Theodor.

"You are a fool if you think you can stop me, Theodor,"

the beast of a man said in a powerful tone. The beast's thick accent was foreign to Anders; he'd never heard anything like it.

"You will not find what you're looking for, Thargon," Theodor said firmly.

Anders, both astonished and confused about what was happening, had a host of questions pulsing through his mind. All he could do, however, was wait to see how the events would unfold.

"I know he is here, I can smell his blood," Thargon shouted, sniffing the air with his black disfigured nose. "You will bring him to me or die!" Thargon ordered Theodor.

"He is far away from here," Theodor said. "Somewhere where you will never find him."

"You lie!" Thargon bellowed. "I know he is near. If you don't bring him to me, believe me when I say, I will kill you."

Theodor stood silent in the road.

"Die, you fool!" Thargon bellowed as he kicked his hound forward, leaping toward Theodor.

Theodor drew an arrow from his quiver and let an arrow fly at the giant beast. For the second time the arrow stopped right before hitting its target and fell to the ground. Anders couldn't just stand idly by and watch his uncle be attacked by the beast, so he ran out of the woods in an attempt to help Theodor. But as he did so, the giant hound was already mere feet from his uncle. Anders watched horrified as the hound came down hard on Theodor and sank its sharp teeth into his chest.

Bursting forth from the darkness, a man wearing all black came rushing from behind where Theodor had been standing. The man shot a brightly colored sphere from his palm. The small circle of light flew through the air and exploded just before hitting Thargon in the chest. The explosion sent a bright-radiating flash of energy out in every direction. Anders attempted to shield himself from the explosion, but the shockwave hit him, knocking him backward. Everything went dark.

FOUR

PURSUIT

Anders awoke; as he opened his eyes, he found he was peering straight up at the clear blue sky. Daylight. The bright light warmed his cheeks as he attempted to remember what had happened. Confused and disoriented, Anders thought the sky was rocking back and forth. Thinking his mind was playing a trick on him, he tried to make it stop, but the rocking wouldn't go away. His body hurt, and his corded muscles stiffened like steel when he attempted to move.

Remembering the Grandwood Games, everything afterward came rushing back to him. The games, the attack, and, "Theodor!" Anders yelled, bolting upright and looking around. To his surprise, he wasn't on the forest floor where he had fallen the night before. He wasn't even on land. In fact, he was on a cot at the aft of a ship. He began to panic.

How did I get here? he wondered. *Was I captured? Where are Theodor, Thomas and Kirsten?*

All of the memories of what had happened swirled in a collective jumble as he tried to make sense of his surroundings.

I must have been captured, he thought, coming to the only conclusion that seemed possible. Yet he thought it odd that he was the only prisoner that he could see. He double-checked to see if he was restrained or bound in any way. He was not.

Crouching low as he rose from the cot, he crept along the ship's stern. Peeking over the railing, he looked down on the main deck. Nearly two-dozen people worked below him. Their dark skin and tribal tattoos gave their identity away instantly.

This is a Rollo Islanders' ship, he realized.

Using the railing to lift himself to his feet he could take in the entirety of the ship. He took a deep breath in and exhaled with the relief of knowing he wasn't a prisoner. Anders examined the faces of those onboard and recognized the large, dark-haired man as Red. Max stood near Red, as did the strange man who he had seen arguing with Theodor in the woods a couple of days earlier. Anders searched through the rest of the faces on deck, but Thomas, Kirsten, and Theodor were not among them.

Max was the first to notice Anders standing at the railing looking down at them.

"I'd better go tell him what happened," Max said to Red and the man in black, at the same time nodding toward Anders. The two followed Max's gaze and saw Anders had awoken.

Catching him by the shoulder, the man in black stopped Max, who was on his way across the deck to fill Anders in on what had happened. "I'll tell him," he said. "I know the most about why this happened and what it means for him." Max nodded in agreement and let the man proceed.

Already on his way to confront him, Anders walked

squarely up to the man in black and violently shoved at his chest. "Where's my family and who the hell are you?" he demanded angrily.

The man in black put his hands up to show he meant no harm and said soberly, "Calm down, Anders, I am not your enemy. I helped prevent the soldiers from capturing you."

Anders was about to attack the man again, not believing his claim, when Max rushed in and wedged himself between them. "Whoa. Anders, settle down."

Anders' eyes darted from Max, to the man, and back to Max again. Max saw Anders' shoulders relax and said in calming tones, "Listen to what he has to say."

Anders didn't trust this man, but he did trust Max. He also needed answers about what happened after he was struck unconscious, so he decided to listen.

Anders nodded, and Max stepped out from between them, "I'll give you two some alone time," and walked away.

"I'll hear what you have to say," Anders said, his gaze steadily glaring at the man in black. "But first tell me where my cousins are and what happened to my uncle."

"I don't know exactly what's become of your cousins, but I can tell you what happened to your uncle," the man matched Anders' gaze as the two stood face-to-face. "Theodor did not survive the attack," the man said, not letting his expression change.

Instantly Anders felt sick to his stomach. When he heard the news, he broke eye contact with the man, and stared vacantly to the side.

"He did the best he could to keep all of you safe and away from the reality he wasn't willing to face. Your uncle bravely sacrificed his life to make sure Thargon didn't find you."

Anders barely heard the hollow words as the memory of the giant hound attacking his uncle flooded his mind. "You were the man in the woods with my uncle that night you met in the clearing behind our house," Anders said.

"I was," he admitted to Anders. "And you were spying on us in the trees."

"How did you know?" Anders asked confused, because he was positive the man couldn't have seen him that night.

"It's not important now," he said. "I did what I could to save your uncle from Thargon, but I was too late to stop his death."

"You were the one that shot the ball of energy," Anders said.

The man nodded.

"You're a sorcerer," Anders said. "My uncle told us all those who could wield magic died long ago in The War of the Magicians."

"He had good reason to think I was dead after that terrible war, but that is not what I'm here to talk to you about," said the man.

"Why are you here?" Anders asked, partially blaming the man for his uncle's death.

"Let me explain myself. My name is Ivan," he said. "I knew your uncle well. Theodor and I were good friends before you and your cousins were born. We served together in The War of the Magicians. We were both sent to the same military training camp and became fast friends. Over the years we watched as a great and powerful evil nearly tore this world apart. A very formidable sorcerer whose dark shadow almost crushed out all hopes of peace led these evil forces.

"Near the end of The War of the Magicians, Theodor decided his life as a soldier was over, so he moved to Grandwood. It was there where he became the humble man you knew him to be. He created a comfortable life for you and your cousins, but he did not completely escape the realities of his former life.

"Thargon and his master have been searching for what your uncle kept secret from them for all these years. Thargon's master will stop at nothing to find what Theodor was hiding; that is why they came to Grandwood. When you saw us arguing in the woods, I was trying to warn him, but he refused to believe the threat was real. I may have been unsuccessful in saving your uncle from Thargon's wrath, but I was able to keep them from finding you."

Anders sat in silence for a moment trying to understand all of what Ivan had just told him. Finally he looked at Ivan and asked, "How can I trust that what you're telling me is the truth?"

"I know it's hard to believe, Anders. You can choose to believe what I have told you or not, but know that I was a dear friend of your uncle's and he would trust me to guide you along the path where you have been placed," Ivan said to him.

"What happened to Kirsten and Thomas?" Anders asked. "Are they on a ship as well?"

"Unfortunately, I couldn't save all of you from Thargon; your cousins have been taken by him. I promise I will do everything in my power to help you get them back," Ivan said with conviction. Anders' stern poise slackened at the disheartening news. A pale look of dread washed over his face as he slouched in silence, Ivan added, "I'll give you some time to think this all through," and left him.

Leaning against the side of the ship, Anders looked over

the edge at the coastline fading in the distance. He pondered the death of his uncle, who had been like a father to him, and watched as the thin strip of land where Grandwood lay bobbed away, slowly disappearing behind the blue horizon.

Max, seeing Anders alone, joined him by leaning on the ship's railing. "I'm sorry about your uncle."

"If what Ivan said is true, that my uncle was hiding something from Thargon and his master, then I feel like I hardly knew him," Anders quickly wiped a single tear from his cheek with the cuff of his sleeve. "I grew up thinking that Theodor was an honest man. I knew he served in The War of the Magicians, but I had no idea of the extent of his actions. I wish he'd told me more about all this. What am I supposed to do now?" Anders asked through watering eyes.

"I know we hardly know each other, but from what I know about your uncle based on the brief time I knew him, he was a good person who risked his life to save ours' and your cousins'. You may not have known much about his backstory, but what really matters is you knew the person he was and not the soldier he had been," Max said placing his hand comfortingly on Anders' shoulder.

Anders knew he was right. His uncle was a good person and he knew Theodor would never intentionally bring harm to either of his kids or Anders.

With his voice a little shaky, Anders took a deep breath and said, "You're a good guy, Max," and looked out at the curved horizon. Grandwood had become unrecognizable and the thin sliver of land disappeared behind a blanket of dark blue water. "The last thing I remember from last night was trying to run to Theodor's aid. I saw a bright light exploding near Thargon. Then it all went dark. What happened after that?" Anders asked.

"Yeah, you went down hard," Max said, his eyebrows pinched together and raised high. "After you were knocked unconscious by Ivan's blast of energy, Thomas, Kirsten, and I ran out to get you. Thargon wasn't affected much from his ball of energy. He had some kind of invisible shield protecting him. It more distracted him for a moment than anything. Thargon saw that you had tried to rush out from your hiding place and ordered his soldiers to capture you. We tried to drag you to safety while the soldiers were knocked down from the blast's shock wave, but they quickly regained their composure. I picked you up, in an attempt to escape. Thomas and Kirsten were right with us and we fought the advancing soldiers off as best we could. Somehow you and I got separated from your cousins in the chaos.

"Just when the soldiers had us pinned, a group of the Rollo Island warriors charged up the road and attacked the enemy from behind. Most of the soldiers were distracted and Ivan took out the rest. I carried you on my back as Ivan led us through the woods. I stopped to look for your cousins, but the soldiers had already captured them. Thargon and his men took them as his prisoners and they returned to Grandwood.

"After a short while, we came out of the woods and joined up with Red and his warriors on the road. He informed us that the enemy had captured many people at the festival and had taken them aboard their ships as prisoners. Unfortunately, your cousins were among them.

"Thargon and his men out-numbered us five to one. When we got back to the ships on the beach, we attempted to rescue those who were taken by the soldiers. We were not successful, however, and the soldiers boarded their ships and left as quickly as they'd arrived.

"The Rollo Islanders' clan chiefs, along with Ivan's influence, agreed that Red would take three of their fastest ships along with enough warriors to pursue and attack the enemy ships. The rest of the Rollo people would sail back to their islands and assemble the rest of their warriors and mount the full naval fleet. Our mission is to track down the enemy, rescue the prisoners taken, and sink their ships. The rest of the Rollo Island forces will join us to defeat any of the enemy's remaining ships." When Max had finished recounting what had happened after the initial attack, Anders was surprised to find that he'd missed so much.

"I understand it's a lot to take in," Max said to him, breaking the uncomfortable silence.

"Yeah, no kidding. What happened to your brother? I remember he was in the crowd at the start of the mountain race. Did you ever find him?"

Max looked down at his feet as he scuffed them against the wooden deck, "No, I didn't." His gaze rose skyward. "All I can do now is hope he made it out of that mess alive."

Anders' life had changed drastically in the last twenty-four hours. He wished he could just blink and make it all go away, make it go back to the way it was before the attack. He wanted to feel the comforts of having a father figure around and the joy of laughing with his cousins at their home above Highborn Bay. This was no longer an option. He couldn't make the events of last night disappear and have his old life back. He was going to have to face this problem head on. He was going to have to trust Ivan and attempt to rescue the only family he had left.

Anders worked his way through the crewmembers on deck, moving toward Ivan. Facing him, he said, "I'm grateful for what you did to help me last night. Max told me about how you helped us get to safety. But do you know how I really feel?" He leaned over and whispered in Ivan's ear, "I don't want to trust you, but it looks like I have to if I want to see my family again. They had better be alive when we catch up to Thargon and his soldiers. If they aren't, I'll kill you myself." After he and Ivan exchanged crossed glares for several deep breaths, Anders walked back to the other end of the deck. Running his hands through his unkempt shaggy hair, he looked out at the water isolating the ship and realized he would not see his home for a very long time.

THE SALTY OCEAN waves crashed over the ship's bow as they pursued their enemy through turbulent water. In the distance, billowing storm clouds developed in the warm afternoon air. Anders stood near the bow alongside Max and Ivan. The wind washed over their faces as the smell of rain filled their nostrils. They eyed the looming clouds warily.

"Enemy ships, dead ahead!" a crewman shouted from high up the center mast.

Anders clambered around a group of people sharing a telescoping lens to see the ships more clearly. He scanned the area to see if he could catch a glimpse of the fleeing ships.

Spotting them in the distance, the ships looked like tiny specks far away on the horizon. With just his naked eye, he couldn't quite see the ships clearly. A female warrior passed the telescope to him. There, through the circular optic lens, he saw three tiny ships with black sails bobbing across the water.

"We're gaining on them," Anders said to Max passing him the telescope.

"We'll be able to engage them before nightfall," Red said as he came to stand alongside them. "Our ships are far superior in speed. At this rate we'll surely overtake these three ships before too long."

"Have you constructed a battle plan?" Ivan asked Red.

"I have faith our crew will easily overtake these stragglers," Red said confidently.

"Perhaps we should go to the Captain's quarters and plan a strategy. I have some insight in the ways of this particular enemy and I think I could be of help to you in this matter," Ivan suggested. Anders could tell by the look on his face that Red was insulted by Ivan's recommendation.

"You don't trust the strength of my warriors?" Red asked.

"I don't doubt your crew's skills in battle," Ivan said, attempting to reason with him. "I fought an entire war against Thargon and his master. I just want to make sure we have a clear plan before engaging with those in his command."

Red pursed his lips and waved over the higher-ranking members in his crew to discuss their strategy. Ivan followed them to the rear of the ship and into the cabin.

Anders and the others waited for them to come up with a plan for the upcoming naval attack. The suspense mounting of the fight to come loomed over them. Anders could hardly stop his nerves from getting the best of him.

As the day grew longer, they closed the gap on the enemy. Anders noticed the ships they were pursuing sailed directly toward the storm that had been building all afternoon.

"The ships are going directly into that storm. Are they mad?" Anders asked Max, his face contorted with concern.

Max saw the trajectory of the ships as well and said, "We need to tell Red."

Anders agreed and the two of them went back to the cabin where Red and the others were deliberating on a battle strategy. Opening the door and entering the cabin, Max and Anders gained the attention of everyone in the small room.

"There is something you need to see," Anders urged them. The seriousness in his tone drew the attention of the leaders and Red and Ivan rose from their seats to follow them. Max and Anders directed them out of the room.

"Look, their ships." Anders said pointing off the end of the bow. Ivan and Red squinted and watched the ships for a moment. Worry clouded Ivan's face, but Red's expression remained unchanged and didn't seem concerned by what he saw.

"They're heading right into the heart of the storm," Max urged.

"That doesn't scare me," Red bolstered. "We have the fastest and most well-made ships in all of Kartania, or any other world for that matter. We'll fight through the storm." Red said confidently.

"Are you sure you want to do that?" Ivan asked. "This could very well be a trap."

"What trap is that? They're just trying to lose us in the rough waters of the storm. Our ships are far superior to those of our enemy. We'll continue our pursuit and over-take them by nightfall."

"Ivan's right, this could be a trap," Anders said, angry at Red's decision.

"How is it a trap?" Red asked. "They're running scared and think we won't follow them into the storm. They're trying to avoid a fight with us because they know we'll defeat them. I've seen desperate crews do the same thing before, trying to flee the wrath of our ships. Each time we've overtaken them because our ships are much faster and can out-sail any storm."

"What if you're wrong and it is a trap?" Anders asked. "If your ships are truly as fast as you say they are, what more are we risking sailing around the storm and running them down on the other side?"

Angered at Anders and Ivan's questions, Red said, "We will continue our course and defeat them in the storm. I'm your Captain and that is my final decision on the matter." Red stomped back to the cabin, grumbling angrily in his native Rolloan tongue.

Ivan spoke to Anders without looking at him, and kept his eyes on the ships sailing into the outer edge of the storm, "This is no doubt a trap and we need to be prepared for the worst. However, if this wasn't a trap and we did sail around the storm, we'd run the risk of losing their trail. If we lose sight of them now, we might never find out where they're going. The ocean doesn't leave a set of tracks to follow and it's easy to lose a ship in the open ocean if you don't know where they're heading."

"I don't like it," Anders said to Ivan.

Ivan turned to Anders, "Me either." Then he, too, followed Red back into the cabin.

Anders and Max were frustrated by Red's dismissal of their concerns. Anders was also angered by Ivan's decision to allow Red to sail into the storm even though he knew it was a trap as well. Once they were alone, Anders said, "If Thargon is truly as clever and evil as Ivan says he is, wouldn't he send these three ships from his fleet to lead us in the wrong direction? If he is that evil, what would he care if a few of his fleet were sunk by our cannons or wrecked by the storm?"

"I think you're right," Max said. "They could've slowed down intentionally to allow us to catch up to them, just to create this dangerous predicament."

"I can't believe Ivan is allowing him to go through with it," Anders said, frustrated.

Max shrugged, "You're probably right. I just hope they know what they're doing. We're stuck with their decision either way."

Exhaling heavily, Anders kept the rest of his opinions to himself. Instead of talking about something he couldn't control, he began to prepare himself for the storm.

As daylight faded to dusk, they caught up to the three ships; the others in their fleet were nowhere to be seen. Red dismissed the fact that they couldn't see the other ships, suggesting that these three were sent back to destroy the Rollo Island ships so the others could escape, but Anders had his doubts.

Anders noticed Ivan standing at the rear of the ship, muttering to himself. Anders thought Ivan was praying and didn't pay much attention. Instead he focused on what Red was ordering them all to do, engage the enemy ships with cannon fire.

As they advanced on the ships in the stormy waters, they had to wait for just the right moment to fire because the rise and fall of the waves disrupted their clear line of sight. The crew would have to wait until the ship was at the peak of a wave before taking aim and firing. If they didn't fire at exactly the right moment, their cannon balls would splash ineffectively into the rough ocean waves.

The fleeing ships shot their stern cannons at Red's ships;

each time they missed. Anders was helping the gunner load and fire the cannons. They struggled to keep the cannons from rolling out of firing position while being tossed by the storm. Every time they came racing down into the trough of a wave, a burst of water would pour in through the cannon doors. The water would rush out again once they began to climb up the next wave. Many times the crew struggled to keep themselves from being swept off their feet and out the hatch doors.

After waiting for what seemed like a lifetime, Anders heard the order to take aim. They pointed the cannon directly at the ship in view off the starboard bow. He watched it climbing the wave in front to them.

"Fire!" The order was given.

One of the gunners lit the fuse. The cannon roared as it released its explosive contents. The ropes holding the cannon snapped tightly as they caught the steel barrel on wheels before it could roll across the floor and smash into the other side of the ship. Through the hatch door, Anders saw the cannon balls blast the rear end of the enemy ship. His ears rang from the explosions of firing cannons in close quarters. Wood splintered off the outside of their target and Anders thought he saw a cannon ball hit one of the masts before the ship disappeared beyond the peak of the next wave. He heard muffled cheering from his crew.

The ship rocked forward, and he knew they were racing down toward the trough once more. This time Anders closed the hatch door before they reached the bottom. The force of the water rushed in through the doors of those who were unable to close them. The water swelled in and flowed out with great force. It took several men off their feet and swept them out the doors. Anders felt the ship tilt upward again and opened the hatch door, ready to take aim and fire once more. They battered the enemy ships several more times before one of them lost its main mast and was swallowed by the storm's waves.

Red's ship turned to engage another enemy ship. A wave hit them with such force it nearly knocked everyone off their feet. A cannon rolled hard against its restraints and broke through the ropes. The heavy steel cannon rolled across the floor and smashed hard into the wall on the other side of the hull, pinning a warrior who was unable to escape its path. It crashed right into his chest and Anders knew he must've died instantly.

The storm had increased in magnitude; their ships couldn't last much longer. Picking himself up off the floor, Anders searched for Max who was working another cannon down the line. He heard the order to take aim and fire. The cannons roared once more. Anders saw Max struggling to grab his hatch door before the ship swelled with water again. He ran over to him and together they closed the hatch just in time to avoid becoming victims of the ocean's deadly pull.

Max thanked him, and Anders shouted over the ringing in his ears, "This storm is going to sink us! We can't last much longer! Let's go up to the deck and find Red! Perhaps we can convince him to disengage the enemy! Their ships are battered and will be destroyed by the waves soon enough!"

"Alright. Let's go!" Max shouted.

Anders and Max ran across to the stairs that led up to the main deck. Once they opened the hatch, the storm blasted them with saltwater. The wind raced with gale force as it threw stinging pellets of water into their faces. Climbing out and closing the hatch door behind them, Anders squinted, searching for Red. Staggering to hold onto a rope tied to the ship's mast, Red was barking orders at the crewmembers steering the ship. Max and Anders could hardly hear Red's shouting over the howl of the wind. Waves crashed over the deck, sweeping them off their feet as they tried to make their way across to Red. Several times they were nearly swept overboard by the water rushing off the deck. Finally, they made it to Red and got his attention.

"Red!" Anders shouted. "We won't last long in this storm! The waves will wreck us if we keep pursuing the enemy! They're defeated, and their ships will sink! We must disengage before we share their fate!"

"No!" Red growled and stared at him with a crazed look in his eye. "You know nothing; we can outlast any storm! This ship will not sink! I will not give up the fight now. Go back below deck and keep loading cannons!" he shouted.

"You're a fool, Red!" Anders shouted then turned back and began to walk toward the hatch door to go below deck.

Staggering at the stern of the ship, Anders saw Ivan still lost in a trance. He wondered what he could be doing up there. Just before Max and Anders reached the hatch door, a sudden blast of wind came down from the clouds and raced across the deck, snapping the ship's masts in two and blowing overboard any who were not holding onto something. Many who were tied on with safety lines were able to climb back onto the ship, but Anders, Max and Ivan were not. The unnatural burst of wind sent them flying off the deck. Anders watched the wooden floor beneath his feet disappear and he was cast violently into the water.

They came down hard into the waves. Anders gasped for air as he reached the water's surface. Each wave was so large that he couldn't see anything but walls of water all around him. The very next wave picked up the ship they'd just been standing on and brought it crashing down. Now that the masts were broken off, the ship was at each wave's mercy. A powerful wave flipped Red's ship, smashing it apart in its immense force. Anders, Max and Ivan looked on at the destruction from the surface of the water. The roaring waves came crashing onto them and pushed them down, deep under the water. Anders tried, but couldn't hold his breath long enough to reach the surface. Before he could reach the surface for air, he blacked out.

CHAPTER
FIVE
CAPTIVES

"**T**homas," Kirsten said in a hushed tone. "Are you there?" She couldn't see anything through the coarse fabric that cloaked her eyes. Soldiers had placed burlap bags over their heads before carrying them onboard the ship. A terrible odor emanated from her surroundings and slowly oozed its way inside the scratchy burlap sack. Kirsten tried her hardest to avoid gagging. She didn't hear a response from her brother, only heavy breathing from someone lying nearby on the floor.

Raising her voice slightly, but careful not to raise it too loudly, she said again, "Thomas, is that you?" The body on the ground next to her did not respond.

If that's Thomas, Kirsten thought, *he's not conscious.*

She wondered if it was safe for her to attempt to take the bag off. She didn't want the soldiers to see her try, because Kirsten had seen what they would do to those who didn't obey their commands. One young girl with fiery red hair and green eyes had thrown a fit when the soldiers separated her from her mother. A soldier clad in dark leather armor lacking any insignia or clan identification shouted at her to calm down, but she kept screaming, kicking and clawing at him trying to break free from his vice-like grip. Without hesitation, the soldier raised his wide grimy hand and silenced her. Kirsten didn't want to have a terrible thing like that happen to her, so she was careful to not make any noise.

Her hands were chained behind her back so to take the bag off her head she would need to get them in front of her body. She figured it was safe to attempt it because she hadn't heard any footsteps come back since they tossed her onto the cold hardwood planks of the ship and closed a gate before walking away.

Carefully she moved her wrists down below her waist. She could now lift her legs up, one at a time, and backward through her cuffed hands. Trying once but instantly having to place her foot back on the ground, Kirsten learned balancing was a little tricky due to the rocking ship and being blinded by burlap. Once she had successfully moved her hands in front of her body, she quietly reached them up to her head and took off the bag covering her face.

Her eyes took a few moments to adjust in the dimly lit room. She could see bars on the cell door and knew she wasn't going to escape anytime soon. Light peeped through cracks in the wood panels above her head. She was in the hull of the ship. Pushing her face up against the bars of the cell door, she looked in both directions down the dimly lit hallway running the length of the ship's belly. Prison cells lined both sides of the narrow passageway. An open door at the far end revealed a set of stairs leading up to the ship's deck.

Having assessed her surroundings, Kirsten quickly turned to the person who had been lying silently on the floor next to her. She could tell right away from the dark silhouette that this wasn't Thomas. The person's figure was slender in shape; it was a girl. Bound in the same way she had been, the girl also had a burlap sack over her head. Dropping to her knees, Kirsten lifted the bag off the girl's head. To her surprise, Kirsten recognized the girl, but she couldn't remember from where. It was hard to know for sure in the dark, but she thought she remembered seeing the amber-haired girl in the crowd at the festival cheering loudly for Anders.

Kirsten shook the girl lightly by the shoulder and said, "Hey, are you okay? Hey girl, are you alright?"

The girl weakly opened one of her eyes and made a feeble noise. By the look of her, she needed serious help. The left half of her face was bruised badly and one eye was almost completely swollen shut. Kirsten's first instinct was to call for help, but she stopped herself before shouting. Trying to recall what her father had done to treat Anders after a steer gored him nearly ten years ago, she remembered Theodor bringing him inside and laying him on the couch. He kept Anders warm and made sure he was breathing until he regained consciousness. Then he made Anders drink a lot of water.

Kirsten searched the cell for anything that might be helpful to her. She noticed the girl's clothes were tattered and wet. It was damp and cold on the floor of the cell so she decided to try to dry her off. A pile of wicker baskets and a moldy sack of grain were stuffed haphazardly in the corner of their cell. She found a dry spot along one of the cell walls. Flattening out several baskets, Kirsten placed them neatly on the floor. Satisfied, she took off the girl's wet clothes and wrapped the two burlap sacks meant to be their blindfolds around her body like a blanket. Kirsten moved the girl onto the dry pad she had created.

Feeling better about the girl's condition, Kirsten thought next about the challenge of getting some water.

I could wait until the soldiers bring us some, she thought. Then she figured they wouldn't be so kind as to provide their prisoners with that luxury. Seeing small puddles of water on the floor of their cell, Kirsten had an idea.

This must be rainwater, she thought to herself. *The water seeps in through these cracks when it rains.* She looked up at the cracks in the wood above her head where thin strips of light shone through. Feeling the cracks with her fingers she was able to locate a spot in the board that was saturated. She knew this was where most of the rainwater dripped down.

Now how do I collect it if the rain comes? Kirsten asked herself. She looked around the small cell, but didn't see anything that would hold water. *At least we have this pile of moldy grain,* she thought. This was the source of the stench she smelled. She sat down on the ground next to the girl and rested her head against the wooden wall that separated them from the next cell over.

I hope she wakes up soon, Kirsten thought. *It's awfully dull sitting here with no one to talk to.*

After what felt like several hours to Kirsten, she heard someone begin to shout. It was a man's voice. Judging by his Rolloan accent, Kirsten knew him to be one of the Rollo Island warriors who had been competing in the Grandwood Games. He was calling out the name Tabitha. He shouted over and over again. Fellow prisoners in the cells near him tried to hush him up, telling him the soldiers would come if he made too much noise. Shortly after the man began shouting, soldiers came running down the stairs. Kirsten heard them throw open the cell door.

The man's demands to see his daughter at once went

unanswered and Kirsten put her hands around the bars of the cell door and watched as they dragged him out of the cell, down the hull and up the stairs. Shortly after the man was taken way, she heard the footsteps of someone walking down the stairs and watched as a soldier locked the door to the empty cell. Kirsten knew the man they dragged away would not be returning.

What kind of people are these, she wondered, *to rip families apart and beat them when all they want is to be reunited. Nobody raised in the great nation of Westland would treat their fellow humans with such cruelty.* Kirsten wanted to find out if her brother, Thomas, was on the ship with her, but she wasn't about to get killed over it.

After the Rolloan left, it was quiet and dark for a long time. She could hear the waves rushing along the side of the ship. It rocked up, at first making her feel sick, but after a while she got used to the constant motion. Eventually she heard another pair of feet thudding their way down to the hull and she feared for herself and the other prisoners, but to her surprise the person was carrying a bucket and a stack of empty bowls. They placed a small bowl outside each door and then spooned in fresh drinking water before returning to the deck above.

Someone must want us alive, Kirsten thought, curious at the random act of generosity.

She took a sip from the bowl. The cold water soothed her dry, throbbing throat. Kirsten had to force herself not to drink all of the water, saving some for the girl who still lay unchanged on the floor. If she was this thirsty now, Kirsten could only imagine how thirsty the girl would be when she awoke.

The bright light of day had faded, barely peeping through the cracks in the ceiling when the girl finally awoke. As she opened her one good eye, her face belied her confusion as she examined her surroundings. When the girl's scan of the cell landed on Kirsten, she attempted to speak, but her voice was so hoarse Kirsten couldn't hear her. She handed the girl the bowl of water.

Kirsten whispered to her as she took small sips from the bowl, "We have to be quiet. The soldiers have been punishing everyone who makes too much noise."

The girl nodded, letting Kirsten know she understood.

"I'm Kirsten," she said quietly placing her hand on her chest. "You were soaking wet and the ground is cold, so I took your wet clothes off and put you on the dry pad. I hope that was okay?" she asked, trying to make sure that the girl knew the soldiers weren't the ones to remove her clothes.

The girl pointed a shaky finger at herself, opened her cracked lips and whispered in a hoarse voice, "Maija."

Kirsten smiled, "I remember seeing you in the crowd at the competition." The girl nodded and took a small sip from the bowl before placing it back on the floor.

"I was one of the people working the event," she said quietly sounding a little better after drinking some water. "Thank you for helping me. I'm very grateful."

"Don't mention it. I'm sure you would've done the same for me." Kirsten said. "My cousin was competing in the games. He wasn't in town when the attack began. He eventually found us but that was when..." she trailed off. "Well, never mind about that, we're here now. Do you know anything about the people who took us and where they're headed?" she asked.

"I don't know who they are," Maija said. "I saw their ships had black sails lacking any banners or sigil and they don't wear any of the colors associated with the other nations of Kartania. Nobody saw them coming. Whoever they are and wherever they came from, they didn't want anyone to know who they are associated with."

"Why did they attack such a peaceful event?" Kirsten asked. "It doesn't make sense. Grandwood has always been a peaceful place."

Maija shrugged, "I don't know. The attack came so suddenly. All I know is that they fought without honor. They killed unarmed men, women, and even children. I was trying to save a child when they captured me."

"Is that how you got the bruises on your face?" Kirsten asked.

Maija nodded. As she nodded, a guard came down the stairs. They looked at each other wide-eyed and worried the soldiers knew they were talking. Nobody moved or made a sound as the soldier walked down the hallway. With a club gripped firmly in his hand, he looked into the cells for whoever made the noise he'd heard. Kirsten and Maija held their breath and tried to look asleep when the man peered into their cell.

They heard shouts coming from above. The soldier hustled back above deck, responding to the commotion and slamming the door behind him.

Within a matter of minutes, the ship began to rock more fiercely than before. Waves crashed over the deck and water spilled through the cracks in the ceiling. The shouts from the men above them were now drowned out by the howling wind.

"The sounds this ship is making don't instill confidence," Kirsten said. "I hope the ship doesn't come apart at the seams."

Night came and Kirsten and Maija closed their eyes hoping everything would be okay.

Kirsten awoke cold and dehydrated, her head throbbed. Water seeped through the crack overhead. She watched as the liquid formed into droplets and fell splashing into the small pool on the floor. The air in the hull was thick with damp wood and vomit. The storm had sent many people over the edge unsuccessfully fighting off seasickness. She tried to avoid thinking about the smell. Maija and Kirsten hadn't been among those who became ill from the ship's motion. Kirsten worried about some of the prisoners' living conditions and feared that many of them wouldn't survive. She could only guess at how long they would be locked up down in the ship's hull. All she could do was take her captivity one day at a time. *Make it through today*, she kept telling herself. *Just make it through today.*

Once the ocean waves stopped crashing over the side of the ship, Kirsten and Maija heard rain begin to fall on the deck above. They figured the fresh water dripping through the cracks would be safe to drink. Using the bowl the guards had given them, they collected the rainwater. Over the course of the night, they collected enough to fill the bowl and took turns drinking its contents. Drinking the water helped Maija hydrate again and she seemed to be faring better than the day before.

Downing the last of the water from the bowl and placing it back under the slow drip, Kirsten said, "I didn't sleep very well last night. It was the first time I've been on a ship during a storm. I thought we were going to sink."

"I didn't sleep that well either. Mostly because laying on cold hard wood that's constantly wet isn't exactly comfortable," Maija said. "I overheard some of the soldiers talking late last night after the storm passed. They said three of their ships trailing us did not emerge from the storm."

"Really?"

"I hope they weren't carrying any of the people who were captured," Maija added.

"I can't imagine how scary that would be," Kirsten said concerned. "I wonder where they're taking us?" She looked up at the light now showing between the boards.

"I'm not sure," Maija responded. "But wherever they're taking us, it can't be somewhere good."

"I hope we're not going to be cooped up in here much longer. I just want to stretch my legs and walk around. It's hard to do that in this small cell," she said as she demonstrated that it only took her three steps to reach the wall separating them from the next cell.

The two of them went silent when they heard several pairs of feet come stomping down the stairs and open the door. Two leather clad soldiers were dragging someone who looked to be unconscious. Kirsten watched as they dragged the person down the hall toward their end of the hull. They opened the cell door and tossed the person into it. She heard the limp body thud as it hit the ground. One of the men saw Kirsten was watching them from her cell.

He slammed the bars with his club and said with a thick foreign accent, unrecognizable to Kirsten, "What're you looking at, darling?" Kirsten looked away trying not to provoke the soldier. The man said, "That's what I thought," and closed the cell door next to them. They left just as quickly as they came, remarking how bad the smell of caged humans had become.

Kirsten thought there was something familiar about the person they stuffed into the cell next to them. "I think that was my brother," she said to Maija once the soldiers were out of the hull. She pressed her face up against the bars and whispered loudly, "Thomas." She waited, listening intently for her brother's voice to respond. For a moment there was no response.

She was about to call his name again louder when she heard his voice say, "Kirsten?"

"Oh, Thomas, it's you!" Kirsten blurted out. Just then the door at the end of the hallway cracked open. A soldier popped his head in and listened for the noise he thought he'd heard. It didn't take long before the soldier cursed the foul smell of the hull and gave up trying to catch whoever had made the noise.

"Shhhh," Thomas urged her. "Keep quiet, Kirsten. It will anger them if they know I'm talking."

"What did they do to you? Are you okay?" she asked him in a more hushed tone.

"Yes, I'm fine; a little banged up I guess, but I'll be fine," he replied. "When they brought us onto the ships, they didn't bring me down here with the rest of you. They brought me to Thargon."

"Is he the beast that killed father?" she asked.

"Yes," Thomas sighed still coming to terms with what had happened to their father. "He questioned me for hours on end, torturing my mind with some kind of magic or something. He kept asking me where I got my powers. I didn't know what he meant. It didn't make any sense; I don't have any special powers. I was so worried about you because he kept telling me he would kill the rest of my family if I didn't tell him. Finally, when the storm came, something distracted him and he stopped interrogating me. I tried to escape when they weren't watching, but they knocked me out and I just woke up when I fell on the floor down here. How are you doing, did they try to get anything out of you as well?"

"No," Kirsten said. "They just put a bag over my head

and tossed me in here. I've been trying to stay out of their way. The soldiers will beat you just for talking too loudly."

"I don't know who they are or what they want with us, but I'm glad they didn't do to you what they did to me," Thomas said. "They must think I'm someone else."

"Did you happen to overhear anything about where they're taking us?" Kirsten asked.

"There was some kind of two-way mirror or something that Thargon used to talk with someone. Unless he was just talking to his own reflection, which he very well could have been, because he's clearly a psychopath."

Kirsten chuckled a little at Thomas' description.

"I didn't understand most of what he was saying because he's been speaking a strange language that I don't recognize. It could be the soldier's language, because Thargon speaks Landish with the person in the mirror but addresses the soldiers in the foreign language. When he was talking to the mirror, I heard him mention something about Dark Water Bay, I'm not sure if that's a real place, but it could be where they're taking us?"

"I've heard that name before," Maija said, chiming in on their conversation.

"What does it mean?" Kirsten asked her.

"I remember my grandfather saying something about it being in the east. I can't remember exactly, but I think he said it was along the Marauder Sea's shoreline."

"Who is that with you?" Thomas asked.

Kirsten answered, "Her name is Maija; she was working the competition when the attack started."

"Thanks for the information," he said. "And it's nice to meet you."

"Thank your sister," Maija replied.

"I helped her out a bit," Kirsten said.

"A lot, a bit," Maija said. "I probably would've died had you not helped me."

"I wonder what they're going to do with us when we get there?" Kirsten asked. Neither of them responded to her question because they didn't know what awaited them. *One day at a time*, Kirsten reminded herself.

For the next week, the three whispered back and forth. They kept a positive attitude considering the grave situation. One day, a soldier brought down several more prisoners and jammed them into the cells with others. The three were not the only ones whispering to each other. Soon there was conversation flowing among all of the people in the hull. They quickly found out who was in each cell and how they were faring. Many people were beat up, but didn't have life-threatening injuries. Those who weren't going to make it had already passed.

Kirsten and Maija had torn up part of their burlap sacks, tying them off to create smaller bags. They filled them with the rotting grain that was in their cell and passed it through the bars to those who needed it the most. Several people talked of escaping the cells, but their conversations didn't last long before someone would dismiss the idea. Once a man had attempted to tackle a soldier who was putting a prisoner into his cell. The soldier was much stronger and apprehended the starving man. The soldiers took him up to the deck and he didn't return. After that incident, many of the people who had whispered of escape stopped. They were beginning to lose hope that they'd ever get off the ship.

ALMOST TWO WEEKS had passed since they were forced onto the ship when Kirsten had the idea. She was thinking about how the man who had tried to tackle the soldier completely took him by surprise. Had the Westland prisoner been stronger, they might've succeeded. She knew their ship would eventually reach its destination and then the prisoners would be offloaded. When the soldiers came to accompany them off the ship, the prisoners would most likely be taken up as a group and then placed somewhere else. If all of the prisoners took on the soldiers at the same time when they were being brought off the ship, they might be able to take the soldiers by surprise. Kirsten estimated there were now about twice as many prisoners as there were soldiers. If she could convince the rest of the prisoners to follow through with her plan, they would outnumber their enemy two to one.

She shared her idea with Maija, who seemed to think it was about as good an idea as any.

"What do we have to lose?" Maija asked when she heard Kirsten's idea.

Kirsten told Thomas next, who asked her more in-depth questions about timing and the signals that they would need to communicate with one another. Kirsten was feeling better about the plan already and now had something to look forward to.

The three of them began spreading the idea around to the other prisoners. It took a few days for each prisoner to get a clear idea of what he or she would be doing and how to do it. When they got the point across, it seemed like they had a good showing of support. All they had to do now was wait for the day they all would be transferred. Once they were above deck, the signal would be given and their rebellion would begin.

Nearly three weeks had passed since they'd been abducted when one evening the ship came to a complete halt. Maija and Kirsten woke to the sudden lack of movement. The prisoners began to whisper, asking each other what was happening. Kirsten knew this was it; they were going to be transferred off the ship. She listened intently, but no noises came from the deck above. Nobody came down to escort them up to the deck. Confusion and worry began to sink in.

"What's happening?" she asked Maija.

Maija shrugged, just as confused as Kirsten.

A loud crash made them jump. The ship shook with tremendous force, so much so that they thought it was going to fall apart. Kirsten heard footsteps cross the deck, march down the stairs, and kick the door open violently. The light of the moon shone down through the opening and a dark outline of a person stood backlit in the doorway.

Kirsten held her breath in anticipation. This wasn't how she'd imagined the transport to go. Usually several soldiers had come to take them away one at a time.

The man held out his arm and swiftly flicked his wrist. All of the locks on the cells simultaneously sprung open with a loud 'CLICK.' Those who weren't already standing at their cell doors, ready to exit, were forced to rise and stand at the ready by some mysterious energy. Kirsten tried to move, but she was frozen in place. The more she struggled against the invisible force, the more strenuously it required her to obey its will. She panicked, unable to move a single muscle voluntarily.

What the hell is happening to me, she thought. How was she going to lead a rebellion against their enemy if she couldn't even lift her finger?

All of a sudden, her arms shot outward and her hands

pressed together like she was going to be shackled. All of the other prisoners experienced the same forcefulness and their hands collectively made a loud clap that echoed through the otherwise silent hull. The dark, shadowy figure in the stairwell commanded them. In an ominous voice, he said, "Come." He walked back up the stairs to the top deck.

Single file the prisoners were forced to march out of their cells and up onto the deck. None of them could do anything to stop their bodies from marching. They were clearly under some kind of spell. When they emerged from the hull, the silver moonlight blinded them. They had been in darkness for so long that their eyes weren't used to the light. Kirsten found she could do nothing, however, to cover her eyes from the bright light of the moon. Her eyes swelled and tears began to run down her face. Suddenly, all she wanted was to put something over her eyes, or close them, but the powerful spell she was under wouldn't allow it. She thought the pain from the bright light would never go away.

The men and women held prisoner stiffly lined the ship's deck. Kirsten didn't know how long they'd been standing, but it was long enough for her eyes to adjust to the light. She couldn't turn her head, but she could use her peripheral vision to see what was around them. To her right was open water. It looked unnaturally darker than she remembered. In front of her was the bow of the ship. The men who had once commanded it were nowhere to be seen. On her left, was a shoreline with dark cliffs rising from the edge of the rocky beach. It looked like the ship was docked at a large open gate at the base of the cliff walls. Beyond the gate stood some kind of castle or fortress. She couldn't see much of it, but she could see dark stone spires climbing up from behind the cliff walls.

Kirsten strained her eyes to see who had come out of the gate and was walking up the dock toward the ship, but she couldn't tell who it was. She heard the person come aboard the ship. Walking to the front of the ship and standing in front of them, Kirsten recognized it to be the same person who had descended the stairs and placed them under this spell. Her heart raced; yet she still couldn't move a muscle. The mysterious man was accompanied by several other soldiers who stood just at the head of the line of frozen prisoners. The spell-caster looked at them and for the first time Kirsten saw his face.

The lines on his face told her he was older, but his strong jawline and proud cheekbones made him handsome. He wore his tawny brown hair slicked back across his head. His eyebrows, the same shade as his hair, came to a point. He had a short, well-groomed beard. Around his shoulders he wore a black cloak clasped together by an emerald jewel high on his breast. He was of average height for a man, and well dressed. Around his neck he wore a thin silver chain with several crystal-like stones attached at the base. He carried no weapons on his belt. He spoke for the first time directly to Thargon, who stood at his side.

"Which one is he?" the man asked in refined Landish tones.

Thargon snorted and walked down the line of prisoners. He stopped next to Kirsten and said, "This one." Kirsten could not move her head to see who he was referring to.

The cloaked man stood at Thargon's side silently looking at the person behind Kirsten. He said slowly at first, "You are correct. He is not the one I am looking for, but he does share the boy's blood. I thought their family would produce more dominant specimens. This one is rather thin and shorter than I would expect."

"I questioned him thoroughly, invading his mind for hours at a time. He does not possess the gift," Thargon said.

"Were there any others?" the man asked.

"There was one other, but another hostile sorcerer showed up and I was unable to defeat him," the beast said.

"I have a good idea who that was," the man said, clearly irritated. "They will no doubt be searching for this boy. You did not totally fail me, Thargon. We can still use this one to our advantage."

Without another word, the man made a flick of his wrist and the whole line of prisoners began to move. They were forced down the dock and across to the shoreline. Once on the beach, they were led through the gates and into a narrow stone entryway. After passing through the entrance, buildings rose up on either side of them. Kirsten couldn't lift her head to see how tall the buildings stood above. The line of people was forced into a large courtyard.

The marching stopped and the dozens of Westland, Rolloan and Southland prisoners were put into a new row of cells that faced the courtyard. As the cell doors closed behind them, the spell was lifted and they were given back their own bodily control. Kirsten was placed in a cell with Maija again. She looked out of the barred cell door at the courtyard in front of them. At the far end of the courtyard, the cliff walls that surrounded the fortress rose high into the sky. To the right of their cell, Kirsten could see a large pit at the end of the courtyard. Kirsten called out her brother's name, hoping he was still nearby. He responded from the next cell over. Kirsten sighed, as she knew they were going to be stuck here for a long time.

CHAPTER

SIX

THE TRAIL TO BROOKSIDE

nders awoke to the trickling tune of shallow tidal waves sifting through porous sand. The sun's heat bore down on his face as he lay on his back. With his body half beached in the sand and half adrift in the shallow surf, he ached like he'd been beaten with a bullwhip. The scent of the salty ocean filled his nostrils as he gasped for air and coughed up water, forcing him to roll onto his side. Finally able to breathe easily again, Anders could hear birds singing in the trees on the hillside above him. A slow breeze swept over the ground, chilling his wet body.

With a tired heave, he rolled himself onto his back and felt the slightly warmer temperature of the salty water flow up and down along his waistline. All he wanted to do was lay still and ignore his problems, letting them wash away and be carried out with the ebbing tide. He wished in that moment for his old, uncomplicated life, the comfortable life before Ivan appeared at the family farm.

With his legs slightly suspended in the waves and his back nestled in the soft sand, Anders let go of his grasp on

79

reality. His mind wandered freely. Becoming in tune with his surroundings, he felt as though his mind was reaching out and communicating with the soul of the world, a resonating energy passing harmoniously between his body and his surroundings.

Like a crack of thunder, a voice sucked him back to reality, *Anders, Anders! Are you okay?* Angry to have been ripped out of his blissful state, Anders sat up and looked around for whoever had disturbed him. The voice called to him again, *Anders, I can sense you, are you okay?* The shock of the sudden voice, combined with dehydration and stress, made him cringe as the slow throb of a headache crept its way into his consciousness. Anders squinted to shade his eyes with his bushy brown eyebrows and scanned his immediate surroundings for whoever was calling to him, but he couldn't see anyone. He was confused.

Am I going insane? he thought to himself.

Anders, it's Ivan. You can't see me right now, but I know you can hear me. Are you all right? the voice said.

Anders responded out loud, "How are you doing that? I can't see you. Where are you?"

It's something sorcerers can do. I'm extending my mind into yours, so we can talk to each other. I've been searching the area for hours with my senses but haven't been able to feel your thoughts until just recently. All of a sudden you showed up like a beacon, Ivan's voice said.

"How is that possible?" Anders asked, his headache growing from a slow throb to a pulsating stab of pain.

It's a part of the magic I can still control. I need to know where you are so we can find you. For some reason I cannot sense your location, I can only feel the presence of your mind. Our ship was destroyed and most of the crew was lost. I was able to reach Max; he's with me now. Others survived as well, but they're scattered along the shoreline and their thoughts are too distant for me to sense clearly, Ivan said.

Anders rose to his feet stiffly. Still somewhat groggy, Anders examined his surroundings and attempted to get his bearings. Behind him stood a large hill covered in thick trees and vegetation. To his right down the coastline a broad section of cliffs jutted up, protruding skyward from the water's edge. As he looked at them, he began to focus on the sharp outline of the rock formation.

"Ouch," he said aloud, wincing at the sudden intrusion of Ivan's voice as it sounded in his mind once more.

I know where you are. We'll meet you at the top of those cliffs down the beach from you.

"You have to stop that," Anders said out loud, knowing Ivan was still reading his thoughts. "I have a splitting headache and every time your voice comes into my head it sounds like a thousand bells are ringing all at once."

Sorry, Ivan said, *but it's the only way I can communicate with you right now. Can you meet us at the top of those cliffs?*

Anders responded, this time in his thoughts, *My body hurts something awful, but I think I can make it there all right.*

Good, Ivan said. *It will take Max and me about a half hour to get there. We are on the opposite side of the cliffs from you.*

Anders felt the pain in his head subside slightly as Ivan left his mind. Feeling stiff as a board, he half-heartedly attempted to stretch out his limbs before starting for the cliffs.

It took him longer than expected to walk through the thick vegetation carpeting the slope. Scrambling along the wet hillside covered with moss and ferns, Anders zigzagged uphill along the cliffs. The slope steepened as he climbed higher. Out of breath and weak in the knees, he finally made it to the top to see Ivan and Max waiting patiently. The two were sitting on a downed tree just upslope of the cliff's edge. Anders was slightly irritated by how comfortable they looked.

Max waved him over to join them. He sat down heavily on the log, tired from his climb. Not saying a word, Anders looked out over the vast view of the ocean. The peaceful expanse from atop the cliff was spectacular. It cleared Anders of his irritation with Max and Ivan. The marvelous view was, however, an illusion of what had been and not what is. He sat for a moment in silence absorbing the singular moment of beauty before he would have to face the harsh reality of their predicament.

"What do we do now?" Anders asked Ivan, giving him a look as if he were truly lost.

"The only thing we can," Ivan said seriously.

"And what exactly is that?" Anders was frustrated with the situation.

"We must find Red and any others that may have survived the wreck. Then we will continue our journey on foot." Ivan got up off the log without looking at Anders or Max and began to walk down the hill from the top of the cliff.

"Well that sounds about right," Anders said to Max.

"What do you mean," Max asked.

"I don't know what's real anymore," he continued. "Everything I thought I knew about my life has just been flipped upside down. An evil beast riding a giant hound attacks my home, murders my uncle, and kidnaps the only family I have left. Now this guy shows up blasting energy from his hands and he can even read my thoughts. Everything is all screwed up; it's like a nightmare I can't escape.

What's next, dragons and demons?" Anders said in a half-crazed voice.

"Be real, dragons haven't been seen in the five kingdoms of Kartania since long before The War of the Magicians. They either went extinct or are too busy sleeping in caves to be bothered with the problems of humans," Max said. "I know it's been hard to face the reality of all this, but for now we need to accept what happened and move on. Pretending it never happened or running away from it won't bring back the people who were taken from us. I don't know if my brother is dead or alive, but I'm going to assume he's alive and I'm not going to give up until I free him from the soldiers who took him." Max was on his feet breathing heavily after letting his emotions rile him.

"You're right," Anders said, pushing his tired body off the fallen tree. "I need to accept that what happened is real and I need to do whatever it takes to find my cousins."

Anders and Max caught up with Ivan on the beach after swiftly scaling down from the cliff with a rejuvenated sense of determination.

"Do you know where Red is?" Anders asked, once they were walking alongside him. He assumed Ivan could sense Red using his mind.

"He's far away, so it's hard to tell the exact location," he pointed in the direction they were walking. "All I know for sure is that he's alive."

"Where will we go after we locate the remaining survivors of the wreck?" Max asked Ivan.

"We need to reach a spot where we can send a message to the Rollo Islanders before their warships sail past us. If we can send a messenger to intercept them with a planned location for a rendezvous, we can join forces and continue our search for Thargon's ships."

"Brookside is only a few day's walk from here," Max said. "I have family there who could help us."

"Yes," Ivan said as if he were remembering something he had forgotten. "There is a man there who goes by the name of Solomon, do you know of him?"

"Of course I know Solomon!" Max exclaimed. "He's a dear friend of mine. Why do you ask?"

"He has a great wealth of knowledge and may be able to answer a few of my questions," Ivan said.

"Are you sure we're talking about the same Solomon?" Max asked.

"I know he is odd at times, but he's been around for a long time and has helped me before," Ivan said, confident that the old man would be of assistance to their quest.

"Sounds like a plan," Anders said.

Together the three of them walked along the coastline searching for Red and any other survivors. Anders squinted to see a couple figures far off in the distance, moving along the beach. "Look!" he remarked pointing down the sandy shoreline in front of them.

"Yes, that would be our bull-headed captain," Ivan said seeing Red's silhouette in the distance. "And there are two others with him. Part of his crew."

"That's creepy how you can do that with nothing else but your mind," Max said.

"Helpful, not creepy," Ivan corrected him. "I'm not nearly as formidable as I once was. At one time in my life I could sense people from much greater distances, among other things. But those days are farther from me than I like to think."

"Creepy, but amazing," Max said, and Ivan gave him a look.

Anders felt better knowing that Ivan could tell whether

the people far down the beach were friends or foes, although he was still unsure how he felt about the idea of having a sorcerer around. He wondered what had convinced his uncle that Ivan was dead; because he'd always told Anders since he was little that magic no longer existed in the world.

Did that mean Ivan was the last magician? No, because Thargon had used magic in Grandwood. Thinking about it made his head hurt, so he dismissed the thought to another time when he could devote more energy to it.

Red, along with two other men, had been surprised to see all three of them alive and well.

"The gods were good to let us live," Red said, grabbing each one of them and embracing them with a soggy hug. "We drifted ashore late last night. After the ship went down, I found a piece of wreckage and was able to grab these two lads before they drowned," Red said pointing to the men. "We have been up and down the shore, but didn't see any sign of other survivors, until you."

"It was a long, cold night. We were all lucky to survive it," Ivan said trying to guilt Red a bit for sailing them into the storm. Red forced a cough, realizing Ivan's implication. "We need to send word to your people before they sail past us where it will be harder to join them," Ivan added, ending the awkward silence.

"I agree," Red said. "I'm not familiar with this area. Is there a town close by where we can send a messenger bird?" he asked.

Ivan explained their plan to make the multi-day trek to Brookside.

"It's about three or four days from here," Max said. "I traveled to Grandwood on the trail just north of here. Once we bushwhack our way to the trail, the going will be easier than walking through the sand."

"That sounds like as good a plan as any," Red agreed, happy to have the next part of their adventure prepared for him.

"I have heard reports of goblins emerging from caves along the base of the Sharpstone Mountains, near Brookside," Ivan added.

"Goblins? Seriously, you believe in goblins?" Anders asked.

"After what you've seen over the last several days, I'm surprised you don't take my word more seriously," Ivan said glaring icily at Anders.

"He's got a point," Max said.

"Yeah, but come on, goblins are just folklore," Anders said. "They're stories to keep children from wandering out of their beds at night. They don't really exist..." he trailed off into his own thoughts, considering the horrifying possibility of an actual horde of goblins rooting around in the foothills bordering Brookside.

"I have heard stories of them from reliable people," Max said. "I didn't have any trouble on my way over from Brookside, so they may have moved out of the area."

"Either way, we should get a move on if we want to reach Brookside and send word before my people sail past us," Red said.

Anders and the others followed Max as he pulled apart the thick growth of bramble and brush and led them toward the trail that meandered from the Grandwood Mountains to Brookside. Reaching the hard-packed dirt path, Ivan pulled Red aside while the others continued on ahead.

"Listen, and you listen good," Ivan said sternly, gripping Red by the collar of his tattered shirt. "You almost cost all of us our lives back there on that ship. It took me nearly every ounce of magic I possess to ensure the four of us didn't die when Thargon's wind wrecked our ship. My magic is nearly depleted and it will take me several days to regain my strength, so we'd better not run into any goblins because I won't be able to do anything to stop them from slitting our throats while we sleep. I didn't spend a good portion of my life fighting in a war that nearly ended Kartania's existence and travel all this way to be led into a death trap by an inexperienced, eager-to-prove-his-self-worth child! From now on, I'm in charge of this outfit and you'll do as I command. Is that perfectly clear?"

Red furrowed his brow and clenched his jaw. Grumbling, he said, "Yes, sir," and the two of them continued on behind the others.

THE NEXT MORNING Anders watched the sun slowly rise out of the eastern horizon, reflecting a golden hue off the water's edge. Mountain snowmelt fed into the lake where they'd decided to camp. Kneeling, Anders bent down and cupped cold lake water into his hands. Splashing it over his face, he found himself momentarily engulfed by its icy grip. It sent a chill through his body that invigorated him. He thought it might have the same effect on him that caffeine did, pulling him out of the sleepy fog that clouded his mind during the early morning hours.

Anders was alone. He'd awakened early and couldn't fall back asleep. Letting the cold water trickle down his face, he noticed a rustling in some tightly grouped willows to his left. Suddenly alert, he sat still, listening intently. His now-sharp eyes darted around the area as his body remained perfectly still. He was fully awake now, but hoped the noise was a figment of his imagination stemming from his lack of sleep. Slowly reaching his hand to his waist where his knife was holstered, he prepared for the worst. Blade in hand, he turned to face the brush where the noise had originated. A squirrel sprang out and scurried up a tree. Cursing himself for being so on edge, he took several deep breaths and slowed his heart rate. Then he laughed for having been so worried and tucked his blade back into its sheath.

Feeling foolish, he walked back to camp. Ivan, Red, Max and the other two Rollo warriors were now awake and preparing to leave. Anders gathered what few belongings he had: his bow and three arrows, a canteen, a small pouch of coins, and some flint for starting fires. The only other things he possessed were the clothes on his back and the knife holstered to his belt. He'd found the canteen and pouch of coins among the wreckage that washed ashore, but decided to leave some larger items behind. The group was anxious to make good time, so they'd decided to travel light.

"You ready to hump it all day?" Max asked enthusiastically.

Anders looked at him with a slightly confused and embarrassed look, and asked, "Wha... What do you mean by hump it all day?"

"You know," Max said, gesturing to his legs. "Hike across the hills for the whole day. We still have at least two days of humping to get to Brookside. I know my feet will need a good soaking in hot water when we're through with this one. What did you think I meant?" he asked Anders, recognizing the strange look on his face when he'd first asked him the question.

"Oh, nothing," Anders said quickly. "I knew what you were talking about." He raised an eyebrow and nodded at Max, hoping he wouldn't keep digging into it.

The roughneck crew of shipwrecked men walked all day. They crossed countless rolling hills, trekking through green grass and lush trees. They'd been walking for an unusually long time without anyone saying a word, when Max broke the silence.

"Hey, Ivan," he said.

"What?" Ivan replied shortly. Anders could hear the irritation in his voice when answering Max's questions over the last several days.

"Tell me a story about when you were in the war," Max said cheerfully. "How about when you first joined the army, what was that like?"

"I don't feel like talking about that," Ivan replied gruffly. Max's disappointed sigh could be heard nearly a mile away.

"What about how you and Theodor met? You served with him, didn't you?" Ivan glanced back at him as he spoke. "How did you two become friends?" Max continued, hoping Ivan would break and divulge something about his past.

Ivan paused for a moment, struggling to find words. He began to speak, slowly at first, and faster as the story flowed out.

"Theodor, Anders' uncle, and I... were from different towns in Southland. Back in those days, the King's army sent recruiting officers to get young men to sign up and join them. When they came to each town, the recruiters would set up obstacle courses in the town square and hold contests. As one can imagine, each contest was physically demanding and catered toward those who were the strongest and fastest. I won most of the competitions each time they came to my town. Ever since I was old enough to think for myself, I wanted to be soldier. When I became of age, I didn't even blink twice before signing up for the King's army.

"All of the recruits within Southland went to the same training camp. After six weeks of training, the recruits were assigned to divisions. Most people were placed into the infantry or cavalry, as more bodies are needed at the front lines during a war. Numbers were typically what won wars back then.

"Theodor and I were sent to the same camp and were both placed in bunkhouse thirteen, which became our training squad. During our first week of training, it became clear that I was going to be our squad's leader. Theodor, however, needed some encouragement and drive to do what was expected of a new recruit. You see, he was underperforming and didn't take the training very seriously. I was very committed to my role as our squad's leader and began to help Theodor. When you have to rely on each other in a setting like that, you are only as good as your weakest person.

"Theodor told me briefly after meeting that he was forced to join the army by his father, who would strip him of his family rights if he didn't do his part for the war effort. He didn't want to dishonor his family name, so he joined reluctantly.

"Looking back on it now, I was a little harsh with him at first. We spent extra time in the mornings and evenings going through the drills. I helped him find his role in our group and after several weeks his improvements were leaps and bounds above any other person at the training facilities.

We became quite close during those six weeks," Ivan paused for a while, looking up at the sky.

With a long exhale he continued, "Once our squad's training was complete, we were assigned and placed into our new roles. Theodor and I were posted to different divisions and didn't see much of each other for a long time after that."

"I thought you two served together during the war?" Max interrupted.

"We did serve together when the war reached its peak. But after training camp, we both went our separate ways for several years before our paths crossed again," Ivan said succinctly.

Ivan quickened his pace to put some distance between himself and the others and walked in silence, clearly not wanting to say anymore. Anders wondered if there was something Ivan wasn't telling them, and he wanted to know, he deserved to know.

"Please continue," Anders urged Ivan as he jogged to catch up with him.

Anders could tell Ivan didn't want to continue but knew Anders wouldn't let him end where he'd attempted to, so begrudgingly he picked up where he'd left off.

"Theodor was placed in the cavalry as a marksman. He had a special talent with his bow that not many could rival. I was sent off to an officers' training program to further my role as a leader," Ivan stopped at a small stream flowing across the trail. "Red," he hollered at the Rollo warrior who was walking with his men several yards in front of them. "Let's hold up here for a moment," Ivan commanded.

Max and Anders took this opportunity to sit and rest their feet. Ivan stopped and drank from the stream.

"Theodor never talked about his time during The War

of the Magicians," Anders said. "Thank you for talking about it with us. It seems there's a lot about my uncle that I didn't know."

Anders felt Ivan was holding something back and wasn't telling him everything about his uncle's part of the story, but reading the current situation, he knew now was not the time to ask. If he did and wasn't sensible about it, Ivan might clam up and never talk about his uncle with him again. Anders had the over-whelming feeling that Ivan knew things about his family that could help him discover where he came from, perhaps even who his parents were.

"We have about two more hours of daylight; we should consider making camp soon," Red said to the group.

"There's a place coming up where I've camped many times before," Max said.

"We will camp there," Ivan said, speaking as if Max's idea were his own.

Max rolled his eyes and sat next to Anders on the side of the trail. Whispering, he asked, "Did you get the feeling he wasn't telling us the whole story?"

Anders nodded and replied, "He's hiding something all right."

Once they'd set up camp, Anders and the four others set out in search of firewood while Ivan went hunting for their dinner. By the time they returned with armloads of sticks and sizeable broken branches, Ivan was already preparing a small deer he'd killed. Anders noticed that the deer didn't have any arrow wound like he'd seen in the deer he'd hunted. The deer was definitely dead; Ivan had already begun slicing off pieces of meat for their meal.

Anders and the others sorted the wood they'd gathered into piles according to size and diameter.

"The key to preparing a good fire is first to have four

different-sized wood piles ready when you go to light it," Red said as if he were showing them how to build a fire for the first time. "First you need two large handfuls of straw-sized twigs, then a bundle of finger-sized wood. Next, a bundle slightly larger in diameter goes on the fire. And finally, once that's burned and you have your bed of coals, put on your larger logs." He demonstrated by lighting some dry grass and placing the bundles on one at a time as he spoke.

Anders leaned over to Max and whispered, "I'm not a child. I know how to build a fire." They both rolled their eyes and tried to ignore Red's arrogant demonstration.

"Or," Ivan said. "You can do this." He pointed to a log that was not on the fire and whispered to himself. The log burst into flames and he chuckled.

"Not all of us are magicians," Red said angrily.

"Thank the gods for that," Ivan said in response. "That is the last thing this world needs, more sorcerers to mess up what the natural world already provides. And only non-magical people call us magicians; the proper term is sorcerer."

Anders thought it was strange that he had that kind of outlook on magic, seeing as he was someone who could wield it.

"I see the magician has regained his strength," Red said mockingly.

Ivan shot him a deadly glare that made Red turn away from him and continue to put wood on the fire. Ivan went back to preparing the meat for the six of them. Soon all of them had bellies full of fresh venison. They washed it down with the crisp cold water gathered from a nearby creek. Exhausted from the day's travel, they were all sound asleep before long.

The next day they walked across the base of the Sharp-stone Mountain Range. Anders hiked at a distance from the others using the time alone to ponder during their trek. He was angry with Red for not seeing that the storm they sailed into was a trap and Ivan for not stopping it, but mostly he missed his cousins. They were like brother and sister to him. Anders controlled his anger by keeping his thoughts to himself and staying away from the others while he fumed in solitude.

He also used this time to think about Theodor and Ivan's shared history. He wanted to know if Ivan was born with the ability to use magic or if he became magical through some kind of transformative process. Anders could tell there was more to what Ivan told him about his rela-tionship with Theodor and considered asking him about it. Before he did, Anders remembered that Ivan told him there was a time and a place where he would tell Anders every-thing, besides Anders was still irritated with Ivan, so he decided to wait.

Anders found it difficult to trust Ivan because he didn't know much about him, but it did seem as though Ivan was doing everything in his power to help as he had agreed on the ship. Anders found himself realizing that he only really trusted Max, who had never given him any reason not to.

Ivan had them set up camp that night in the center of a long narrow valley. He wanted Anders to accompany him while he hunted for their supper, so Anders agreed and brought along his bow and three arrows. They hadn't been gone long before a thick fog surrounded them. It wafted through the air and blanketed the two so they couldn't see much farther than their immediate surroundings. Ivan told Anders not to worry about getting lost as long as he stayed close to him, because he could sense where camp and the others were.

The setting sun could only be seen as a bright orange circle through the fog. It dropped steadily lower, nearing the horizon. Ivan had killed three rabbits with his mind, snapping their necks as they tried to escape. It was getting dark when he suggested they head back to camp.

Anders bent down to pick up the last dead rabbit. As he scooped it into his hand, he thought he saw a person standing in front of him through the fog. When he looked closer, it was gone. Anders got Ivan's attention by making a 'psst' noise.

"I think I saw someone in the fog just now," he said.

"That's strange," concern flooded Ivan's voice. "I don't sense anyone."

The two of them peered intently toward where Anders had seen something or someone. Then Anders saw the dark shape again, this time moving. It slunk low to the ground and darted from behind a boulder to a nearby tree.

"There!" Anders said, pointing to the shadowy figure as it moved across the misty foreground.

Ivan shot a burst of energy from his hand toward it. Anders saw chunks of bark blow off the tree and knew he'd missed. Anders drew his bow and aimed toward the tree where he'd last seen the figure. He moved closer toward it, arrow nocked and ready to fire. The shadowy figure bolted as soon as Anders drew near. He let his arrow fly; shooting in the direction he saw it fleeing. There was a screech and he knew he'd hit it.

The two of them approached the figure with caution. Anders had struck it right in the side, mid-ribcage. Getting a good look at it, he didn't know what kind of creature it was. He'd never seen anything like it. It had two arms and legs in the same way humans do, but its skin was dark green in color and the creature had wiry gray hairs covering most of its body.

"What is that?" Anders asked curling his upper lip in distaste.

Ivan knelt down beside it and began searching its pockets for anything of value. "It's a goblin," Ivan said. "My guess is it's a scout, probably one of a group of scouts. There will be more, lots more. Goblins travel in hordes and move quickly. We need to go."

He paused at the sound of light footsteps trotting up behind them. Ivan turned and to see another goblin and swiftly shot his hand out, snapping its neck with an accurately placed flow of energy.

"We need to get back to the others," Ivan said. "The only reason we're not already dead is because of this fog."

Together they ran back down to camp. Seeing them come sprinting from out of the fog, the others rose to attention.

"Put that fire out and get your things, we need to leave now!" Ivan commanded, kicking dirt over the flames of their newly made campfire.

"What's going on?" Red asked, confused but helping stomp out the fire because of Ivan's serious tone.

"Goblin scouts," Ivan said quickly. "We killed two of them in the fog. There will be a horde behind them."

"The rumors were true," Max said as he scrambled to find his few belongings.

Within a minute they'd erased any sign of having made a camp. Ivan used his magic to disguise the smoldering coals as a pile of rocks. Together they moved down a shallow gully and ran as fast as they could in the direction of Brookside.

Soon it was pitch black and Ivan figured they had run far enough to stay hidden and out of the way of the goblins behind them. They found a small cave to sleep in for the night. The group went without dinner or the warmth of a fire.

While lying on the cold rocky cave floor, Anders whispered to Ivan, "Why couldn't you sense the goblins when they were so close to us?"

Ivan responded, "They are magical creatures, Anders. Though their magical abilities are primitive, the powers they do possess are very strong. If a goblin is trained, he or she can be a very skilled wielder of magical energy. All goblins can instinctively prevent their minds from ever being discovered by other magical beings. They're truly nasty creatures and are always causing mischief wherever they go. They only possess one weakness; goblins will do almost anything for gold. Did you notice I searched the one you killed? He was carrying gold, but I never feel bad taking gold off a goblin, because you know they did something terrible to get it in the first place. The way I see it, taking it off their dead bodies puts it back into the hands of hard-working people; I'll use it to buy and trade at markets. Do you know what those goblins would've done if they had captured us?"

Anders shook his head.

"If those goblins had gotten ahold of us, they would've tortured us for fun, then killed us and taken anything of value for themselves. It was lucky that fog hid our presence, otherwise we would find ourselves in much different circumstances."

Anders shuddered at the thought of being tortured by one of those nasty creatures. The world outside Grandwood was all very new to him and he was just trying to get through it to save his cousins.

"Get some rest. We'll need our strength for the last leg of our journey tomorrow," Ivan said rolling onto his side and closing his eyes.

The following morning, the tired group filed one-by-one out of the cave. The six of them walked low staying below the skyline so they wouldn't be seen by any goblins that may be wandering nearby.

"They'll be on the lookout for whoever killed their two scouts," Ivan said to the group before leaving the cave. "So we'd better stay low and stick to the gullies."

By noon they had made it a good way across the base of the mountains west of Brookside. Looking down into the valley below, Max was the first to spot the small town.

"We should be safe to walk on the road now that we're closer to Brookside," Max said. "We have patrols who keep the outskirts of town safe from bandits and other nasty things."

They found the road that led to town and stuck to it for the rest of the day. They passed several small farms and people riding in wagons full of early-season harvested goods as they came into town. At the gate they stated their names and business to the guards, who let them in.

"I'm tired. Take us to an inn where we can get a good meal and hot bath," Ivan said to Max upon entering the town. "We'll attempt to send word to the Rollo warships and find old man Solomon tomorrow."

Max nodded and took them to the Brookside Inn where they devoured a warm meal and scrubbed the journey's dirt and bad luck off in a hot bath.

SEVEN

SOLOMON THE WISE

Anders and Max nestled up at the pub on the main floor of the Brookside Inn and ordered a couple of pints. The frothy brew was a refreshing delicacy they hadn't had since before the Grandwood Games. The only indulgence they'd had since leaving Grandwood was an occasional sip of mead with Red's crew back on the ship, but that was hardly comparable to the luxury of a full mug of brew.

Anders took a sip of his brew and asked, "So who is this old wise man we're going to see tomorrow?"

"He's been around these parts for as long as anyone can remember. Some say he's a sorcerer using magic sparingly to keep himself alive. I think that's a bunch of hooey, though. He lives in the hollow of an old oak tree just outside town. My folks used to tell me Solomon would hang out in this pub and tell strange stories. He got a reputation for being a bit loony; no one takes his tales seriously. I felt bad for him because he stopped coming here when I was little so I used to go keep him company, letting him entertain me with his wild stories. He likes to chitchat. If you let him, he'll talk your ear off," Max said and sipped the frothy foam layer from his mug.

"And Ivan thinks he can help us to track down Thargon?" Anders said it more as a statement than a question. Slugging down the rest of his brew, he pulled the mug from his lips, slammed it on the bar top and said with a smile, "I think I'll have another."

Max gulped down the last of his mug to keep up with Anders. With an audible belch, Max said, "I could do with a second as well."

Soon the two had downed six pints between the two of them and were feeling in high spirits.

"We should probably get to our rooms before we aren't able to wake up with the others. Ivan wouldn't be happy with us if we weren't able to make the walk to Solomon's," Anders said, rising from his seat.

"Yeah, you're probably right," Max replied, stumbling a bit on his way off the stool. "Wow," he said, catching himself on the bar. "Either that was a strong batch or I haven't had a decent drink for far too long."

The following morning Anders woke before dawn, the streets below their small room at the Brookside Inn lay silent as the town slumbered. The early morning sky was at its blackest just before sunrise. A thin layer of frost had formed around the window in their room. Ivan was already up and adding kindling to the wood stove. Anders stayed in bed half asleep until he heard the teapot whistling.

Pulling the covers off the bed and forcing himself up right, Anders grumbled, "Tea ready yet?"

Ivan extended his arm out and handed a hot mug to Anders who continued to slouch on the edge of his bed.

"Thanks," he said and wrapped his hands around the warmth of the mug. The water spread a comforting sensation to the rest of his body as he sipped the hot tea. "Are we going to Solomon's place soon?" he asked once the caffeine had begun to take effect.

"We leave in ten minutes, so you'd better get your boots on," Ivan answered. He walked over to Max, who was still asleep in his bed and shook him by the foot, saying loudly, "You hear that boy? We leave in ten minutes."

Max groaned, rolled over to face the wall, and pulled the wool blankets over his head. "Five more minutes," he said in a muffled voice.

"We will leave without you," Ivan said and walked back over to the stove.

"We should probably get the Rollos up if they're coming with us," Anders said, stuffing his feet into his boots.

"Red and his two men have another important task to complete today," Ivan said. "They need to send word to their people's ships to let them know what happened to us. Hopefully the warriors haven't already passed here or we'll have some catching up to do."

With one minute to spare, Max rolled out of bed fully clothed and poured a mug of hot tea, "Ready," he said, burning his mouth on the hot water and trying to shake the heat off his tongue.

Together the three walked out of the inn. Max lagged behind sipping his tea, blowing gently across the surface before bringing the rim to his lips for more of the caffeinated drink. The sun had risen enough so they could see Brookside in the early morning light. Anders was glad to be back in a community again, even though he'd never been to this town before. There was something familiar about the place that brought him comfort.

Max talked as they walked through streets lined with

small houses and businesses. Anders discovered Brookside's namesake when they reached a brook flowing along the edge of town. The thatched roofs faded away behind them through the trees as they walked away from town. Max seemed happy to be back in his hometown, a new spring in his step as they walked along the lightly worn path.

"How far into the wood does this old man live?" Anders asked, looking intently at their surroundings and remembering the goblins they'd seen on the other side of town the previous day.

"Not much farther if I remember correctly," Max said. "Just over this next hill."

As the three rounded the top of the hill, Anders saw a small opening in the forest floor. At the bottom of the hill, on the edge of the opening, protruding from a large oak tree was a thatched awning. Wood smoke piped out from a broken branch serving as a chimney of the wise man's tree house. A beam of sunlight brought a glow to the grass surrounding the front door at the base of the tree.

"There it is," Max said as they looked down on the cabin.

"It looks cozy," Anders said, impressed with the way it was built nicely into the large tree.

"Come on," Ivan said. "We haven't got all day." He was the first to keep on walking down to the home.

"Is he expecting us?" Anders asked when they drew close to the front door.

"I don't see how he would know of our visit? Last time I was here, he told me that I was welcome back at any time, and meant it," Max said. "He doesn't get a lot of company out here. A friendly face is always welcomed at Solomon's."

Ivan reached out and rapped on the wooden door with his fist. Anders heard the shuffling of footsteps and the mumbling of an old man as he scuttled over to open the door. The knob turned and the door opened with a squeaky swing inward. Standing there was a short, bearded man, almost dwarf-like in stature. His long white hair was nappy and dreaded from years of not being groomed. The different length clumps of hair poked out in all directions from under his pointy hat. Tattered wool cloths and his felt vest tied the humble hermit together. Anders smiled widely seeing the strange-looking man.

"Not at all what I was expecting," he whispered to Max.

Solomon squinted at them through half-moon spectacles. Upon realizing who was standing on his doorstep, his white eyebrows rose high on his brow and he cracked a large smile.

"Ahhh," he laughed. "Max, my boy, alas you have returned, and with friends as well I see. And let me get a good look at you. Oh, I remember you as well," he said looking at Ivan. "But I don't believe we have met before," he said looking at Anders.

Anders introduced himself and stuck his hand out to greet the man.

Solomon put his arms up and motioned for him to come in for a hug, saying, "Shaking hands is for making deals; friends hug."

Anders embraced the short man with a hug.

"Come in, come in! Excuse the mess, I haven't had company in a long time," he said ushering them inside.

The three of them crammed into the cluttered home. Many piles of books were stacked almost to the ceiling and scrolls of parchment lay unorganized in heaps on the floor. Anders saw a table thick with maps layering its top, places he'd never heard of or seen before. The maps had strange markings drawn on them, coating the original pictures with the dark ink drawings.

"Oh, excuse me and my clutter. Please make yourselves at home," he said brushing books off some chairs. "Don't mind the mess," he said to Anders and pointed to the freshly exposed upholstery and nodded. "Go on, sit, sit."

Anders sat down where Solomon directed him, "Ouch!" Anders exclaimed and jumped up. He nearly whacked his head on the cabin's center beam as he leapt out of the chair. Rubbing the sore spot on his rump, Anders looked down to see two small creatures covered with sharp, needle-like spikes skitter off the seat. Their little legs carried their horned bodies across the floor and behind a pile of parchment stacked near a desk.

"Oh, there you little ones are," the old hermit said. "I have been looking for you two for three days. I thought they were out on a walkabout," he said to his guests.

"What are they?" Anders asked, rubbing his tender bottom.

"Those are Lumbapi Razor-Backed lizards," the old man said. "They are quite rare. I found them in the woods. I suspect a rotten-hearted tradesman had them. Probably dumped them out here when he realized how hard they are to care for. You see, the thing is, once you gain their trust, they basically take care of themselves. Come on out my dears," he said bending down and placing his hand flat on the floor, letting them crawl up his arm and onto his shoulders.

Anders' jaw dropped in astonishment upon seeing the creatures more closely. "They are quite cute, aren't they," he said, forgiving them at once.

"Yes they are, and magical creatures as well. This purple one is Ulgna, and that green one is Rufus," Solomon said pointing to them one at a time. He placed them back down by the desk and they scurried off. "Well now, what is it that brought you out here to my quiet home?" he asked. "I can tell from the looks on your faces that you're on some kind of mission, unless I'm mistaken, and you've traveled all this way just to have a chat with me?"

The silence that followed made the room feel a tad uncomfortable as Solomon looked around at the expressions on their faces. Anders felt uncomfortable explaining what had happened during the last week. He was still mourning the death of his dear uncle and thought it wasn't his place to tell such details of his life, no matter how decent Solomon seemed.

"Okay, Sol," Max started talking. "There was this competition that I went to in Grandwood... You know the one, right?"

Solomon nodded his head, but Ivan interrupted Max before he could continue, "Thargon attacked Grandwood last week with a fleet of ships at his command. He was looking for something of great value to him and his master. It led him to Anders' uncle's place. He killed Theodor, Anders' uncle, over it, right in front of Theodor's own children."

Solomon gasped at the wickedness of Thargon's wrath.

"Despite my efforts to save Theodor from this fate, I was unable to stop it. By the time I arrived, Thargon had already attacked. I engaged him and was able to save these two," he pointed at Anders and Max. "Thargon and his men retreated, thinking they had captured what they had come for. They took many people who were in Grandwood at the time of the attack as prisoners. We pursued his ships with the help of the Rollo Island warriors, but a storm and some powerful magic left us ship-wrecked."

So that's what he was doing back on the ship, Anders thought to himself. *He must have been attempting to counter the massive gust of wind that sent us all overboard.*

"The Rollo Islanders sent for the rest of their naval forces and are currently crossing the ocean. Red, our Rollo companion, is sending word to his people informing them of what has happened to us. When Thargon's master discovers that he failed to retrieve what he was sent to capture, they will return to Westland and kill countless people to find it. We must find out where Thargon is going, so we can prevent him from causing further destruction. Do you have any knowledge of where he's going?"

Anders noticed Solomon eyeing him as Ivan spoke, making him feel a little uncomfortable.

"I haven't heard talk of Thargon for many years. I was under the impression he'd been defeated near the end of The War of the Magicians and had departed from this world," Solomon said, stroking his fingers through his nappy beard as he looked to be searching carefully for his next words. "Yes, you were wise to come to me before you got too tangled in this web," Solomon said in a much more serious tone.

Max gave Anders a worried look as they realized the situation they found themselves in was something much bigger than they had anticipated.

"I am aware that you, Ivan, are well versed in the past of your enemy, but from the look these two just gave each other, they are less well informed," Solomon said to Ivan.

"I was trying to keep them on a need-to-know basis. I thought it would be easier for them if they didn't know what they could possibly be getting into," Ivan said as if he were trying to protect them. "I'm more than happy to inform them about Thargon's past, since it appears they now do need to know," Solomon said as if he were scolding Ivan. "But first, I will need to put a fresh pot of water on and pack my pipe," Solomon said pulling a pipe from his pocket and searching for his teakettle.

A THICK HAZE began to fill Solomon's cabin as he puffed and pondered how to begin the history lesson. Once he'd smoked most of his pipe bowl and had a hot cup of tea in his hand, he sat down on a wooden chair ready to begin.

"To give this story proper justice I must first give you a brief history of magic; then I will tell you how Merglan came to be so powerful," Solomon began.

"He's the one in charge of Thargon, right?" asked Max.

Solomon nodded and then opened his mouth to begin.

Ivan interrupted, saying, "Is that really pertinent to what we're dealing with right now?"

"Yes, it is," Solomon said matter-of-factly.

"This is a waste of time," Ivan muttered to himself under his breath.

"I heard that, boy," Solomon said glaring at Ivan. "Now where were we...? Ah yes, Merglan. To understand his power you must first understand that there is universal energy that flows within and through all living things," he began again. "It's what binds us with the world around us. You cannot see it, but it's there, and if you're lucky, maybe one day you'll feel it. This energetic force can be used to do inexplicable and unimaginable things. What I'm talking about is what we humans refer to as magic," he said opening his hands as if he was about to cast a spell.

"No human, elf, or any other species of this world has ever been able to harness this energy on their own. Except for dragons, that is. Anyone or thing that has ever been able to use magic was given the gift by dragons alone. Many people have devoted their lives searching for a way to conjure up this ability without the help of dragons, but not once has it been done."

"I thought it was something you were born with. Isn't it passed on by genetics?" Anders asked.

"That is what many people believed; however, that's simply not the way it works. Why that is has boggled the minds of those who've studied it throughout each of the five civilized nations of Kartania, Westland, Eastland, Southland, Mount Orena, and the Everlight Kingdom, for as long as anyone can remember. The only way to gain the ability and control the energy within all things is if a dragon gifts it to you."

"Hold on," Max said stopping Solomon. "Dragons are wild beasts that only bring death and destruction. Rarely do they venture far enough south to be seen. How does anyone get close enough to a dragon to let it give you something?"

"Yeah, come on, dragons aren't exactly known for being friendly," Anders added. "This all seems a bit suspect to me. Dragons are best known for devouring humans and anything else they see as a quick meal. Besides, there hasn't been a dragon in Westland since they destroyed the royal castle along with everyone inside that used to sit atop Highborn Bay. That was over seven hundred years ago."

Ivan chuckled to himself quietly as pipe smoke expelled from his mouth.

"What are you laughing about?" Max asked, looking over at him. "I thought you said this was a huge waste of time."

"There are many things you spring chickens do not know," Ivan said with a smirk.

"Believe it or not," Solomon continued, "although the dragons of Nagano are wild creatures, they have an exceptionally long life span. Mind you, when they form a bond, it can only be broken by death. Dragons have keen senses that can see a creature's deepest truths. When a dragon connects with you on that level, something unexplainable happens."

"So you're telling me, anyone who can wield magic has befriended a dragon, including Merglan, Thargon, and Ivan?" Anders said, turning to face Ivan.

"In a sense," Solomon said.

"What does that mean?" Max said, confused.

"Ivan and Merglan were fortunate enough to form bonds with dragons, yes. Thargon, however, was not."

"Then how come he used magic during the attack?" Max protested. "That contradicts everything you just told us!"

"It is a mystery indeed," Solomon said, puffing on his pipe. "Merglan is the most powerful sorcerer this world has ever seen. In bringing Thargon back into this world, he must've figured out a way to transfer some of his abilities to Thargon. Since you have survived Thargon's attack, it's safe to assume he doesn't possess the same skills as his master. If he had, none of you would be here today," Solomon said, raising his bushy eyebrows for dramatic effect.

"I didn't want to believe it until I heard it from someone else," Ivan said. "We would all be much better off if he had somehow found a dragon evil enough to give him the gift."

"If Merglan has figured out how to give magic to anyone he desires, he could easily and swiftly destroy anyone or anything that opposes him," Solomon said gravely.

For the next hour, Ivan and Solomon debated what this could mean for the fate of humanity.

"At any rate, that is how one acquires the gift of magic," Solomon said finally, turning his attention back to Max and Anders, who had been playing with Ulgna and Rufus, the two lizards, while Ivan and Solomon quarreled.

"Come on, playtime is over. Let's continue the history lesson," Solomon said. "Where were we before I went off on that tangent?"

"You were about to tell us about Merglan," Anders said, gently setting Ulgna down and watching her scamper off across the floor.

"Ah yes, that's right. The tale of Merglan and how he came to power has been told many ways and in different forms, but the one that I will tell you is the one that is the most accurate.

"Merglan grew up in Kingston, the royal city of Southland. At the time, this was where the king of both Westland and Southland ruled. King Koufen was an honest and just man who ruled both human nations fairly. It was a time of peace and prosperity among all five civilized nations. Without any of the distractions of war, King Koufen was able to spend his time dabbling in other areas. He was particularly fascinated with science and philosophy. The king did not believe in magic, because, as Anders said, dragons hadn't been seen since they destroyed the old kingdom's capital at Highborn Bay. No human had been gifted with magic for hundreds of years. King Koufen thought all things caused by magic could be explained with science.

"Merglan's father was Koufen's alchemist. As a boy, Merglan spent his childhood in the King's castle. For better or worse, Koufen had a son around the same age as Merglan. His name was William. Merglan and William were the best of friends. They played together every day and became very competitive with each other at an early age.

"King Koufen made sure his son had lessons in morality and knew when the boys' little competitions were getting too extreme. Merglan's father, however, was too obsessed with perfecting his work and did not pay close attention to his son. So the son developed a dark and twisted sense of right and wrong, focused on winning. After all, the only praise he received was from his friend, the prince, when Merglan bested him at one of their games.

"One day, Merglan came up with a game to see who could catch the most cats around the castle before lunch. When William returned, he found his friend with a bag full of strangled cats. He was horrified and told Merglan that what he'd done was not okay. Merglan was a clever child and acted remorseful in response to his friend's dramatic reaction. He lied, promising the prince he would never do such a thing again and said he misunderstood the rules of the game. William was innocent and naïve to such a trickster, so he believed Merglan and promised not to tell his father.

"By the time the two were young men, Prince William had made Merglan a squire of sorts. Merglan helped the prince in all things, his favorite duty being William's training to be a leader during times of war. It was during these years that Merglan developed experience in battle strategy and the art of war. Merglan was also being groomed by his father to become William's alchemist when King Koufen stepped down and gave William the throne. Certain aspects of the ancient art drew Merglan's curiosity, like creating a potion that would grant those who took it eternal life, or crystals that could house the spirits of the dead, among other things. Merglan felt alchemy wasn't his true calling and wanted to be a soldier most of all. Death and killing were all the young man truly cared for.

"One day, the prince came back from traveling with a young girl who he desperately wanted to marry. William began ignoring Merglan, preferring to spend his time with the young lady. Having no time to strategize for a war that did not exist, Merglan grew very jealous of the girl. He made several attempts to get rid of her, but was unsuccessful. Each time he tried, either William would get in the way and ruin his timing or he was unable to find the prince's fiancé.

"Fed up with the situation, Merglan left the castle without any explanation of his destination. We now know he went north to find the dragons. Some say he ventured to Nagano, east of the Everlight Kingdom, while others say he went all the way to Northland, a place from which no one had ever returned. No one knows exactly how it happened, but one day he came back to the kingdom with malice in his heart and an unquenchable thirst for power. He killed King Koufen and then went after William and his new wife. The two of them escaped and Merglan couldn't find them. Using his new power, he began conquering as much of Kartania as he could.

"The free races of the five nations banded together, forming alliances among elves, humans, dwarfs, and several dragons. They fought against Merglan for many years. The war was dubbed The War of the Magicians. Merglan never relented in his search for Prince William and his wife. After their initial flight, whispers of their survival were told throughout the kingdoms. Despite the rumors no one knows what happened to the prince and his wife. Some say they went into hiding and bore a child, or perhaps Merglan killed them shortly after fleeing Kingston. Others say they disappeared into Northland and were never seen again. Many believe the last to be what drove him to altogether disappear. Suddenly he vanished and released his grip on the world, bringing the long war to an abrupt end. There are those who believe he's still wandering the vast wilderness of Northland in search of them." Solomon raised his eyebrows and looked down into his empty mug. "My cup has gone dry," he muttered and got up to refill it.

"That was the war you and my uncle fought in," Anders said to Ivan.

Ivan was still standing with his arms crossed and leaning against a wall. He shifted and cleared his throat, saying, "Yes. Those were dark times. Your uncle was brave and helped bring a halt to Merglan's forces."

"Wait. What do you mean Merglan just disappeared?" Max asked.

Solomon rejoined the conversation, "I believe he went mad and sent himself into a deep exile after realizing he'd killed his only friend in the world."

"I too, have a theory about what happened to him," Ivan said. "It is my opinion that Merglan has once again become obsessed with power and world domination. That's why he's suddenly made his presence known. He has found his passion and needs to quench his thirst for it."

"Well, you would probably know more about it than I," Solomon said. "I was just guessing. I wasn't in the War of the Magicians like you were."

"So," Ivan said. "Do you have any idea of where he is now? Where Thargon is heading?"

"There is a place far to the east of here that has begun to draw some inquiries from the elves. Perhaps he has taken up residence in one of the abandoned castles along the Eastland coast," Solomon said.

"I explored parts of Eastland when we first heard of his disappearance. I remember searching several abandoned castles along the coast of the Marauder Sea. Wherever he is, we know he has a small army, perhaps a larger one. But with the entire force of the Rollo Islanders at our side, we should be able to defeat any force he has managed to muster, as long as we act quickly." Ivan straightened his body and thanked Solomon for his counsel. "Come on boys, we need to be getting on our way," he said.

"Take care and don't hesitate to come back anytime," Solomon said as he escorted them out of his tree house.

Anders followed Ivan and Max out the door. Solomon grabbed him by the arm as he passed. Anders looked at the old man, surprised to see his eyes were rolled backward into his head.

Anders was about to call to Max and Ivan for help when Solomon said, "The journey ahead is a dangerous path. Do not follow its every turn, for there is an evil that hunts behind you, but do not stray too far from the path. If you get lost, you will never come back. Follow your heart and your truth will be revealed."

When he was done speaking, his eyes came back to their normal position and he seemed confused as to why he was gripping Anders by the arm. Releasing his grip, he patted the young man on the shoulder and said, "Take care then."

Anders pulled away, giving him a strange look and ran to catch up to the others, unsure if he should tell them what had just happened.

EIGHT

THE WAR OF THE MAGICIANS

Max had led Ivan and Anders nearly half way back to the inn when Anders finally decided he should mention Solomon's cryptic trance and what he'd said to Anders just before leaving the tree house.

"Something strange happened between Solomon and me right as we were leaving," he said to his two companions.

At that, Ivan stopped in his tracks. "What exactly do you mean by strange?"

Looking perplexed, Anders said, "I mean what he did was very odd. As I was walking out the door, he grabbed my arm. When I turned to see what he wanted, his eyes had rolled back into his head and he looked as though he was in some kind of trance or something."

Ivan stepped closer to Anders and earnestly asked, "Did he say anything to you?"

"Yes," Anders replied, concerned at Ivan's serious reaction. "He said something about the path ahead being a dangerous one. That there was an evil hunting me, so that I shouldn't follow every turn because it will find me but not to stray too far from the path or I'll never find it again. Or something like that... What do you think it means?"

Ivan pondered this warning for a moment, then answered, "I have no doubt the evil he is referring to is Merglan. It would be wise for you to try to remember every word of the message and heed its warning."

"What do you mean 'the message?'" Anders asked. "He was just having an episode and talking nonsense, right?"

"I'm afraid not," Ivan said lowering his brow. "Solomon's body was being used to transmit a message to you. Whoever sent it must be trying to warn you. It's not to be taken lightly or ignored."

"Should I be worried? Who would want to send me a message like that?" Anders asked, shaking his head in confusion.

"Don't dwell on who sent it too much; I doubt it came from someone or something that meant you harm," Ivan said, dismissing Anders' concern.

"How do you know that?" Max interjected.

"Why would someone who wanted to do Anders harm go out of his, her or its way to warn him about it?" Ivan responded rhetorically.

"I guess that makes sense," Max said, looking skyward and coming to terms with what Ivan said after giving it a second's thought.

"He said something else just before the message or whatever it was ended," Anders said. "He said, 'Follow your heart and your truth will be revealed.' That doesn't sound much like a threat; more like advice, I guess."

"That's pretty vague," Max said mulling over the words.

Ivan started walking again. "Keep the message fresh in your mind. There's nothing we can do about it now. We need to get back and see what progress Red and the others have made. We have spent too much time talking."

Max shot Anders a look of surprise at Ivan's sudden grumpiness. Anders responded with a silent shrug, delivering his, 'who knows what's up with him' message. The two quickly caught up with Ivan as they followed the trail back to Brookside.

Red and his two men were waiting for them in the pub on the ground floor of the Brookside Inn. They had a round of drinks in hand and were talking loudly.

Joining them at the table, Ivan asked, "Were you able to send word to your people?"

Red nodded while gulping down his brew and added in his gravelly accented voice, "This morning we went to the docks hoping to catch the fishermen before they went out for the day. We began asking if anyone had seen or heard of the Rollo's naval fleet sailing past here. None of the fishermen had ventured out very far from the reef, so they were of little help. Next, we tracked down local merchants who'd just docked their ships. By noon we found the news we were hoping to hear. A captain who'd just sailed from Argon City landed this morning. He had seen the warships being prepped and loaded when he left the Rollo Islands' capital. He told us they were going to leave the following morning. That was three days ago. We didn't have much time to get a carrier falcon with a message. If there aren't any hang-ups, the falcon will intercept them, but they'll still have several days to go before they make it here to the Brookside area. The best option for all of us is to continue on foot to the Statue of Old Kings."

Ivan looked at Red sternly, "Good," he said, seemingly satisfied with Red's decision. "How long will it take for the ships to arrive at the statue?" Ivan asked.

"About two days," Red said. "I saw the location on a map and it doesn't seem too far to walk from here. We'll be able to meet them there with plenty of time to spare."

Ivan shook his head, saying, "The Statue of Old Kings may look close on a map, but we have to cross part of the Bareback Plains. It's the largest grassland area in the world."

"So, you're saying it will take longer then?" Red asked.

Ivan nodded, folded his arms across his chest and said, "To walk there would take twice as long as riding. If we get horses and leave tomorrow morning we will be there in three days. I hope you mentioned in your letter to allow us at least a day or two to meet up if we are not there when they arrive."

"I did just that," Red said with a smile, realizing he hadn't totally messed up their plan. Ivan seemed to relax a bit after hearing this and let his arms drop back down to his sides.

"I know someone who can sell us some horses," Max said cheerful to be able to help. "My family has a herd of horses on the outer edge of town. I haven't talked to them in a while, but I'm sure they would help us."

"Very well," Ivan said. "We will go there in the morning. I'm sure your family will be happy to see you."

Max looked down at his feet and didn't acknowledge the remark.

"You all know how to ride, don't you?" Ivan asked.

Anders and Max nodded their heads, each having plenty of experience on horseback. Red and his men, however, looked at each other and shrugged.

"How hard can it be?" Red said.

Max and Anders burst out laughing. "You'll see," Max said and laughed more.

A bartender with a weathered face walked past their

table. Ivan motioned swiftly with his arm, stopping the man before he passed. To Anders' surprise, Ivan coughed up enough coin to order meals and a round of brews for them all.

When the drinks arrived, Ivan said in a cheerful tone, "Here's to a successful day. We may not have had the best luck on our journey, but we did something... well, mostly right today." He raised his glass and the others clinked their mugs together in salute.

After a hearty meal of steak, eggs, potatoes, and pound cake along with several more brews, the stories began to flow between them. Anders listened as Max bragged about his many travels. Clearly he was proud to have visited so many places at such a young age. He reiterated to Anders that he wasn't one to back down from a tough challenge.

Red told stories of training for battle back home on the Rollo Islands. He and his men boasted about their sailing and naval tactics. When Ivan asked if he'd ever been in any battles other than the attack at Grandwood, Red told him about several smaller skirmishes, none of which last more than a day each.

"Nothing like the days of my father, when they were fighting in The War of the Magicians against the dark navy," Red said, reveling in his father's accomplishments.

Anders decided to chime in, "The only thing my uncle ever said about the war was that those were dark times. Ivan has told me more about him than I ever knew."

"That's not entirely true," Ivan said. "The Theodor you knew was the man he always was. During the war, all he wanted to do was return home and become a farmer. You knew him better than anyone from the war. He was his truest self when he was home at Highborn Bay."

Anders smiled slightly, remembering his childhood

with his uncle. "How old was he when he went off to war?" Anders asked.

Ivan finished his ale and said, "He must have been about your age, I'd wager."

Anders imagined what it would be like going to a training camp and then off to fight a war you didn't know much about other than that you were fighting evil forces the world had never seen before.

"A lot of people lied about their age back then, so they could join the King's army. We were all eager to serve. I tried to do it, but the training officers knew my face too well from recruiting in my hometown for so long. Seeing as how Theodor didn't much want to be there in the first place, I bet he was of age when he joined. Let's see," Ivan said, pushing his jaw to the side and looking up at the ceiling. "That would put him at around eighteen or nineteen."

"You mentioned he was assigned to a cavalry division," Anders said, trying to get Ivan to tell him more about his uncle's time spent in the war.

"Theodor was sent to the cavalry, yes," Ivan said taking a sip of his freshly poured pint.

"And what about you? I forget," Anders asked, remembering full well what Ivan had told him several days ago, but he wanted Ivan to tell him more about their history.

"I was one of several selected to be a part of a special task force. I did not see Theodor for many months after that. The special task force I was assigned to was top secret at the time and I was cut off from all communication with the outside world. We trained rigorously day and night in the Everlight Kingdom."

"You got to train with the elves!" Max exclaimed wild-eyed.

"I hate elves," Red said, gritting his teeth while the other two Rollo warriors scowled at his mention of elves.

"Yes I did, Max." Ivan continued ignoring the Rollo warriors' dissatisfaction. "We were tasked with attempting to bond with dragons. Dragons and elves have coexisted going back to before any human had seen a dragon. The elves had made an alliance with the dragons that young hatchlings would be paired with new recruits in hopes that some of them would form bonds and be gifted magic."

"I always wondered how someone came to possess magic," Red said, looking into his pint to see if any liquid was left.

"It's pretty hard to believe," Max said, still unconvinced that was how it worked.

"How did the elves forge an alliance with some of the dragons?" Anders asked.

"When Merglan had begun conquering nations with his new power, the elder dragons saw what he was doing to his own kind. They did not approve of the way in which he treated his fellow humans. Younger dragons, however, that only knew foul stories of humans and disliked our race, remained indifferent to Merglan's destruction of so much of our history and culture. The dragons eventually decided to align with the elves and those humans who opposed Merglan. With the help of his dragon, Merglan began to turn younger dragons against their elders and started a civil war in Nagano. The dragons referred to this as The Dragon Wars, but we call it The War of the Magicians. The Dragon Wars are not talked about much among our culture, mainly because very few were there to witness them. Only the elves and those of us who were paired with dragons were aware it was going on. After a few others and I bonded with our dragons, we were able to put an end to the civil war in Nagano."

"How did you manage to pull that off?" Max asked, believing all that Ivan was saying was a bald-faced lie.

"A dragon that flies into battle with its partner is much more powerful than a lone dragon," Ivan said as though this was common knowledge.

"What about Theodor? Where was he during all of this?" Anders asked, trying to keep Ivan on track.

Ivan continued, "After the civil war among the dragons ended, our task force was assigned to defend the elves' borders, because Merglan had shifted his focus and attacked their lands while we were off dealing with the dragons."

"You should've let them burn," Red said.

Ivan ignored him, "It was here that I reunited with Theodor. He'd seen many battles at this point and risen through the ranks. We fought boldly along the elven front, unable to drive away Merglan's forces. One day an epic battle took place at the base of the Frozen-Tip Mountains. The enemy had pushed us back into the foothills leading up to the mountains, giving our army the field advantage. The enemy would have to fight uphill, tiring their forces more quickly than ours. Riderless dragons were sent to distract me from my duties of commanding our forces. The infantrymen on foot were our first line of defense, leaving Theodor with his cavalry in command. The enemy fought through them with impressive strength. The ancient elven city has always been protected by the magic woven into the walls surrounding it. If we failed to stop Merglan's army, he'd gain unobstructed access to the kingdom and could begin dismantling that ancient magic protecting the elves. If the elves fell, so would all of the nations," he leaned closer to

Anders for dramatic effect, "dragons, humans, and dwarfs alike."

Ivan paused, leaned back and took a sip of his pint. Then he looked at Anders and said, "We fought hard that day. While I dealt with the dragons, Theodor fought Thargon in single combat, defeating him, but not before Thargon could deliver a terrible blow rendering him unconscious for the remainder of the battle. When our forces were left leaderless, a warrior among them stepped up and led us to victory."

"Let me guess," Max said. "It was you."

Ivan smiled and said, "Anders, it was your father."

Anders' jaw dropped in disbelief. "You knew my father?"

"Yes," Ivan said. "This could be the ale talking, but your father was the finest soldier I ever knew. He was a very brave man, a natural born leader. He knew when to pull out of a fight he would not win, but he also never hesitated in the face of danger. We drove the enemy back and sent them running scared. Even the kurr among them fled in terror."

"What's a kurr?" Anders asked.

"Kurr are part elf, part beast. They are wild creatures and not easily trained. Thargon is a kurr. Merglan has been the only person in history to get a group of them to fight for him," Ivan said.

"How well did you know my father?" Anders asked, switching the subject back to what he really cared about.

"I knew him well," Ivan said. He looked out a window along the wall next to their table and seeing that the sun had gone down and it was dark outside, he said, "We should get some rest; we've got a long day ahead of us tomorrow." He pushed his chair back and rose to his feet. "Meet here at sunrise," he said to Red.

"Yes, sir," Red answered.

Anders wished Ivan had kept talking; he wanted to hear more about his father. He thought it was strange that Ivan mentioned him and then was quick to end the conversation when Anders asked more about his father.

Max and Anders followed Ivan up to their room. Anders lay awake in bed unable to sleep, thinking about all he'd learned that day. Dragons, strange messages from an old man, what a kurr was and his discovery that Ivan had known his father.

Why didn't he tell me sooner? Anders wondered, as he lay awake. The more he found out about Ivan, the more he discovered how little he knew about the strange man.

NINE

MOONLIGHT WALK ON THE BAREBACK PLAINS

At first light, Anders and the others followed Max as he led them toward his family's place just east of Brookside. Before leaving town, they stopped at the market to gather the supplies they thought they'd need while crossing the plains. Anders carried with him the small sack of coins he'd found among the ship wreckage along the beach. Though the money from the pouch wasn't a fortune, it was enough to purchase several items from the eclectic Brookside Market. The first of his purchases was a lightly worn saddlebag he picked out from a stand selling leather and leather-made products. After searching through many vendors, he came across a man selling hunting arrows and bought enough arrows to easily restock his quiver. Before walking away from the man's booth, Anders noticed a sword roughly the length of his arm. Taking advantage of Anders' curiosity, the man offered him a decent price on it, so Anders once again emptied more coins from his small pouch.

Walking among the many people wandering through

market, Anders noticed how clean their clothes looked compared to his. It didn't take a keen eye to see his clothes had become ragged and were beginning to smell of filth. With the remaining sum of his coin, he decided to buy several new clothes and pants for his travels.

Wool was best for spring traveling because if wool got wet, which often happened during spring rain showers, it stayed warm. He had his eye on some silk shirts, but the rich material was too costly, so he turned his attention elsewhere in the market. He purchased several clean shirts and a pair of wool pants. To his surprise, he'd negotiated quite well and had just enough money left over to buy some extra food. He placed his food and new cloths in his saddlebag and scanned the crowd for his companions.

Anders and the others waited impatiently while Max searched the market for a particular style of shirt. Taking notice of their aggravated scowls, Max gave up the effort and resumed leading them toward his family's house at the opposite side of town.

The small ranch was centered in a large grassy field that bordered the edge of the Bareback Plains. Anders took in the endless expanse of gently rolling hills. The plains consisted of golden waist-high grass extending beyond the horizon. Upon their arrival at the sod-roofed log house, several members of Max's family came out to greet them.

"Max!" a young girl exclaimed, running and jumping into his arms.

Two others, a young man and an older gentleman followed her at a short distance. Anders assumed Max's entire family would be excited to see him. To his surprise, however, the older man Anders assumed to be Max's father, didn't show the same level of enthusiasm as the young girl.

Holding the young girl in his arms, Max let out a

chuckle as she said in a squeaky voice, "Oh, I've missed you! Where's Bo?" she asked, looking past the others, but not finding Max's younger brother.

Max's face turned pale at the question. Fumbling for a moment, he found the appropriate words, "He decided to stay a little while longer."

"Max!" the older of the two men barked coldly as they approached, looking warily at the strangers. "Who are these men? And where's Bo?"

Max put the little girl down and told her calmly, "Go inside and tell your mom I'm here." He waited until she was out of earshot to say anything more.

"What have you done this time, Max?" the older man asked.

"Tony, it's not my fault. The Grandwood Games were attacked by invaders," he said.

The older man scoffed, cutting him off, "I knew I shouldn't have let you go to that stupid race."

"It wasn't my fault," Max protested.

"Sure, nothing bad ever happened to you or anyone you loved because it wasn't your fault," Tony said angrily. "Don't even bother telling me your lies. I want you and your thieving friends off my land," he said pointing his finger at Max and the others. He stormed back to the house.

The younger man stayed behind and asked, "What happened?" He looked over his shoulder making sure Tony wasn't listening to them.

"Grandwood was attacked during the last event of the games; Bo and I got separated. I'm almost positive he was captured. These men saved my life. We're trying track down those who attacked us so we can free those they took hostage," Max said, quickly summing up the events that had transpired since the last time he'd seen his family. "We need six horses. Can you help us out?" he asked.

The young man looked back at the house to be sure Tony wasn't watching and said, "Make it look like you're leaving and I'll meet you down at the swimming hole in a half hour. I'll bring you the horses."

Max nodded and the younger man waved as though he was saying goodbye to Max, then he walked back to the house.

"What the hell was that all about?" Red asked Max as he led them back the way they came.

"I'm not exactly on the best terms with them right now," Max said.

"That was obvious," Red said.

"Come on, follow me. We'll get our horses and then we can be on our way," Max said, walking faster to get away from Red's pestering.

They walked to a small spring, bubbling fresh water from the ground, and waited for the young man to bring them the horses they'd need to cross the plains.

Anders sat down in the tall grass next to Max and asked, "So that was your family?"

"Kind of," Max said. "They adopted me and Bo when we were young. The older man's name is Tony. He was against taking us in and has never liked us very much. Evans, Tony's son, is bringing us the horses. He's much nicer than Tony."

"I see," Anders said.

They weren't waiting long before Evans emerged through the grass leading six horses, saddled and ready to ride. Ivan handed him a sack of coins in payment for the horses and thanked him for his help. Before they left, Ivan had to give the Rollo Islanders a quick riding lesson. Anders laughed as he watched one of them mount a horse and try to ride it onward. The horse wandered over to a clump of lush grass along the edge of the spring and put its head down to graze. The warrior cursed in Rolloan and shook his hands in the air, frustrated that the animal wouldn't obey him.

Ivan yelled after him, "Pull his head up with the reins as I showed you and press your heels into his sides!"

"This is going to be a long couple of days," Ivan said to Anders and Max as he rode by them.

Ivan took the warriors ahead with him while Max said his goodbyes to Evans. Anders waited for Max and then they were off to catch up with Ivan and the others. Red and his two partners trailed behind Ivan, shouting 'yeehaw' and 'yahoo'! Max and Anders shook their heads simultaneously. The two were glad to know nobody was around to see how embarrassing these big men were.

The three Rollo Islanders rode haphazardly, following Ivan, Max and Anders into the Bareback Plains.

Anders had something on his mind and finally mustered the courage to ask Ivan, "So where is your dragon?"

Ivan didn't answer him. *Maybe he didn't hear me?* Anders thought. Asking him again, this time louder, "Ivan, where is your dragon?"

Ivan looked at him with a lack of expression on his face. "Dead," he said bluntly.

"I'm sorry," Anders said.

"Don't be. It wasn't your fault," Ivan replied.

"If you don't mind me asking," Anders continued. "How did your dragon die?"

Ivan paused for a while not saying anything. Anders waited patiently. Eventually Ivan responded, "It was after

Theodor left the war. I was trying to find a way to eliminate Merglan once and for all. I rushed into a situation blindly, taking her with me. She warned me not to do it, but I could only see my desires. It was a trap. The spell was too strong for me to break. The only way to escape was by sacrificing a life. Before I knew what had happened, she gave her life in exchange for mine." He brought his cuff up to his face and wiped away a single tear.

Anders didn't know how to respond to Ivan's confession.

"The death of your dragon is one of the hardest things to overcome," Ivan continued. "Most often those who are left behind end up losing their sanity trying to bring back their other half. I considered attempting it, but knew my duty to both her and myself would not end until Merglan's threat to Kartania no longer existed.

"After she was gone, my powers diminished significantly. It took me many years to be able to tap into what little magic is left in me. I understand you have suffered the loss of loved ones Anders, but the death of your dragon is a pain I cannot describe."

They didn't talk for several hours after that revelation. By midday the sun's overwhelming heat caught up with them.

"The horses need a break. We'll get off there," Ivan called to them, pointing to a stand of trees, a lull in the topography of the plains. Upon a closer look, they could see water pooling near the base of the trees. "The horses can get water and rest for an hour or two. Once it's cooled off a bit we can continue."

Red groaned as he hoisted his legs and slid down out of the saddle, hitting the ground hard. "No one told me how badly horses makes your loins hurt. I won't be able to walk straight for a week!" He and his two companions waddled over to a shady spot, griping to one another about their sore crotches. Anders and Max laughed as they slid down off their horses.

"I told you it wasn't as easy as it looks!" Max shouted after them. "You're lucky these horses were already broken. Try learning to ride a horse that has never been around a person, much less letting someone sitting on its back pulling and poking it around."

Anders and Ivan sat down in the shade, watching the horses drink from the pool. "It seems like what happened in Grandwood was ages ago."

Ivan lay back on the grass under the trees and said, "A lot has happened to you in this last week."

"I think about what my life was like before the attack, simple and happy. Now it's so complicated, I don't know what to think. For all I know my cousins could be dead. All this stuff about magic, dragons, and creatures I thought only existed in stories is hard to believe," Anders said looking up at the leafy branches above them.

"Your cousins aren't dead. Thargon will know we've got what he failed to retrieve and will keep them alive to draw us near. I know this is all overwhelming at first," Ivan said. "When I first learned about magic and dragons I didn't think it was real either. Just remember why you're making this journey - to get your family back. Try not to get too caught up in all of the details. You need to keep your focus on the big picture."

"That's sound advice," Anders said.

For the next couple of hours the six of them rested in the shade. When Anders and Max saw Ivan get up they helped him gather the horses. The three Rollo Islanders snored loudly in the grass.

"Get up you lazy sailors," Ivan said kicking water at them. "Time to go." Red and the other two looked angered by the rude awakening, but knew better than to challenge Ivan.

As they rode, Anders tried to tune out Red and the others talking about battle tactics and war. He was sick of the stress of it all weighing him down, so he let his mind wander. He found himself continually coming back to Maija's kiss, before the race. He was glad to have met her the day before at the registration tent. He wondered what would have happened to the two of them if the attack had never happened, what his life would be like now.

Every once in a while Anders would be pulled out of his thoughts when Max broke through the talk of war and battle with some obscure joke or sarcastic remark. Anders was quickly realizing how much he appreciated having Max in their group. Max was usually in a positive mood and more often than not offered them comic relief with his jokes and smartass remarks.

Before the sun set they made camp and went about their usual routine of building a fire, eating dinner and falling into their temporary beds. Ivan had been giving Max and Anders sparring lessons nearly every night ever since their ship had wrecked. Instead of using their swords, they used freshly cut tree branches so they wouldn't hurt each other too badly. Back on the trail to Brookside, Anders and Max used dead branches they'd found along the trail, breaking them almost instantly when they began their spur of the moment sparring match. Max wasn't as good a fighter as Anders, but the two had made good progress since they'd left Grandwood.

The second day of riding across the plains was more arduous than the first. Often, in the heat of the day, they got off and walked alongside their horses to make sure they weren't overworked. After midday, for the first time since they left Brookside nearly two days prior, they saw the forested coastline in the distance. Ivan suggested they ride along the tree line as long as they could before they had to cross more of the shade-less plains.

That night, sitting around their campfire and eating a dinner of dried meat and bread, Anders realized he didn't know how the Bareback Plains got its name. He asked if Ivan knew how it came to be.

Ivan began to speak, but Max cut him off before he could say anything. "I think I can answer this question best. I did grow up on the edge of the Barebacks after all. The plains are home to the largest group of wild horses in the world. The first nomads to tame and ride the wild horses in this area did so without saddles. Over time, saddles were developed to make controlled riding easier, but the tradition of riding without saddles was already deeply imbedded in their culture. As more and more traveled across the plains, the name 'bareback' stuck."

"Huh," Anders said, through a mouthful of bread. "Where are the nomads now?"

"Not many nomadic tribes exist anymore. With the development of agriculture, the nomads congregated in a city they built in the center of the plains. It is now known as the City of Equine. That's where most people in this area live now," Max said.

"Do you think we'll see any wild horses?" Anders asked Max before they lay down in their temporary beds.

"It's possible," Max said. "The Barebacks have the largest population of wild horses in the world. Back at the ranch outside Brookside they'd sometimes come by and our horses would take off to join the herd."

"Really?" Anders said.

"Yeah, once they join the wild horses, it's really difficult to get them back. Even if you can find the right herd and manage to wrangle your horses in again, they're more difficult to break. Once they've had a taste of what it's like to be with the wild herd, they always want to go back," Max explained.

"That's crazy," Anders said.

"If we do see a group of wild horses, I hope it's at a distance. Otherwise ours might want to bolt and run with them," Max added.

Anders went to bed imagining what it would've been like to live on the plains as a nomad. He lay awake unable to fall asleep, tossing and turning. The harder he tried to find a comfortable position, the more uncomfortable he became. He tried looking up at the stars and clearing his mind for a while, but the light of the rising moon washed out many of the constellations. Thinking he might be able to clear his mind if he went for a walk, Anders quietly peeled off his blankets, trying not to wake anyone. He slipped on his boots, rose to his feet, and slowly began to tiptoe away from camp following the tree line.

Once in the cover of the trees and far enough away from his sleeping companions, he didn't worry about making noise as he walked. He stayed close enough to the edge of the forest to see the grassy edge of the plains.

I wonder how far these trees go? Anders thought. *There's only one way to find out.*

He walked by the light of the moon taking his time to observe many of the smallest details in the natural landscape that he usually passed by without noticing. Anders felt liberated to be by himself in such a peaceful place.

This is just what I needed, he thought.

After the chaos he'd endured over the last week, he longed to forget it all and be stress-free. He looked down at some bushes nearby and was focused on their bowed branches, heavy with bright purple berries, when he heard a loud 'CRACK' behind him.

He froze, his mind flooding with fear. He thought back to the many times when he was hunting in the forest behind his house at Highborn Bay. He would often spook deer or elk that made loud crashing noises when they ran away from him. Whenever that happened, the fleeing animal usually made more noise than one loud crack. Anders stood still looking into the dark shadows among the trees, hoping it wasn't anything dangerous.

Once he'd seen a cougar stalking a fawn in the Grand-wood Forest. It moved slowly making sure its prey wouldn't see it. But cougars are such stealthy hunters that they wouldn't make a loud noise like the crack he'd heard. Suddenly, another loud 'CRACK': this time closer. All at once it hit him, he knew what kind of animal could make that noise.

"Bear," he said out loud.

He began to slowly back up, knowing that if the bear could see him he didn't want to startle it, provoking its instinct to chase. He kept his eyes fixed on where the noise came from, but did not see a bear. Then he saw something shift in the shadows.

Anders lost sight of it for a moment, but pinpointing the movements once more, he could see whatever it was as it drew closer. Through the darkness, he still couldn't tell for sure whether it was a bear. He thought he noticed something different about the way it stayed in the shadows, unlike a bear's thoughtless wandering.

If it were a bear, wouldn't it just come stumbling through instead of hiding in the shadows? he wondered.

Anders stopped dead in his tracks when he saw it begin to emerge from the shadows. Shimmering dark green and purple light reflected off its body in the moonlight as the creature showed itself to him.

Anders' gulp was audible. He whispered aloud to himself, "That's no bear."

EMERGING from the shadows and into the silver light of the moon, Anders saw something he'd never before hoped to see. A dragon stepped cautiously from behind the trees. It moved carefully, holding its head low to the ground, while keeping its dark-purple eyes fixed on Anders. He didn't move. He had no idea what to do. His heart raced, and he thought, *This is it, this is how I die.*

Exposing the entirety of its body, Anders could see the dragon was a truly beautiful creature. The silver moonlight reflected off its iridescent scales. The scales transformed from green to blue to purple as its muscular limbs effortlessly moved its body without a sound.

The dragon's large nostrils sniffed the air as it slowly approached Anders, who remained completely still. The creature exhaled so forcefully it shook the ground around it, sending a chill up Anders' spine. He imagined how powerful its attack could be. Its sharp teeth and razor claws could slice into his flesh with ease if it decided to attack him. For now, it seemed only to be curious about what he was.

The dragon came closer, letting out a low growl, *or was it a purr,* from deep within its throat. Anders took a step backward and stopped when the dragon hopped sideways, startled by his sudden movement. It rose up on its two hind legs, standing tall above him. Anders tilted his head back to look at the entire length of the dragon's body. With its neck outstretched and head tilting from side to side, looking at him with one eye at a time, Anders guessed it stood over fifteen feet in height, and had a tail extending another seven or eight feet behind its back legs.

He remembered from his childhood that the dragons that attacked the Royals at Highborn Bay were said to be sixty feet in length and stood fifteen to twenty feet off the ground when they were on all fours.

This must not be a full-grown dragon, he thought. Still, the creature was pure muscle and could easily devour him if it wanted to eat him for dinner.

Anders remained still, kicking himself for not bringing anything he could use to defend himself. The dragon dropped back down to all fours. It came closer, more hesitant this time, pulling itself back whenever Anders failed to remain perfectly still.

When the dragon was right in front of his body, Anders closed his eyes, fearing the worst was about to happen. He felt the warmth of the dragon's breath was over his skin, raising the hairs on his neck. He heard the sound of lips parting and opened his eyes to see the dragon's mouth cracked open inches away from his face. From within its deadly cage of teeth, Anders watched the creature's forked tongue extend out beyond its jaw and lick the side of his face. His skin pulled along, sticking to the dragon's barbed tongue. Anders wouldn't have imagined what the dragon did next, not in a million years.

To his surprise, the dragon began to nuzzle him with its snout. It purred softly as it brushed its head up and down against his body. Its tail flicked back and forth like his uncle's barn cats did when they rubbed against his legs back at the family farm. Anders nearly fell over backward from the pressure of the dragon's head against his body. The dragon seemed to be snuggling with him. He extended his arm out over the massive head and stroked its scaled neck from the ears down. The moment Anders laid his hand on the dragon; he felt something happen inside him. His body flooded with a warmth and strength he had never experienced before. In that moment, Anders felt truly happy.

He let out a laugh as he stroked the dragon's neck and it playfully nuzzled him back. All of a sudden the moment ended as fast as it started. The dragon pulled away from him. It raised its head; ears pointed upward on alert in the direction of Anders' group's camp. Anders heard his companions' shouts as they called his name. He turned his head to see where they were. He looked back expecting to see the dragon still at his side, but it was no longer there. Only the slow movement of a low-hanging tree branch was proof of it having been there.

Was that real? he asked himself, looking at the branch swaying among the otherwise motionless vegetation. He raised his hand to his cheek feeling a wet streak on his face. *It was.*

Anders looked back toward the shouting as it grew louder. He turned his head once more to where the dragon had been and smiled. He rushed back to the others who searched for him along the tree line.

"Over here!" he yelled when he saw them in the light of the moon.

They came rushing to his side, blades drawn. Upon seeing he was okay, they began to question him.

"What are you doing out here?" Ivan asked.

"I couldn't sleep and thought a walk would be nice," he replied not lying but not telling them the whole story.

"Why didn't you let anyone know where you were going?" Max asked.

"I didn't want to wake anyone, and figured I wouldn't go far and would be back before anyone woke up," Anders said.

"How is it that I couldn't sense where you were?" Ivan asked.

"I don't know?" Anders replied. "I was walking along the edge of the trees."

"I have always been able to sense you, even when you were much farther away from us after the shipwreck," Ivan said. "Just now when I awoke and noticed you were not in your bed, I reached out to sense your presence, but felt nothing. How could that be if you were just walking along this close to camp?"

Anders shrugged and thought, *The dragon must've blocked Ivan from sensing me.* "I don't know. I was just trying to clear my head is all, honest," he said.

Ivan looked at him strangely, "All right. I'm glad you weren't devoured by goblins or something," he said. "Let's go back to sleep. We have a long way to go if we are going to make it to the statue tomorrow."

As they walked back to camp, Anders wondered if he should tell Ivan or Max about the encounter. He was finally beginning to feel that he could really trust them, but his heart was telling him to keep it a secret. Remembering the message Solomon had given him before he left Brookside, he decided to follow his instincts and keep it a secret for now. If he'd just seen the dragon off in the distance, the situation would be different, but this wasn't your average run-of-the-mill dragon sighting.

Back at camp, Anders lay on the blanket he'd laid out for his bed, though now he was even more wide awake than before. He couldn't go to sleep, not after what had just happened. He rolled his head to the side and stared toward the tree line, peering through the moonlight for a glimpse of the magnificent creature with which he'd just had such an intimate encounter. As he watched, his eyes grew heavy and the next thing he knew he was lost in a dream.

Anders cracked open his eyes when he felt the morning sun shining through his eyelids. He smelled fresh meat cooking and looked to see Ivan and Max preparing a rabbit leg breakfast. The sun was rising and he could feel the heat of the day beginning to warm the ground around him. Looking out at the plains, the grassland glowed in the golden morning light.

"Not a bad way to wake up," he said.

"I prefer to wake up on an island beach, looking out at the ocean," Red said sitting up from his bed.

Anders didn't really care for the Rollo Island warriors; they were stubborn and close-minded, at least Red and his two comrades were. Luckily, he didn't have to spend much time alone with them.

After they ate, the crew set off across the plains. They rode in their usual formation, Ivan up at the front leading the expedition, Red and his men following behind, and Anders and Max bringing up the rear. This way they had an experienced guide in the lead and some experienced riders behind the Islanders making sure nothing happened to them if they fell off or fell too far behind.

"Come on. What were you really doing out there in the woods last night?" Max asked Anders once they'd ridden far enough to let some distance get between them and the Islanders.

"I couldn't sleep, so I thought I'd take a walk along the edge of the trees." Anders said sticking to his story.

Max brought his eyebrows together with a look of suspicion, "Okay... You could've been attacked or captured by goblins; you know they're in the area. We barely escaped them coming into Brookside the other day. I wouldn't be surprised if they were roaming around out here as well."

"I know. Next time I'll let you know," Anders said. "What do you think made Ivan wake up?" He was curious why Ivan would notice that he was out of his bed. Up until now, Ivan had slept soundly through the night. Anders knew this because he often woke up in the middle of the night to relieve himself, usually making enough noise that anyone having trouble sleeping would wake up. Ivan, however, never even moved, remaining sound asleep.

"I don't know? He probably just had to pee or something," Max said, still giving him a suspicious look.

"I was just trying to relax," Anders said, "honestly."

"Okay, well, you know you can trust me if there's something you want to get off your mind," said Max.

"Thanks," Anders said. While they were talking, they'd let their horses lag behind the others. Ivan had stopped his horse and the others to wait for them to catch up.

"Everything all right?" he asked, concerned.

"Yeah, Max was just telling me a funny joke," Anders said.

Ivan shook his head and sighed, "You always have something to joke about, don't you Max." Then he turned his horse back around and continued on his way.

The crew rode hard and only got off to walk their horses twice that day. By the time the sun began to set behind them, they could see the Statue of Old Kings protruding from the coastline. At its base a large, sandy beach swept down the crescent-shaped coast. Lining the beach were the Rollo Island Navy warships.

"Look," Red said, pointing to the statue.

"The warriors, they got the message!" Max exclaimed.

"I knew they would," Red said proudly. "You can always rely on the Rollo Islanders." He straightened his posture and puffed out his chest.

As they made their way across to the statue, Anders noticed something out of the corner of his eye moving swiftly across the plains.

"Wild horses," he said pointing toward the herd galloping through the grass in the distance.

"Hey, we did see some," Max said, happy to see them at a distance. Anders watched as the herd ran freely across the open land.

"It is truly a beautiful sight," Ivan said, acknowledging their excitement at seeing the herd.

The night's darkness had descended by the time their small group reached the beach beneath the statue. Red and his two comrades hopped off their horses and rushed to greet the Rollo war party's leaders.

The Islanders embraced one another and one of the leaders said to them in a thick Rolloan accent, "I never thought I would see the day when my son would become a master horseman."

"He most definitely isn't a master," Max said leaning over his saddle and looking around for a laugh. Instead the warriors gave him cold looks that told him they were not pleased with his comment.

"Tough crowd," Max whispered to Anders, as he sat back into his saddle. Anders chuckled and shook his head, then dismounted to join the others.

"Chief Jorgen," Ivan said, bowing his head slightly, showing Red's father more respect than Max had.

"Welcome to our camp. We've been eagerly awaiting your arrival. Come, we have much to discuss," Red's father said, taking Red under his arm and walking back toward their camp.

TEN

ZAHARA

Despite their presence, Anders and Max were not invited into the tent where the Rollo Island leaders were discussing their next plan of action. Instead they went to set up their own campsite near the edge of the cluster of warrior tents. The size of the camp rivaled the size of most towns in Westland. Anders remembered reading in a book in Theodor's library that in the Rollos' culture anyone brave enough to fight was allowed to join the warriors. He passed men, women, and even children as he and Max walked across the sprawling camp. The youngest child looked to be about fourteen years old. Anders greatly respected the women who'd come on their journey. He did worry that the youngest of the children were too young to see battle and could possibly be a hindrance in a fight.

After Max and Anders set up a spot for themselves, they wandered through camp in search of food. Many fires blazed, most smelled of roasted meat. They joined in with a group who were handing slices of lamb cooked over a spit roast. Anders introduced himself and sat down to soak up the warmth of their fire. Max and Anders enjoyed the savory meat.

Anders struck up a conversation with a woman sitting next to them. She introduced herself as Britt. "I was surprised to see such young warriors with your party," Anders said to her through a mouthful of lamb.

"It's common in our culture to go on your first war party when you're very young," Britt replied, the thick Rolloan accent Anders' had grown accustomed to from listening to Red was nearly absent in her speech. "Most of us have seen battle by the time we're fourteen. I went on my first raid when I was thirteen," she added proudly.

"Weren't you scared?" Anders asked her, imagining what he would have felt going off to fight strangers to the death when he was only thirteen years old.

"Fear is something that we do not see in battle," she said strongly. "It is the greatest honor for our people to die in the glory of battle. We do not fear death in battle; we welcome it."

Anders was shocked at this thought. "Why is that?" he asked.

"If you fight hard and prove yourself to be a brave warrior and die in battle," she said, "the spirit within your body will leave this world and join the spirits of others of our people who have gone before us. All of the finest foods are waiting in a giant feast when your spirit arrives at the Great Hall. A giant goat sits at the head of the table and its udders produce endless amounts of brew..." she trailed off smiling up into the night's sky. "If you live your life as a brave warrior you will be granted a seat at the table. If you cower from battle or fear being killed in battle, then you will be damned for eternity and spend your afterlife wandering the endless skies outside the Great Hall's gates, starving and thirsty, but never able to die from starvation or dehydration. That is why we don't fear death in battle, it's far worse to die afraid."

Anders thought the feast and endless brew didn't sound that bad. "That is pretty amazing," he said and turned to Max. "Did you hear that?"

"Yeah. The great hall sounds like somewhere I could spend an eternity," he said jokingly.

Anders and Max thanked Britt and the others for their hospitality and walked back to their campsite.

"That whole not being afraid to die in battle thing is nuts," Max said when they reached their campsite. "Do they really think that being killed in battle is the best way to die?"

Anders shrugged, "It could be an effective way to form a mindset for some people to be fearless in battle, even in the face of overwhelming odds."

"I want to die old and in my sleep," Max said. "Preferably next to a beautiful woman."

"That sounds like a better way to go than being sliced open by a sword," Anders said, settling into his blanket at their campsite.

"Yeah, that is much better," Max mumbled as he closed his eyes with a grin across his face.

Anders was extremely tired from his lack of sleep the night before and then traveling all day, but he couldn't stop thinking about his encounter with the young dragon. He decided to wait until Max was sound asleep and then go for another walk. Maybe the dragon would find him again. Anders wanted to feel the warming sensation the dragon gave him once more. He was desperate enough to wander away from camp to have a chance at finding it again.

He dozed in fits, nodding off to sleep and catching

himself before he was all of the way out. He again stared up at the washed out stars hoping the attempt to find constellations he knew would keep him awake. He found himself thinking back to the girl from the competition again, Maija. He replayed their kiss again in his mind. Just then he heard a rustling in the grass nearby.

There isn't any wind tonight. Maybe the dragon is letting me know that the coast is clear to come and meet with it, he hoped.

For the second time in as many nights, Anders slowly climbed out of his makeshift bed. He could tell from the quiet snoring that Max was asleep, so he snuck off into the tall grass toward the rustling sound.

He heard it again and moved closer. When he saw what it was, he dropped down out of sight. It wasn't the dragon. It was Ivan.

I knew there was something weird about him being up in the middle of the night, he thought.

Surely if he was going to the bathroom, as Max suggested he was doing the night before, he would have stayed closer to camp. Anders made sure to keep his distance, but kept a visual on where Ivan was going. He followed him as he continued away from camp. Anders hoped that the number of people in the camp would be too overwhelming for Ivan to sense Anders trailing behind him. From a distance, Anders watched as Ivan walked to a pile of boulders scattered on a small hill.

Ivan crouched down behind a rock and pulled something small from his coat pocket. A bright light shone, illuminating his silhouette against the darkened night. Ivan began to talk to it. He was too far away for Anders to hear what he was saying, and after the last time he spied on Ivan having a secret conversation, Anders decided it was best not to listen in on whatever he was doing.

Instead, Anders decided to take a different route back to camp. He didn't want Ivan to catch him out of bed again on his way back to camp. He made sure to stay low out of sight, creeping toward the beach through the tall grass. He wondered if he should continue to look for the dragon. Anders decided to find a place to sit and watch the waves. The last time the dragon found him, he was enjoying his natural surroundings. Solomon told him dragons could sense things in people and thought if he did it again, perhaps the dragon would return.

He walked until he could no longer see the glow of the campfires still burning along the beach. The sound of the crashing waves reminded him of being back at home at Highborn Bay. He found the repetition of the waves relaxing. He sat down on a log to enjoy the peacefulness of the coast. Looking down, he noticed baby sea turtles on the other side of the log crawling out of the sand. He smiled as he watched them use their paddle-like flippers to push themselves through the sand to the ocean's breaking waves. Anders had never seen this phenomenon before. He felt happy seeing the baby turtles make it from their nest all the way to the water, where they could begin their life's journey.

As he watched the last of the hatchlings crawl out from behind the log, he heard a swooshing noise behind him. He swiveled around to see the dragon gliding just above the ground, coming straight for him. He ducked behind the log, but the dragon made a soft landing next him instead of swooping over his head. Anders peeked out from behind the log and saw the majestic creature sitting back on its hindquarters and looking down at him with purple eyes.

Feeling a little bit foolish, he propped himself back up on the log. He looked over to the dragon. It watched him intently. Anders reached his arm out slowly toward the dragon. It bowed its head to meet his hand. He rubbed its forehead and the dragon purred. He felt the warmth of the dragon coursing like liquid fire into his veins. The feeling was electrifying and charged his body in a way he'd never known possible. It brought a newfound sense of rejuvenation to him, making him feel as full of energy as he'd ever felt in his entire life. Then he heard a voice come from the dragon. It was feminine, gentle and kind-hearted.

I followed you from the edge of the forest all the way to this beach, she said. Anders could hear the voice in his ears yet the dragon's mouth didn't move.

"How are you doing that?" Anders asked.

Well, I made sure not to leave until your group was far out of sight... she began.

Anders interrupted, "No, I mean talking to me. I can hear your voice, but I don't see your lips moving."

Oh, said the dragon. *I can't use my mouth to make words like you humans, but I can use my mind to make you hear what I have to say.*

"That's amazing," Anders said.

Thank you, the dragon said, and purred.

"Why did you follow me?" Anders asked.

When I first saw you walking along the edge of the trees, I noticed something within you that I have not seen before. You were completely in love with what was around you. I could feel your love for the earth and nature, so I followed you. I was so drawn to you that something within me made me show myself to you, the dragon said. *When my body did that, I got a little scared. Your love for nature seemed to disappear when you first saw me. I wasn't quite sure, but I trusted my instincts and when we touched it was like nothing I've ever felt before, almost electrifying, but filling me with a strength I've never had."*

"You felt that too?" Anders exclaimed! The dragon nodded.

When I heard the other members of your group trying to reach you, I decided to leave. I haven't had any close encounters with humans before. The humans I have seen were different. They did not exhibit the same love for nature that I felt when I saw you. Anyway, I was so curious about the warm feeling I felt when we touched that I had to follow you. When I saw you come down here to the beach, I decided that I would come and properly introduce myself. The dragon sat up tall and said, *My name is Zahara. What's yours?*

"I am Anders," he said looking up the dragon. "Judging by the sound of your voice, you're female?" Anders said, hoping this wouldn't offend her.

That is correct. I am a girl, Zahara said.

"I don't mean to pry, but there's so much I'd like to ask you. From what I was told as a child, I thought dragons would be much bigger," Anders said.

Zahara laughed, *That's true that members of my species can grow to enormous sizes, but I'm not yet fully grown. I'm only two years old.*

Anders was surprised to find out that such a young creature could be so intelligent. "What are you doing this far from Nagano? That is what your homeland is called, isn't it?" he asked.

Yes, Nagano is home to us dragons, she said. *I got separated from my group. I've been searching for them, but this land is all new to me and actually I'm very lost.*

"How did you happen to become separated?"

We were flying away from our home because a human

my elders called 'the destroyer' came to Nagano on the back of a black dragon. The destroyer summoned forth anyone who'd aligned with him several decades ago. When nobody answered his summoning, he began killing and torturing those who wouldn't answer his call to action. It wasn't safe for us to live there so we left to find the elves and stay in their realm, but a storm arose out of nowhere. My wings weren't strong enough to keep up with the group. I have never met an elf, so I didn't know where to look. I just began to wander, trying to keep out of sight while I searched for my family, she said.

"How terrible. I think I might know someone who could help you. He has stayed with the elves before."

You mean the man you were following through the tall grass? she asked.

"Yes, his name is Ivan."

I have a funny feeling about him. He's hiding something and I don't want to put my life in the hands of a stranger who's keeping secrets. I trust you. I have felt you and seen you with my mind, Anders could hear the fear growing in her tone. *I don't want to go with that man.* Zahara shifted her weight uncomfortably from one side to the other. Ruffling her wings she said, *I have to go now.* Spreading her wings, she took several steps back and took flight. *Meet me tomorrow night,* Anders heard her voice in his head as she flew off into the night. *Just make sure you're alone, I'll find you.* With that she was gone.

Anders shook his head to make sure he wasn't dreaming. Then he stood up and walked back to camp. He crawled back into his blankets and fell asleep, eager for their next encounter.

The next morning, the Rollo Island warriors' leaders announced their plan to continue sailing east along the coast and around the Bareback Peninsula. From there, they would enter the Marauder Sea and begin to search each bay, cove, and inlet for any sign of the enemy's ships. Once word of their decision spread, Anders was surprised to see how efficient the warriors, as a collective group, were at taking down their camp. They were ready to sail within an hour.

Anders and Max found the group of warriors they'd eaten dinner with the night before and climbed aboard their ship. They didn't want to travel under Red's command again, after he'd sailed them into a storm that wrecked their ship. To his surprise, Britt, the woman he'd spoken with by the fire was their crew's captain.

"You two," she said, pointing a dark finger at them when she saw the two on the deck of her ship. Anders worried that she planned to send them away to another ship given the tone she used to address them. "Grab an oar and help us paddle out to open water, then you can help out with the rigging and sail work," she instructed. Anders and Max seemed surprised that she'd given them working orders instead of sending them away. Seeing their hesitation, she added, "If you're going to sail under my command, you're going to work just like the rest of us. Now get to it."

Anders and Max did as they were told and rowed alongside the others as Britt barked out the rowing cadence. They stayed in time with the others rowing on each count. If the crew didn't all row in sync, they wouldn't gain enough speed to make it past the breaking waves just offshore. Anders pulled against the oar as their ship plowed through the six-foot-tall waves, sending the bow of their small ship careening over and out into the open ocean. Anders watched as the other remaining ships did the same. They had to time their launches just right or a wave would crash over the bow and easily turn the whole vessel sideways in the surf. If that happened, it would be hard to stop the boat from flipping. He was impressed that all of the other warships made it out of the break.

These people clearly know how to sail, Anders thought to himself.

Anders and Max were happy to be in new company. They had begun to grow tired of Red's bullheadedness and Anders didn't know if he wanted to be around Ivan after seeing him sneak away from camp for a secret conversation in the middle of the night. It had seemed as though Ivan was beginning to open up to him and he thought Ivan could be trusted, but after seeing what he was up to last night and noting the apprehensiveness Zahara felt toward him, Anders was no longer sure whether Ivan could be trusted.

Being on the new boat with new faces felt different, in a good way. It wasn't long before they broke from rowing and dropped their sail. Britt took control of the ship from the stern. Her black skin beaded with sweat as she stoically looked ahead, gripping the ship's tiller.

"Where exactly are we heading?" Anders asked her.

Wiping her forehead with her sleeve, she said, "East, past the grass-lands and up the Marauder Sea. Once there, we'll begin to search every inlet and cove for the soldiers who killed and kidnapped so many of our people."

"And when we find them?" Max asked.

"We will repay them the revenge they are owed, recapture our loved ones, sail home, and drink till we drop," she said looking at them with her piercing brown eyes.

Max turned to Anders and whispered, "She scares me. In a good way."

When evening came and they didn't beach and make camp, Anders began to worry. Zahara had told him to meet her that night. If he couldn't get off the ship, then she wouldn't be able to talk to him. He asked Britt, "Will we be staying on the ship every night?"

Britt nodded, "It takes too much time to camp onshore every night. We need to keep a fast pace if we're going to have a chance at catching the enemy's ships."

Anders looked over the edge of the ship at the passing shoreline. He hoped Zahara would follow him even though he couldn't meet with her as they'd planned. *What if something happens to her and she can't find me when we do land?* He wondered. Then, pushing away such negative thoughts, he decided, *she's an intelligent creature. If she found me twice, she can find me again.*

ELEVEN

MERGLAN'S FORTRESS

Thomas and Kirsten once again found themselves in separate cells, while Kirsten and Maija shared one for a second time. Kirsten found this one to be a little bit nicer than the cell on the dingy ship where they'd spent the last week. This one had a dirt floor and was above ground; in Kirsten's eyes that was an improvement. Still no toilet, but at least she could look out the doors and see the sky again. Theirs was among a line of cells that ran along the side of the large tower, built in the center of the compound. Large cliff walls surrounded the outskirts of the structures. Several other tall buildings sat within the walls, but the prisoners only had the luxury of observing them out of the corners of their eyes during their forced march into the fortress. The cell doors faced a courtyard and beyond that a path that wound downhill into an enormous pit. Entrances to shafts lined the steep sides of the pit; the prisoners could see it was being mined for something.

"What do they want with us?" Kirsten asked Maija when they were out of earshot of the guards.

"Forced labor it looks like" she said, hands gripped around the iron bars of their cell as she peered out at the large pit. "What is this place?" she asked Kirsten, not really expecting an answer.

"It's some kind of fortress," Kirsten said eyeing the cliff walls. "The man in the dark cloak had us locked in some kind of spell or something?"

"He must be a sorcerer," Maija said.

"I was told that all the sorcerers were dead and gone, but I guess that isn't true. I saw a man fight Thargon using magic just before he captured us and now this guy in the dark cloak can just wave his wrist and we have to obey his commands. I have never seen anything like it," Kirsten said, frustrated.

"I've seen one once before," Maija said.

"When?" Kirsten asked.

"It was when I was little," she began. "I don't remember much about who they were or what they did. I just remember sitting in a house that looked like a tree. A man there could make plants grow from nothing, make things move with his mind, and even control someone else's thoughts. I try sometimes to remember more but I can't."

"How old were you?" Kirsten asked.

"It was when I lived with my birth parents. I don't know how old I was exactly, maybe six?" She said bringing her eyebrows together and curling her lip.

"I can remember most things with great clarity going all the way back to when I was a toddler," Kirsten said. "How is it that you don't know if you lived with your parents when you were as old as six?"

Maija seemed to be straining through the cobwebs of her memories, "I can't remember much before I was twelve years old." she said, unsure of herself. "I just woke up one day and everything around me was different. I was in someone else's home. I came out of the bedroom I woke up in to find an old man and woman cooking breakfast. When I asked them what had happened to me, they told me I had lived there for years and they were my grandparents. The strange thing was I did not recognize them and had no memory of anything they said. It took me several months to come to terms with what was happening. They had to be telling me the truth; they were so nice and knew everything about me. They were wonderful people, too."

"So you don't remember anything about your life before you woke up in the house of strangers who claimed to be your grandparents?" Kirsten asked trying to imagine what that would be like.

"Yes," she said.

"What about your birth parents? What happened to them?" Kirsten asked.

"My grandparents told me that it wasn't safe for me to be with them and I wasn't allowed to see them ever again," Maija said sadly. "I can sometimes remember their voices, but that's it."

"So you grew up not knowing your parents or what happened to them? That must've been hard," Kirsten said.

"It was. It looks like I'll never find out now," Maija said looking around at their current situation.

"Don't say that," Kirsten said. "We're going to get out of this." She looked at the iron bars locking them in the darkened cell. "Somehow..."

Kirsten spent the rest of the afternoon and evening trying to make sense of what that man wanted with her family.

Had Theodor been involved in something dangerous that

no one knew about, she wondered. *Did it have something to do with the man she saw fight Thargon during the attack?*

It all seemed very strange to her. She couldn't make sense of it, no matter how she tried to piece it together. All she knew was that a sorcerer, with malice in his heart, sent an army of evil men led by a beastly-looking monster to wreck her life. She hated it, she hated them all and what they'd done to her and her family. They'd killed her father and hurt her brother.

I'm not going to give up on my escape just because my original plan of taking over the ship didn't come to fruition, she promised herself.

That night Kirsten lay on the dirt floor plotting and scheming ways to escape this hell she had been forced into.

A loud banging on their cell doors woke the two girls before sunrise. It was the coldest and darkest hour of the night, just before the sun rose.

Kirsten shivered and rubbed her hands along her cold arms. "What's going on?" she asked, looking over to Maija who was already on her feet.

"I'm not sure," she said, her teeth chattering. "A guard just walked by banging a wooden stick on all of the cells shouting to us to wake up."

By the time Kirsten had mustered the strength to stand up, the guard had returned to open the locked door.

"Out," he said firmly and pointed toward the courtyard.

They staggered out, along with all of the others who'd already been ordered to stand in the dark space. Just as Kirsten was about to ask someone what was happening, loud footsteps came stomping along the fortress hallway. Thargon, the beast that had captured them, moved swiftly toward them. He stood much taller than the average man.

Kirsten thought he looked hideous with dark hair that covered his body and gnarled fangs stained yellow and brown, as if they were rotten and about to fall out of his head at any moment.

"Form a line," he bellowed angrily at them as he walked out in front of them. "Stand tall." He walked up and down the line they had made facing him. He violently corrected their form if they were at all off from his expectations. "I have been granted the task of sorting you worthless pieces of slime into the services you will be providing for your new master, the honorable Merglan."

Thargon took a second look at everyone, walking up and down the line. He started on the far side away from Kirsten and Maija. "Mine, mine, castle chambers, grounds, mine, kitchen," he went down the line assigning the prisoners one by one.

Kirsten bent her head just slightly but not enough to be noticed by the guards or Thargon would've rushed over to violently correct her position as he did with others who'd made the mistake of relaxing their bodies or turning their heads to see what was happening down the line. She could see out of the corner of her eye Thomas' head sticking up over those next to him. He was five or six people down the line to her right, but it was hard to tell exactly in the darkness. When Thargon got to him, Kirsten noticed he stopped and looked at him with a truly hateful glare. He said in a growl, "Mine." Then he continued toward Kirsten and Maija.

When he got to Maija, he paused for a moment, sniffed the air around her and grumbled. "You smell, different. Not like the others." Then he said, "Castle chambers," and continued to Kirsten, dismissing the scent he'd smelled on Maija. Kirsten stared right into his black eyes as he looked her up and down, deciding her fate. "Castle chambers," he said. Kirsten was surprised he didn't put her in the mine with her brother; of course he had no idea she was his sister, but at least she got to be in the same workforce as her new friend and cellmate, Maija.

Stepping back out in front of them, Thargon announced, "You'll be taken to your stations and the other slaves will show you your new tasks. Do not bother trying to escape. These walls surrounding the fortress are laced with magic stronger than anything you will be able to get past. Those who attempt to escape will be reprimanded accordingly. Those who do not perform their duties to expectation will be disciplined accordingly. You will be at your workstations at this time every day; tardiness will be met with reprimand. When your work is complete for the day you will be led back to your cells." When he had finished, Thargon turned and walked out of the courtyard and back up the hallway. Armed guards dressed in uniforms lacking any insignia or recognizable allegiance came to escort them to their new stations.

"Kitchen staff, with me," one of the guards shouted. Another yelled, "Grounds workers, here." A third and fourth shouted, "Miners," and "castle chambers."

Kirsten and Maija walked toward the guard calling castle chambers. As they pushed through the crowd of prisoners assembled in the courtyard, Kirsten found her brother and grabbed him by the arm to get his attention.

"Kirsten," he said, glad to see her. "Where are you going?"

"With the chamber slaves," she said drearily. "I heard they put you in the mine. Listen, tonight when we're back here we should talk."

Thomas looked around, noticing the guards were

watching the two talking to each other. "Okay, we'll talk tonight," he said, then wished her good luck and a safe day. They went their separate ways.

"Follow me," the expressionless guard said. He led them out of the courtyard and into the hallway where Thargon had departed. Wooden torches lit the walls illuminating the darkened hallway. Entering through a narrow passageway, the guard led them up a staircase. They climbed high into the towering building. Stopping at a landing, the guard pointed to a small wooden door next to the stairs and said, "Through this door and you will be with the other maids. Go on, git!" And he pushed them along through the door. As he pushed Kirsten past, he muttered to himself, "Stupid Westlanders." Kirsten raised her arm to hit the guard for the insult, but Maija caught her arm and shook her head, telling her not to react. The guard noticed the two had stopped. Shooing them with his hands, he said, "Go on then, through the door you go, with the other slaves." Kirsten fumed with rage and Maija pushed her through the door into the room with the others.

"I'm going to kill that guard before this is over," Kirsten said to Maija as they gathered around one of the head maids.

All of the others who had come into the room before them were listening to the shrill voice of a tall thin woman. She wore a white dress and gray apron covered in stains. She spoke clear Landish but her silver hair and ghostly pale complexion was more severe than the most fair Westland people. She shouted for them to gather round and pay attention.

"My name is Chantal, the head chambermaid in this castle. Yes, we are all here against our will. But if you do as you're expected, you may survive. Your day will begin by meeting here with the other maids. We then take our baskets and go around to the rooms of all the guards and pick up the dirty clothes and blankets. After that we sweep and mop the floors, clean the bathrooms, and do the laundry. Once each room is spotless, we make up the beds with clean sheets. When the rooms and halls are clean, we set the dinner table for the master. He usually has a feast with several officers in his army. After dinner, we clean up their mess and it's off to bed. There will be lunch at noon and we can eat dinner while the master entertains. Get into groups of two," she said and paused until everyone was standing next to their new coworker. "I will be placing one of the more experienced members who have been here longer with each pair to make sure you do the job correctly."

She went around and placed a more experienced maid with each pair except for Kirsten and Maija. Once Chantal got around to them, she said, "I have been ordered to take the two of you under my watch. You will be learning from me."

Kirsten and Maija both raised their eyebrows ever so slightly as they looked at each other.

Why would Chantal have been ordered to make sure we work with one another? Is Merglan reading our minds and knows my plans of trying to escape? But I haven't even started my plan. I just know I want to do something to get out of this wretched place, Kirsten thought to herself as Chantal led them through the narrow stone halls.

As they followed, Chantal pointed out all of the chambers of the more important members of Merglan's army. They were mostly officers and commanders, the majority of them were human with several male orcs and one female orc tasked with overseeing their grand plan.

Whatever that is, Kirsten wondered.

When they reached the end of the hall, Chantal showed them a set of stairs that led off to a large structure attached to the main building.

Pointing to the stairs, Chantal said, "This is the master's chamber. You are not to go beyond this point. Only I am allowed to clean the master's chambers."

Maija and Kirsten nodded slowly, examining the doorway.

"You two will start by cleaning the rooms here in this hall," she said pointing back the way they'd just come. She paused and looked at them as if she was wondering why they hadn't moved yet.

"Oh, now?" Kirsten said, catching the awkwardness of her gaze.

"Yes, now," Chantal said and shooed them away with her hand.

Kirsten and Maija spent the next several hours of their morning cleaning together. They talked about how strange this place was, what her brother was doing in the mine, and how they were going to plan another escape or attack on the guards.

They were just finishing in the room next door to Merglan's chambers when Maija caught Kirsten's attention.

"Pssst," Maija waved her over to the doorway. Maija had her back pressed up against the wall in their room's entryway. Kirsten rushed over to her and put her backside against the wall next to her friend.

"Shhh," Maija shushed with a finger over her lips. She poked her head around the partially open door for a moment and brought it back in. "Did you hear that?" she asked Kirsten.

"Hear what?" Kirsten asked, not hearing anything.

"The voices," Maija said in a whisper.

"No, I didn't hear any voices," Kirsten said.

Maija poked her head through the doorway again and looked up and down the hallway. Then receding back into the doorway again, she said, "I can hear voices talking out there, but I can't see anyone in the hallway."

"Let me take a look," Kirsten said. She poked her head beyond the door and into the stone hallway and looked first to the left, then to the right. There was no one there, and as hard as she strained her ears she could not hear anything. Bringing her head back inside, she said, "I don't see anyone or hear any voices."

Maija looked at her surprised, "Really? You don't hear the people talking?"

Kirsten shook her head. "What are they talking about?" she asked.

"I'm not sure, it's pretty muffled. I heard something about a prophecy though," she said.

"Let's find out where the voices are coming from," Kirsten said.

Prophecy sounds interesting, she thought.

"What if we get caught?" Maija asked. "We could be beaten or worse if we're discovered."

"It's worth it," Kirsten said and exited the doorway out into the hallway. "Now where are these voices you're hearing coming from?" she asked, looking around the stone corridor.

Maija followed her out into the hallway when she saw that no invisible person or force had immediately reprimanded Kirsten.

"The talking is coming from in there," she pointed to the door leading to Merglan's chambers. The door was cracked open slightly so Kirsten walked over and put her ear up against the crack opening. At last she could hear muffled voices, more like whispers, floating down the stairs to the door. She pulled her head away from the crack and looked at Maija amazed she'd heard them from the other room.

"You could hear that from the other room?" she asked.

"Yeah, I'm surprised you couldn't," she whispered.

"Wow, I could barely tell that there were voices when I put my ear on the crack, and I cannot even begin to decipher what they're saying. To me it just sounds like psssst, psssst, pssst," she said.

Maija pushed her aside and said, "Let me try." Maija stood at the doorway for several minutes, her expressions changing from curiosity to shock and surprise. She pulled away from the door and hurriedly said in a low voice, "Quick, back into the room! Chantal is coming back down."

They rushed back into the room and picked up their cleaning where they'd left off. No sooner had they gotten back to work than Chantal entered the room. She walked around inspecting what they'd been doing. She quickly pointed out some necessary changes and some spots in the room that required further cleaning. Kirsten and Maija wondered if she knew they'd been listening at the door.

Before Chantal left the room, she turned and said, "Ahem." Kirsten's heart dropped for a second, thinking they'd been found out and Chantal was going to send them off to be punished. "You're doing a fine job so far. A bit slow, but better than I expected." Chantal turned and left the room.

Kirsten waited for almost a half hour before asking Maija what she had heard the voices saying. Just as she was about to tell Kirsten exactly what she'd heard, Merglan walked past the door. They heard his footsteps stop in the hallway and heard him walk backwards until he was centered in the doorway. He turned his head slowly and looked at Kirsten and Maija, who stared back at him terrified at what he might do to them. After several long breaths, he turned back to look down the hallway and continued walking, closing the stairwell door behind him. After that, Kirsten and Maija decided they'd better wait to discuss what she heard until they were back in the solitude of their cell that night.

Together they finished their cleaning duties and joined the others in the kitchen to prepare the feast for the master. Once the meal was over and cleaned up, the two returned to the courtyard. Thomas had been waiting for them. Two guards were posted at the end of the hallway near the gates. The three of them were free to talk before they went to bed.

After Kirsten and Thomas had briefly discussed the day's duties, Kirsten asked Thomas if he knew why Merglan had come after their family and what exactly he wanted. Thomas couldn't give her much more information than he'd provided back on the ship.

"He asked me all sorts of questions about our father and whether I was capable of performing magic, but I didn't know what he was talking about," Thomas said. "Thargon's master said I wasn't who they'd sent him to find, but that he was close by when Thargon found us. Do you think he was talking about the young man who was with Anders when he came back with us?" Thomas asked. "If they're still together, Anders could be in danger," he said, concerned for his cousin.

"It's possible. That would explain why Thargon came after us when Anders and the young man returned to the house with father," Kirsten sighed. She had hoped Thomas would provide her with a more solid explanation for why they'd been captured and turned her thoughts to her cousin saying, "I hope Anders isn't worrying himself sick over us."

"I'm sure he's handling it as best he can; he's strong-willed," Thomas said confidently. "And if I know Anders, he'll be trying to find us and free us from this mess. No magician or magical beast will stop him."

"You're probably right, but we can't wait here forever. We need to break out of here," Kirsten said lowering her voice and looking over her shoulder at the guards.

"I agree, but how?" Thomas whispered. "This place is under a powerful spell that doesn't allow anyone to leave. Today a man saw the gates were left open and made a run for it. As soon as he rushed outside beyond the gates, he vanished, poof, just like that," Thomas said snapping his fingers. "All of a sudden he reappeared back where he was before he'd made his escape attempt and the guards quickly took him away. I don't know what happened to him, but it couldn't have been good."

"Geez," Kirsten said, shaking her head. She remembered the strange thing that had happened to them earlier. "Maija and I heard someone talking about a prophecy. I couldn't hear what they were saying, but Maija did."

"What was it? What'd they say?" Thomas asked intrigued.

"At first it was muffled, but once I got my ear to the crack in the door, I could hear them clearly," Maija began. "It was Merglan talking with Thargon. Merglan said something about the son of a king and the veiled daughter of the elf huntress who had been prophesied to become the most powerful sorcerers in history. It sounded as though Merglan was trying to stop them from finding their magic. He also mentioned something about how they would be coming on the backs of powerful dragons. He told Thargon that he'd been close to capturing one of them at the Grandwood Games, but nabbed the wrong person. He went on to say how if he weren't so busy with their operation that he would have gone in Thargon's place.

"After that he said something about how he wasn't able to sense what the boy was thinking when he came aboard the ship. He sounded frustrated as to why he couldn't sense him on the boat or in his cell at night, but can sense his thoughts clearly when he was working in the mine. That's all I heard before Chantal came back and we had to get back to work."

"So there's hope that someone's going to rise up and defeat Merglan and his evil army?" Kirsten asked hopefully.

"Well, I didn't hear them say it was a sure thing, they just said there were two who have the potential to over-throw him, destroying his magic," Maija said. "It sounds like they're worried about them finding the magic and want them killed before they discover it."

"And that's what they wanted with you?" Kirsten asked her brother. " Why didn't they just kill you if they thought you were one of the people who could be powerful enough to overthrow him?"

"Maybe they wanted to try to convert me to their side? But why would they want that? It doesn't much matter now, I'm not dead and they said I wasn't the one they were looking for," Thomas said.

Hearing a scuffle of footsteps in the hallway, the three of them stood up. A group of the dark armored guards came into the courtyard. With filthy hands gripping the hilts of their sheathed swords, they told them through thick accents to get back into their cells or they would be beaten. The three did as they were told and the cell doors were locked behind them.

Kirsten whispered to Maija once they knew the guards couldn't hear them, "I hope Anders isn't in too much danger if Merglan really is after the lad who was with him when Thargon took us. Do you think he'll be okay?"

Maija tilted her head to gaze longingly at the darkened sky. "I don't know."

TWELVE

GLACIAL MELT BAYS

Anders and Max sailed with Britt and her crew, following the Rollo Navy ships along the coast of the Bareback Plains east and into the Marauder Sea. Life on board the ship proved more difficult than Anders could have imagined. Everyone ate and drank only what they needed to get by without falling ill. It would take the ships nearly two-and-a-half weeks to sail around the Bareback Peninsula and into the Glacial Melt Bays area. They didn't have much extra food and water aboard the small ships and couldn't afford to waste much time stopping on land. The only stops the crew made were to resupply their barrels of fresh water and gather more food. Each time they'd leave before nightfall and each time Anders missed the chance to meet with Zahara.

Everyone had to sleep under the blanket of the night sky, because the ships had no cabins or quarters below deck. Unaccustomed to sleeping while sitting up, Anders didn't get much rest during the extent of their voyage. A mixture of saltwater and rainwater formed puddles that pooled in the low points of the ship's floorboards, making the option to lie down for rest more miserable than sleeping upright. He tried sleeping on the deck of the narrow ship the first night, but got so cold he was sure he would freeze to death.

Anders kept a constant eye toward shore, hoping to see Zahara. Though he didn't spot her, he somehow knew she was nearby and keeping her eyes on him. Max caught Anders staring at the shoreline one day and asked what he was looking at. Anders lied, saying he thought he saw some more wild horses, but Max gave him a wary look unconvinced he was telling the truth.

In addition to keeping his encounters with a dragon secret, Anders desperately wanted to tell Max about seeing Ivan sneaking away from camp and Zahara's suspicion that Ivan was hiding something important from them. But he again decided against it, because he knew in the close quarters of the ship someone would overhear him, so he kept his secrets to himself.

After nearly two-and-a-half weeks' travel to the east and one rough night sailing around the choppy waters of the Bareback Peninsula's tip, they at last reached the Marauder Sea.

"One more day with good winds, and we should be at Glacial Melt Bays where we'll begin our hunt," Britt said sounding more than ready to fight against Merglan's soldiers.

"How do you know our location so well?" Anders asked.

"I've sailed these waters several times before," she said. "On my first raiding party we sailed to the southwestern tip of the Eastland Territories. We were going to attack a well-known orc encampment."

"Wait what?" Max stopped her, surprised at the

mention of orcs. "There are orcs in the Eastland Territories?" he asked.

"Oh yeah, loads of them. Thousands," she replied.

"What's an orc?" Anders asked.

"You've never heard of an orc?" Max asked surprised.

"Why, are they well-known?" he asked.

"You could say that," Max said.

"Orcs are a cruel species, the spawn of pure evil," Britt began. "Most are as large as Red, some growing to twice his size. Orcs grow at a very rapid rate. Their children are often indistinguishable from adults by the time they are three years old.

Every orc I've ever seen or heard talk of is boorish and it's impossible to differentiate the males from the females with an untrained eye.

Their dark gray splotchy skin gives them camouflage among rocky and tree-covered areas; however, most orc tribes tend to gather in wide-open areas, like the plains. In the vast expanse of these areas, they can gather in large numbers and see potential enemies coming from miles away. Many orcs have tusks that protrude outward from their lower jaw. A tusk can range anywhere from the size of my finger to the largest of rams' horns.

People say they're the spawn of demons brought to Kartania from the underworld to cause chaos in the lives of humans, elves and dwarves. I don't know about all that nonsense," she scoffed. "I'm not sure where they came from or how they got here; all I know is they are a plague on this earth and should be exterminated."

"I believe they are the spawn of demons," Max said. "I didn't know there were any left, though."

Anders looked at him, eyebrows raised, "You believe in demons, but not dragons?"

"Yeah, so what?" he said with some extra authority.

Britt continued, "Orcs are unnaturally strong for their size but are notoriously slow. Most of them now congregate in the Highland Plateaus in Eastland."

"I heard stories as a child that Eastland is the birthplace of the fairnheir, too," Max said, completely engrossed by what Britt was saying.

"Isn't that what Thargon is?" Anders asked. Britt cocked her head to the side, eyeing him, her brow furrowed in confusion. "Thargon is the one leading the soldiers we're hunting." Anders added to clarify for Britt.

"No," Max said. "He's a kurr."

"Oh," Anders said. "What's a fairnheir then?"

"That beast that Thargon was riding the night your uncle was killed was a fairnheir," Max said. Anders nodded picturing the beast on the streets of Grandwood during the attack and again on the road where Uncle Theodor met his demise. "They're like hounds, but as large as bulls and have the disposition of badgers."

Britt continued to eye them quizzically, "Well, in lighter news and to answer your question, Anders, I've sailed around this part of the world several times." Max and Anders sighed together, remembering the origin of their conversation.

For the rest of the day Anders imagined what it would be like to fight in a battle against orcs, kurr, and fairnheir as his father and uncle had during The War of the Magicians.

"Pull up the sail and get out the oars," Britt commanded the crew when they approached one of the Glacial Melt Bays.

Anders watched from behind an oar, rowing on the count, as the ships entered a narrow bay, lined with thick green vegetation different from that which he was used to seeing back at Highborn Bay. The ships beached along the shoreline and they helped Britt and the others unload gear to set up camp.

"So this is where the elves live," Anders said, admiring the broad-leaved trees and their splayed branches growing off in many directions.

"This is the beginning of the Glacial Melt Bays and, yes, it's the southernmost border of the Everlight Kingdom," Britt said as she hauled several wooden shields onto shore.

"Where are all the elves?" Anders asked not seeing any sign of civilization as he searched the forested land.

"Not here," Britt said. "If you ask me, they aren't as bad as all the others will tell you."

"What do you mean?" Anders asked.

"Oh, you don't know about our relationship with them?" Britt asked as Anders shook his head. "Elves and our people don't exactly get along. It all began about two hundred years ago. Some elves saw our people when we landed on their shores, somewhere in this bay area," she said sweeping her hand along the shoreline.

"It was the first time anyone from our islands had sailed this far east. They were desperate and starving. The elves saw them, had empathy for their ravaged state and invited them into a nearby village. Using their healing spells, the elves brought the Rollo Islanders back to their full strength. Once the warriors were strong again and having seen all the silver and gold trinkets the elves had, the crew hatched a plan to steal all of the precious items that evening. The elves gathered in one of their lodges for a feast. The crew locked the back doors and set fire to the building. They stood at the front of the building and slew all those who tried to escape. When they were done, they stole everything of value they could find."

"That's a terrible thing to do to repay your hosts," Anders said.

"Our people were raiders," Britt said. "The only thing they cared about was wealth and war."

"What happened next?" he asked.

"When they returned home to the Rollo Islands, the crew was praised by our high chiefs. They were seen as heroes for bringing back piles of wealth they didn't know existed before. When the warriors returned to this area to take more, the elves knew what our people had done. The elves were prepared and slaughtered them on sight. Only a few of the warriors escaped to tell the tale. Ever since then our two nations have loathed one another."

Britt could tell her story made Anders feel uncomfortable for being on elven soil with the entire Rollo Navy.

"It has been a long time since our people shed blood," Britt reassured him. "Our quarrels have subsided greatly, no longer resulting in physical violence as often as before."

The rest of the afternoon and evening were quite uneventful. Anders and Max made camp with the rest of Britt's crew. Ivan, Red and Jorgen had meetings with the other Rollo leaders about how to begin searching the area. Anders and Max remained uninvited.

After the meetings concluded, those privy to them passed the word down to those in command of ships. Each lead captain commanded at least five ships. The chiefs passed the word down to the lead captains, who, in turn, let the captains of each ship know the plan. Each captain kept his or her crew members informed of the plans. Somehow Anders knew Britt would be keeping them much better informed than Red ever would have.

During dinner that night, Britt told her crew what would be happening the next day. They were to split up into groups led by each lead captain. One group would search to the east, one to the north, and one to the west. The last group would remain in charge of watching over the fleet of ships and protecting camp.

"I hope we don't get stuck here babysitting the ships all day," Max whispered to Anders. Anders agreed; he would prefer to do something to help rather than sit at camp all day wondering if anything important was happening in the field.

"We will be joining Red's command and going to the north," Britt said. Max and Anders smiled at the news. "We leave at first light. Got it?" she said looking everyone in the eye.

The crew replied in unison, "Yes, Captain."

"Make sure your blades are sharp and your bows are strung," she added.

Later that night as he sat on his wool blankets, Anders sharpened the sword he'd bought at the market back in Brookside. Then he made sure his bow was strung and his quiver of arrows was ready. He said good night to Max and they both lay down to sleep. But Anders was not going to sleep right away. He could feel that Zahara had been following them and he desperately wanted to see her again. Once Max and the others were asleep, he made what was becoming his usual nighttime sneak-away and headed off into the woods.

Once he was far enough away from camp, he used his thoughts to say, *Zahara... Zahara, where are you?*

Emerging from behind a large tree, Zahara showed herself, *Anders, over here.*

Anders crept over to her, *Is everything all right?*

You were on that floating log for a long time, she said.

It's called a ship and I didn't know that we were going to be stuck out at sea for that long. It was a lot farther than I'd thought.

I wanted to tell you, but I couldn't risk the others seeing me or they might have done something to hurt me.

Tell me what? Anders asked.

I flew ahead of your ships and saw far into the distance. There is a large gathering of horrible-looking creatures that are heading this way.

How far ahead of us are they? Anders asked. As the words came out of his mouth, he heard shouts in the distance and saw a plume of smoke beginning to rise above the treetops.

They're here, Zahara said.

THIRTEEN

ORC ATTACK

Anders sprinted back toward camp as fast as he could, leaping over downed logs and bulling through brush as if it weren't there. As he drew near, he could hear the horrible screams and shouts of battle. Clashing iron on iron rang through the night. He wasn't sure if Zahara had followed him or not. Before he made it out of the trees and back to the shoreline where they'd set up camp, he saw a group of ugly creatures chasing one of the Rollo Islanders through the woods. Anders halted when he saw the dark figures, but it was too late to go unnoticed. He made eye contact with one of them. They stood tall like men but had the dark gray mottled skin and large tusks Britt had described.

Orcs, Anders thought.

The one he made eye contact with shouted to the others and three of them peeled off from the group to charge directly at him. Luckily, Anders had brought his hunting knife on his nighttime walk. He drew the short blade and ran toward the orcs head on. This was not a time to be fearful. For all he knew, the orcs had already overrun those he held dear back at camp; he had been lucky to be off in the woods when the ambush began.

Before he clashed with the orcs, he counted on his training for the Grandwood Games and flung his knife at the first orc, hitting him directly in the chest. Hoping to strike fear into the others, he bellowed a gut-felt cry and leapt into the air with both of his feet curled up in front of him. He kicked with all his might as he collided with the second orc, knocking it back so hard it took out the third orc behind it. Now on his back and vulnerable, but just ahead of the orcs, he used his speed to his advantage. He rolled over to the first orc, ripped his knife out of its chest, and pounced onto one of the orcs who was still trying to stand up. Anders swiftly slit its throat just in time to see the third orc rise to its feet. He went to throw his knife at it, but before he could, the orc dropped its weapon. Anders hesitated and then saw Zahara leaping over his head. She bared her dagger-like teeth and in one fell swoop landed on the orc devouring its upper half with her deadly jaws.

Anders' jaw dropped in surprise as he witnessed the sheer power Zahara used to dispatch the orc. She turned and looked back at Anders, crimson blood dripping from her fangs.

Are you okay? she asked him.

"Yeah," he replied, taking a breath. "That was crazy! Thank you!" Anders exclaimed. "I need to get to my things. I need my bow and sword. I won't survive with just this knife." Anders said with urgency.

I hope Max is all right, he thought to himself.

I can check, Zahara said.

"You can hear my thoughts too?" Anders said. It actually wasn't that surprising to him, but he said it anyway.

Yes. I'll look for him with my mind, she paused, and

then said, *I've got him. He is still alive, and not far from here.*

Anders ran the rest of the way back to his campsite, but Zahara didn't follow him this time.

I cannot risk being seen by your people, her voice sounded into his mind when he noticed she hadn't followed him. *I'll watch over you from up here,* she added, showing him a mental image of where she was perched high in the treetops. He could tell she didn't want to leave him by himself to fight, but she needed to protect her identity from those he was traveling with. He understood that many in the war party would want to kill her if they found a dragon was nearby, even if she was helping to kill the orcs.

Out of the trees and onto the beach, Anders could see the attack much more clearly. The rising moon brightened the night sky and the shoreline glowed orange from the light of flames burning many of their ships. The orcs had attacked by land on the east side of the bay, opposite from his campsite. He looked across the bay and watched as several groups of the orcs waded into the shallow water and set fire to two more ships at the southeast entrance of the bay. Anders estimated half the fleet was already ablaze. He saw how the warriors had established a line of defense on the beach to protect their remaining ships.

Anders quickly found his sword, bow and arrows, and began to search for Max. He couldn't afford to lose another friend; panic began to overwhelm him. His vision blurred and fear was beginning to overwhelm his other senses when Zahara called to him. The familiar presence of her voice brought him back to reality; he couldn't see her but he could hear her voice clearly in his thoughts. She told him Max was with a group of warriors who were being separated from the line of defense at the other end of the bay. She sent him a mental image of Max's location in relation to their campsite.

"How are you doing this?" Anders asked searching the treetops, but not finding where Zahara was hiding.

Don't worry about it now, I will tell you more about how I communicate later, Zahara said, sounding a little frustrated with him.

The ships were all docked near the base of the U-shaped bay. Most of the Rollo forces were in their shield wall formation facing the forest, their backs to the remaining ships. It seemed they had secured a solid position that would allow them to fight back while protecting the remaining ships. Orcs attacked in great numbers out of the forest on the eastern half of the bay. Several groups of warriors stood together between Anders and where the assembled warriors of the shield wall held their ground. The smaller groups who'd banded in between battled orcs that must have made their way around to the western half of the bay before the Rollo Island warriors took their position.

Anders decided to make his way along the western side of the bay working north. Max, who he'd seen through Zahara's mind, was with Britt. The two were forced away from the shield wall, taking shelter in the forest. Anders could use the cover of the forest to stay hidden from the orcs as he advanced closer to his friends' aid. Hopefully, he would be able to pick off enough of the orcs with his bow to provide some cover for them to break through the orcs' ranks and rejoin the shield wall with the others. Anders could only assume Red, Jorgen, and Ivan were leading the main Rollo force and did not concern himself with their safety. Both Ivan and Red had plenty of experience; he knew they could handle themselves.

He snuck his way along the edge of the forest, passing

just feet from orcs and men fighting wildly against each other onshore. He could have joined in the fighting here, but the men and women on this side of the bay were already outnumbered and he needed to focus on his task if he ever wanted to see Max alive again.

Anders gathered stray arrows he found on the ground, stocking his quiver with as many as he could fit while he worked his way through the trees. The light from the burning ships combined with the moonlight helped him search for his friends. Soon he saw Britt and Max. They were backed up against the creek bed that led from within the forest and out into mouth of the bay. Taking on twice as many orcs as any other group he had seen so far, he watched as Britt wielded two hatchets and Max struck with his sword to hold the fierce orcs at bay. Anders was within shooting range of the orcs. Remaining hidden behind several large rocks near the stream's edge, he mustered his courage and began shooting arrow after arrow at the orcs attacking his friends. The orcs didn't seem to notice their comrades were being killed by something other than the sharp blades wielded by his two friends.

Anders killed two-dozen orcs before some of them began to look around, noticing someone nearby was shooting at them. Anders foolishly shot one of the orcs in the head while several others around him were searching to determine where the arrows were coming from. They now knew where he was hiding. Most of them switched their focus to him and came running, swords in hand.

That worked, Anders thought.

Realizing he now faced a different problem, a much deadlier one, panic began to overcome him once more. A large group of angry orcs headed straight at him and he had no backup. Fearing for his life, he groped desperately at his quiver. Noticing that it was nearly devoid of arrows, he quickly killed two more orcs with his bow before fleeing deeper into the woods. As he fled, he recalled what Britt had mentioned about orcs being notoriously slow; he could use that to his advantage.

Calming his frantic thoughts, Anders continued through the forest, running deeper into the trees. He called with his mind to Zahara for help but didn't hear a response. He turned around to see the orcs more spread out. He could fight them one at a time. Holding his ground and remaining more confident in his fighting abilities with the sword, he engaged the first of his pursuers. As he exchanged blows, Anders was surprised at the orc's strength, but it was not as fast as he was. He ducked a swing of the orc's sword and drove the tip of his through the middle of the foul creature.

The next four were easier than the first. Anders stuck to what was working: dodge the first blow, and then move in quickly for the kill. Anders kept running farther away to spread out those chasing him. Taking them on one at a time, he worked his way through the mass of orcs following him. The last remaining orcs trailed him at a distance far enough away that he was able take out his bow. The bright moonlight broke through the canopy and made his targets easy enough to see. One at a time he shot the advancing orcs, finishing them off along with the last of his arrows.

Getting back to the battle was easy enough. All Anders had to do was follow the trail of bodies he'd created. He was proud of himself, using his speed to his advantage and taking only one orc at a time. He did wonder why Zahara hadn't responded. He wasn't with anyone else who would have lived to tell about her existence.

Once back at the edge of the forest, Anders could see

that the battle had gone in favor of the Islanders. The warriors had managed to clear the west beach of orcs and were pushing the main orc force back into the forest on the eastern edge. He came out of the trees and onto the beach. He could see through the light of the flames that Max and Britt had rejoined the shield wall and were fighting alongside the main force.

Joining the shield wall, he helped his fellow warriors. From behind the shields, Anders helped the collective group push the remaining orcs off the beach. Soon the orcs began to retreat and the battle was over.

Anders panted heavily, placing his hands on his knees. He was exhausted from all of the running and fighting. He dripped with sweat and his clothes were wet with orc blood. He looked around among those he fought alongside, searching for Max, Ivan and Britt.

Max and Britt had been close by, so he located them quickly. A sense of relief came over him when he found his friends unharmed. Max told him Red and Ivan were in front of the group pointing in their direction. That was enough to ease his worried mind. He and Max joined Britt and the others who had began walking back across the beach.

"I thought you were a goner," Max said. "When the attack began, you were nowhere to be found. I assumed orcs had grabbed you and drug you off into the woods. I stayed with Britt and the people who were near our campsite. We got pushed around and separated from the main group. Somehow, we caught a lucky break and pushed through to the others on the beach. From there the battle turned in our favor. What happened to you? How did you end up in the shield wall?" he asked.

Anders lied and told him he'd gone off to pee when the attack began, so he joined the fighting late. "When I was sneaking back through the woods, I saw that you and Britt had been separated from the others on the beach. From behind a couple of large rocks, I took out two-dozen of them with my bow before the orcs realized I was shooting at them. When they came after me, I led them into the woods, taking them out one at a time," he said, shrugging nonchalantly. "No, big deal or anything," he added with a hint of sarcasm.

"You saved us?" Max sounded surprised. "That was you who led the orcs away from us? Wow, you saved my life!" he exclaimed.

"You saved me back in Grandwood, so I guess we're even."

Max gave Anders a forceful hug, "Even," he released his firm hug and gripped Anders' shoulders at arm's length. "Wait until I tell others about this."

"Well, I don't want any praise or anything. Just keep it between us, okay?" Anders didn't want to draw attention to the fact that he was sneaking off during the night again.

"All right, but I think we should at least tell Britt," Max said. "She should know who saved us."

"Okay," Anders agreed. "You can tell her, but I don't want people thinking I did something more than anyone else in this battle. You all fought harder than I did anyway."

After the battle was over Anders was physically and emotionally exhausted. He tried to get some sleep before dawn, but visions of orcs attacking those he'd grown closest to over the past several weeks kept him up. Although he was worried about Zahara's whereabouts, he didn't know if the orcs that retreated would come back to finish what they'd started. He knew he needed to rest in case the orcs launched a second attack, but despite how exhausted he was, he couldn't sleep.

At dawn Britt came over to their group and gave them an update on the new plan. They were now going to track the orcs that had retreated and find out where they came from, thinking perhaps the orcs had been sent by Thargon.

"Their original location is likely where they're holding our people. Gear up, we leave soon," Britt ordered loudly. She walked over to where Anders and Max were standing. Reaching out and gipping Anders' hand firmly, she whispered so only he could hear, "Max told me what you did. Leading the group of orcs away from us was very brave. We couldn't have made it back to the shield wall without you."

As she released his hand, Anders smiled and gave her a slight nod, then followed her orders and packed up his belongings.

HIS GEAR PACKED, he was ready to go within minutes. From what he could tell most of the camp was not yet ready and most likely would not be leaving for at least an hour or more. With the extra time, he decided to sneak off into the woods to see if Zahara was still watching him. He wanted to make sure she was okay after the battle and thank her for saving him from the orc in the forest.

Anders slowly stepped backward toward the edge of the tree line. When it appeared that no one was paying attention, he slipped behind a tree and out of sight. The morning sunlight glinted off the dew-filled leaves around him. It was strange to think that the battle took place just hours before in such a beautiful place. When he'd gone far enough away from camp that it wasn't likely anyone would find him, he called out in his mind for Zahara.

She answered. The dragon was curled up, her head and tail wrapped tightly around her body like a sleeping dog. She was lying under a ray of sunshine splashing down through the canopy to the forest floor. The light highlighted the brightness of her scales. Anders rushed to her side and hugged her tightly around the neck. The electric burst of energy when he touched her coursed through his veins and gave his drowsy body a much-needed awakening. Pulling away, he noticed her scales were splotched with dried blood.

"Are you hurt?" he asked furrowing his brow.

She sat up on her hindquarters and shook her head and neck sending the twigs and duff that stuck to gooey patches of blood flying. *No, I am fine*, she said with a yawn while spreading her wings to their full span. She folded them neatly against her sides and looked down at him with her head cocked sideways, *I was just enjoying the morning sun. It warms my scales and feels nice. Are you okay?"* sensing his concern for her.

"Yeah, I'm fine. What happened to you after I left?" he asked. "Whose blood is all that?" pointing to the splotches around her neck and just now seeing that her head and paws were saturated with it.

I hate the way they taste, she said, gumming her tongue against the roof of her mouth. *Their blood is as rotten as their souls. I would much rather eat almost anything else.*

"Orcs? You ate one of them?"

That's what you call those hateful creatures? No, I didn't eat one, but when I was biting into them I got their nasty blood in my mouth, she shook her head and stuck her forked tongue out slightly.

"I thought you were just going to watch me from the treetops?" Anders asked, confused why she'd gone off on her own and killed orcs.

You called to me, she said as if he knew she'd responded to him.

"I did, but I didn't hear you reply," he thought maybe she had tried but didn't make the connection with his mind.

I felt someone else watching over the battle with his mind. I didn't want to make myself known to whoever it was, so I shielded my thoughts, she paused to sniff the air for a moment, then continued, *So many orcs were chasing you. I saw a large group following the others you had taken on. I waited until they were far enough in the trees before I attacked them.*

Shocked that she had stopped more orcs from attacking him, Anders said, "I don't know what I would do without you. It's kind of crazy, but I feel..." Anders trailed off not wanting to sound like he was growing too attached to Zahara.

You know I can feel your emotions too, Zahara said. *You don't need to say it Anders, I feel the same way about you.*

Anders sat down on a log next to her, feeling a bit embarrassed at exposing his raw emotions.

You miss your family, Zahara said. *I miss mine, too. Maybe that is why we have grown so attached to each other in such a short time?*

Anders nodded, "You're pretty smart for a two-year-old." He heard her laugh for the first time. The noise came from deep within her throat. "We both have family, but we can't be with them. I just hope they're okay."

Me, too, Zahara added. Suddenly her head shot up at attention with her ears pinned back. Anders knew she'd sensed someone or something approaching. He'd seen her do it once before, the first night they'd met, when Ivan and the others came searching for him.

"What is it? Who's coming?"

It's the man who hides something and sneaks off during the night to talk to a face in the mirror.

"That's Ivan. What's he doing?"

He's trying to sense if anyone is near. I'm blocking us from him. Let's see what he's up to, Zahara said as she crouched and moved behind a tree.

Anders thought it couldn't hurt to see what Ivan was doing, as long as he didn't know Anders was once again spying on him.

Staying out of sight, the two followed Ivan deeper into the woods. Suddenly Ivan stopped and pulled something out of his pocket. It was the mirror Zahara mentioned. They watched as he placed it on the ground and said some words. A voice began to speak out from the small mirror. The forest was calm and silent, so they could hear clearly what was being said.

"You prevailed against the orc tribe," a soothing and at the same time powerful voice said.

"We did," Ivan replied. "I could feel the presence of his mind during the battle. He was searching for him."

"I know it did not seem like the right thing to do but it needed to be done," said the voice.

"I... understand," Ivan said coldly.

"You should know the plan worked; however, it is not safe to talk about with magic. He could be listening in. You know what you must do," the voice said ambiguously.

"Understood," Ivan put the mirror back into his pocket and began to walk swiftly back to camp.

Anders looked at Zahara, "You stay here. I'm going to confront him about this."

Are you sure that's a good idea? Zahara asked.

"I need to know what he's been hiding from us," he said with determination.

Okay, but be careful. It sounded as though he might have known about the orc attack and did nothing to prevent it. I will keep my distance, but if he tries anything, I will jump in to protect you if need be.

"Thanks." Anders hoped that it wouldn't come to that. He had to get to the bottom of what Ivan was keeping from them. If Ivan had known in advance about the orcs' attack and did nothing to prevent it, Anders felt he'd have to tell the others of this betrayal.

Anders ran toward him, calling after Ivan.

"Anders?" Ivan said sounding surprised to see him. "Where did you come from?"

Anders stopped just short of Ivan to confront him. "I saw you the other night, sneaking away from camp to have a chat in private with whoever is on the other side of that mirror," he pointed angrily to where Ivan had pocketed the mirror. "That's also what you were doing the night I was walking along the plains and that's what I just saw you do now."

"Anders, I can explain," Ivan began, but Anders cut him off.

"I heard what they said. You knew about the orc attack and did nothing to stop it?" Ivan looked down trying to think of something to say. He opened his mouth, but nothing came out; he failed to say the words Anders wanted to hear.

"Why didn't you warn us about the attack!" Anders shouted, more enraged now than he thought he would ever be.

"Anders, there are powers at work here that you do not yet understand. The orcs attacking the Rollo warriors was necessary for our mission," Ivan said.

"How was having orcs kill the people who are trying to help me get my family back necessary for our mission? Our mission is to track down the enemy and save the people they took from us!" Anders said with conviction.

"I know it looks bad, but the elves and I have been working on a way to get Merglan to expose his location to us. We have been trying for years to find where he has been conducting his dark magic. We knew it was somewhere east and we know that the Rollo Islanders are involved. The high council of elves and I saw an opportunity. And it worked, Anders. The elves have spies who saw where they were marching. They tracked them to a fortress in Eastland. What you overheard back there was not bad news; it was great news. Now I must go to the Enlightened Forest and meet with the elf king to plan our next move. You must believe me that what happened here was a necessary evil for the greater good of Kartania." Ivan paused, waiting for Anders' response.

While trying to process the information, Anders heard Zahara say in his mind, *He is telling the truth, Anders. I was able to sense him while he spoke to you. He was being honest with you.*

Anders glared at Ivan and said, "Good people died because of this."

"And many more will unless we stop Merglan," Ivan said.

Anders nodded, "All right, I'll keep this to myself, under one condition."

"What's that?" Ivan asked.

"That you take me and Max with you to the elves," Anders demanded.

Ivan paused, scratching the beard that had grown on his chin over the last several weeks. Thinking it over he said, "Okay, fine. You two can come with me."

"Great! When do we leave?"

"As soon as we get back to camp," Ivan said.

Anders used his thoughts to reach Zahara, *You can follow us to the elves, that's where your family and the other dragons you were with were going when you got lost, right?*

Yes. Do you think my family made it there?

It's our best shot at finding them. If they aren't there, maybe the elves will be able to help you find them. They would know more about it than anyone else I can think of.

Thank you, Anders.

Back at camp, he pulled Max aside and told him that the three of them would be going on a separate mission to see the elves, if Max wanted to join in.

"Are you serious?" Max asked, excitedly. "I've never met an elf before. Yes, I'm in! When do we leave?"

"Get your things. We're to meet Ivan by the stream as soon as we're ready," Anders said pointing to the canyon at the mouth of the bay. Max grabbed his travel pack and the two of them said their goodbyes to Britt and her crewmates. Both of them had grown close to their new captain over the last several weeks, so it was a sorrowful goodbye.

Max and Anders met Ivan near the stream. Ivan had explained to Red and Jorgen that he was needed for a different mission and was taking Max and Anders. Their plan was to reunite with the warriors in a week's time. The two Rollo leaders were not happy to see a valuable asset like Ivan leave them now, but none of the three were a part of the Rollo tribe, so they couldn't stop them from leaving. Together Ivan, Anders, and Max set out; Zahara followed, unknown to Anders' two companions.

FOURTEEN

THE EVERLIGHT KINGDOM

With no path for them to follow, neither Max nor Anders knew where they were going, so they trailed Ivan. Anders reached out mentally to Zahara. He felt her presence and knew she was nearby, shadowing them as they hiked up the canyon deeper into the forest.

"How long is the walk to the Everlight Kingdom?" Anders asked as they hiked along the forest floor.

"We are already in the Everlight Kingdom," Ivan said. "We are going to the ancient elf city of Cedarbridge in the heart of the Enlightened Forest."

"Why do they call it the Enlightened Forest?" Max asked.

"Long ago when the elves first built their homes in the forest, they imbedded magic into all of their natural surroundings. The elves and the empowered forest have since coexisted peacefully and harmoniously for thousands of years with this sharing of powers. The magic within the walls is so ancient and powerful that no magician has ever been able to break down its protective barrier, not even Merglan," Ivan said.

"It sounds like a utopia," Max said.

"It's a peaceful place and the quest for knowledge there is never-ending. They hold the largest library in the world. Its manuscripts and scrolls go all the way back to this world's first inhabitants."

"It sounds like a good place to be when the rest of the nations fall to pieces," Anders said.

"The elves are not beyond the destructive grasp of Merglan, but they have managed to avoid it thus far. The location of Cedarbridge disguises itself to those unwelcome magicians who seek to find it," Ivan said. "Though they are protected by powerful magic, the city of the elves has its problems too, just like the rest of the world."

They walked in silence for most of the morning after the talk about Cedarbridge. They stopped to rest for lunch after emerging from the canyon where the Glacial Melt Creek was carving out its path.

"Do all elves know how to use magic?" Anders asked, chewing on a stick of jerky.

Ivan responded, "No, although many can. They are not born with the ability to use magic, like dragons. They have to be given the gift just like we humans. Most elves live very long lives, much longer than a human or dwarf. Elves and dragons share a special connection with nature and all things that come from nature. The elven people have bonded more with dragons than any other race; it has been that way for thousands of years. The land of dragons, Nagano, as named by the elves, is the original birthplace of our world's dragon race. Its borders lie east and north of the Everlight Kingdom. Nagano is surrounded by two enormous mountain ranges, the Ridgebacks to the north and the Eastland Mountains to the south. The Eastland Mountains separate the dragons from the evils that grow in Eastland Territories."

"It sounds like a good place for a young dragon to grow up," Anders said, thinking of Zahara's life when she was younger.

"Yes, Nagano is an ideal place for dragons to thrive," Ivan said looking at Anders, curious about that comment.

For the next several days, the three of them marched through the forest along the base of the Frozentip Mountains, which, according to Ivan, separated Westland from the Everlight Kingdom. Every now and then Anders could see the glacier-capped peaks poking up above the clouds. Each night, Anders would sneak away to visit with Zahara and tell her what he learned about the elves that day. She was just as fascinated by their culture as he was and probably more excited to meet them.

Finally, after several long days with little rest at night, the three travelers reached the camouflaged city gates of Cedarbridge. An expansive wall of tightly woven plants created a living barrier protecting the city's limits. Anders told Zahara to wait until he thought it was safe for her to reveal herself to the elves. He didn't want to take any chances of having Zahara taken away from him until he was sure they would help find her parents.

Ivan spoke a strange tongue that Anders assumed was Elvish, because when he finished the gate swung open. "Welcome to the Enlightened Forest and Cedarbridge, the city of elves," Ivan motioned his arm across his body in perfect timing with the gate as it opened.

Anders and Max stared in awe at the beautiful sight.

Homes built in trees, natural bridges and staircases leading from one to the other. Entire structures constructed of growing plants surrounded them as they entered the city. Beautiful wood carvings adorned each door and each structure's intricate details stood out. Anders took it all in.

Everything is a wonderful work of art, he thought.

Before they'd gone very far beyond the gates, an elf woman walked up to them. She wore her silver blonde hair pinned up at the back of her head, exposing her pointy ears. She had beautiful green eyes and wore a blue dress intricately woven with a pattern Anders had never seen before.

"Follow me," she said in slightly accented Landish and motioned for them to follow her. Max, Ivan, and Anders did as they were instructed.

"Where are we going?" Anders asked Ivan.

"She is leading us to the High Council. There we will discuss the location of Merglan's hideout," Ivan said.

They followed a well-worn path that wound through the forested city. At the base of an enormous tree, they entered through another beautifully carved door. Spiral stairs spun along the inside of the tree's trunk, leading them upward to the canopy. They came out into a large courtyard nestled in the crotch of the large tree. Leaf-covered branches extended out and up from the platform's edges, growing in all directions high above their heads. In the center of the courtyard, seated around a large table, seven elves awaited their arrival. Every one of them looked over at Ivan, Max and Anders when they entered the platform. Only one seat remained unoccupied at the table.

"We weren't expecting you to bring visitors," one of the elves said to Ivan in perfect Landish as he moved into the remaining chair. Anders and Max stood behind him.

"I had to meet certain obligations, Asmond," Ivan said, looking back at Anders and Max as he spoke.

"Very well. We can begin," Asmond said.

Anders and Max listened as the High Council of Elves spoke, though neither of them understood Elvish. They stood behind Ivan and remained expressionless as though they knew what was being discussed. One of the elves pulled out a map of Eastland and began pointing to several locations.

"I have never heard of the orcs and kurr gathering together in such great numbers," an elf woman said, switching effortlessly to Landish so Anders and Max could understand her.

Ivan searched the faces of the elves gathered around the table, his expression serious, "We need to strike now while Merglan is focused on building his army. If what you have said is true, he is planning something big. His armies have never been the size they will be if he can unite all of the orcs and kurr."

"Agreed," Asmond said.

"The Rollo Islanders are tracking the orc tribe that attacked us at one of the Glacial Melt Bays. Together, if we combine our forces, we could launch an attack on Merglan's fortress," Ivan said.

The elves in the room collectively looked on in disgust at the mention of the Rollo Islanders.

"In the interest of our common enemy's demise, I will forgive the feud between our people and the warrior brutes, for now," Asmond said.

Ivan rose and bowed to him, "Thank you, your grace. We will look for your army at the Eastland Mountain front before we march on the fortress."

"I will send my son with you. He can keep me informed of your progress. When it is time, we will send our army," said Asmond.

"That is very generous of you, Asmond. Thank you," Ivan said bowing once more. He turned and nodded to Anders and Max to leave with him.

"This way please," said the elf that had escorted them up to the council meeting.

Once back on solid ground, Ivan told them they'd be leaving once Asmond's son joined them.

"So that guy, Asmond, was their leader?" Anders asked.

"Yes, he is the Elf King. The woman who also spoke our tongue during the meeting was his wife and Queen of the elves. Her name is Lageena," he said. "Their son, who you will meet very soon, is called Nadir."

Max and Anders nodded. They were led to the far edge of the city where they were told to wait for Nadir's arrival. As the elf woman moved to leave them, Anders said to her, "Wait, there's something I need to ask you."

She turned to look at him. Ivan and Max also looked at him, a bit confused about what he could possibly want from her.

"There's a young dragon with us that got lost during a storm. She was fleeing from Merglan when he invaded her homeland. Her family was trying to make it here to seek refuge. She is patiently waiting outside your gates. Do you think it would be possible to see if her parents made it here? Or if anyone knows where they could be?" Anders asked.

Max stood there looking at him with his mouth open in astonishment.

"Let me check. I will be right back," she said and ran off.

"Since when do you know dragons?" Max asked, flabbergasted.

"I met her that night I went for a walk along the forest's edge at the Bareback Plains," Anders said. "I felt bad that she was all alone and lost from her family. After that I snuck off to meet her many of the nights that we traveled when everyone was asleep. She told me how she was separated from her parents on the way here. When you said you had to come here, Ivan, I thought it was a perfect opportunity to come and see if I could help reunite her with her family."

"That's why I couldn't sense you," Ivan said. "You were with a dragon. She must have blocked you from me. I was beginning to think my magic was failing me."

"You have been befriending a dragon this whole time?" Max said.

"Understand that if she exposed herself to the wrong person, they would have tried to kill her or use her against her will. She's just an infant and I didn't want any harm to come to her," Anders said.

"He is right," Ivan said. "Many in the Rollo clans would have harmed her if they knew of her existence."

Rushing back to them, the elf woman, "We have two dragons here at present that claim to have been separated from their offspring on their way to our city. I would be glad to show her to them."

"Great!" Anders said, excited and relieved.

"If you bring her in, we can go together to see if they are her parents. Then I will take you back to your companions and you can go on your way," she said.

Anders looked at Ivan for his approval; he nodded in agreement. Anders went with the elf woman to the gate. When it opened, Zahara stood waiting for him. He knew she had listened in on their conversation so was already aware of the arrangements. She hopped up into the air and did a few loops, then landed back on the ground.

You've found my family! she said excitedly.

"It looks like it," Anders said. "This elf would like to take us to them and make sure they are indeed your parents."

Let's go, she said happily.

Anders looked at the elf woman, forcing a smile on his face, "She's ready."

The woman guided them a long way around the edge of the city. At the far end, they came to a cliff that overlooked a large valley. Anders could see several dragons playfully flying through the air above the valley. He looked up at Zahara and saw the look of pure joy in her eyes. The elf lady called out over the cliff. Two very large dragons, one orange in color and one purple, landed on the cliff in front of them. Zahara threw herself into their embrace, nuzzling their heads and necks and purring happily.

"It looks like you have reunited this family," the elf said to Anders.

"It sure does," Anders said. He felt sad that he had to let her go. He wanted to stay with her, but it was time for him to focus on getting his own family back. Anders knew this was where their paths ended, for now. Hanging his head, he turned and began to walk away from them, the elf woman leading him back from where they'd come.

Zahara saw them leaving and called after him, *Hey, Anders, wait up*. Anders turned and met Zahara as she bounded to him. He hugged her tightly around the neck and she nuzzled him back.

As he held onto her, he said, "Be with your family. I will return someday. I promise." His eyes welled with tears as he pulled away.

Thank you for all you've done, Anders, Zahara said. She watched as he walked away, disappearing along the winding path toward Cedarbridge.

Anders followed his guide in silence back to Ivan and Max. He'd managed to wipe away his tears before rejoining them. Nadir had met up with Ivan and Max while Anders was away; they stood ready to embark on the next part of their adventure.

"I know that was hard for you to do," Ivan said as he patted Anders on the shoulder. "You did the right thing. She will be much safer here with the elves and back among the safety of her family."

Embarrassed at his sniffles, Anders agreed, "I know." As he said the words, Anders found himself gazing longingly at the cliffs. Forcing himself, Anders followed the others as they set off into the vast elven forest once again.

AFTER LEAVING Zahara with the elves, Anders felt his mind become clouded in a gloom he hadn't felt since his Uncle Theodor was killed. While Ivan and Max talked with Nadir, the Elf Prince, Anders wondered if he'd made a mistake in leaving Zahara. In the end, however many ways he mulled it over, Zahara belonged with her parents. She was, after all, just a baby with little knowledge of the world.

Ivan and Nadir knew the paths that would take them to an area where they expected to find the Rollo Island warriors. Once they were close enough, Ivan would be able to sense their exact location, so the small group was confident in tracking down the Rollo people.

When the sun set and then night fell onto the forest, the four built a fire and ate the dried meat and nuts they'd brought along. Nadir went off to gather some leaves, fruits and berries for his meal. Curious about how it would taste, Max and Anders tried the assortment of things the elf was eating. Ivan deferred, sticking with his dried meat and nuts.

"I ate too much of that vegetation when I was training for the war," Ivan said stuffing his hand into the pouch where he kept his rations.

"The greens are pretty bland, but the berries are sweet," Max said, excitedly chewing on a handful of the elf's food.

"All the nutrients the body needs are growing right here in the forest around us," Nadir said humbly.

"That's right," Ivan said. "And the wild protein provided by the animals we eat are just that."

"Carnivores that live in the forest rely on those meats. I will not take a meal away from the hunters of these woods. As long as they keep the deer and other herbivores in check, we'll continue to have plenty of naturally growing foods for all who live here in the Everlight Kingdom," Nadir said.

Anders took a bite of dried meat. Talking with his mouth fairly full, he said, "I think I fall somewhere in the middle of your opinions. I think the greens and fruits complement the meat quite nicely."

"Yeah, I like them both, too. Meat is just too good to give up altogether, in my opinion," Max added.

"Suit yourself," the elf said and finished his meal.

After a short silence, Max blurted out something that'd been bothering him all day. He had been afraid to ask earlier, but now he could not control his eagerness to know. "Can you do magic?" he asked Nadir. "Ivan told us that many elves can perform magic."

"Max," Ivan said in a tone that would be used in talking down to a child. "It is not polite to ask an elf such a personal question. Especially a member of the elven royalty."

"No, it's all right," said Nadir. "To answer your question frankly, no, I am not able to use magic yet. I have been paired with several dragons, none of which shared a connection with me strong enough for me to receive the gift of magic."

"Is it common for dragons to decide not to bestow magic on someone?" Anders asked.

"It happens more often than you would think," Nadir said shortly. "A dragon's likelihood to find a match so strong only happens once in its lifetime, if they are lucky. Most dragons live their whole lives never finding their match."

"How did it happen for you, Ivan?" Anders asked.

Ivan took a sip of some water he had in the bladder slung around his neck, "When I was paired with my dragon the elves had spent many months observing the personalities and behaviors of the dragons and those who went through the army's training camps. The candidates were paired up with the dragon that had a personality most similar to their own. The system had some success, because several of us in the program did find matches.

"My situation was not a normal one. Because of the peculiarity and haste of the match, I feared our connection would not be as strong as most dragon-rider matches that were put together more organically."

Anders saw a tear roll down Ivan's cheek. He quickly wiped it away with his sleeve.

"No matter," Nadir said. "I am sure if Zahara was your match, she would have let you know, what with you being the Prophecy and all."

Flustered by the comment, Anders asked, "What

Prophecy?" He looked at Ivan, who held his forehead in his hands.

Quick to read the situation, Nadir said to Ivan, "You hadn't told him yet?"

Anders struggled to understand why he suddenly felt so confused and angry; perhaps he was just upset after losing another close friend. Perhaps Nadir had misspoken. He looked to Ivan and Nadir angrily, "What the hell do you mean, I am the Prophecy?"

"Let me explain," Ivan said, taking a deep breath. "There is a prophecy that foretells of a human and dragon bond so strong that the two will become the most powerful dragon and sorcerer pair in history. Powerful enough to overthrow Merglan."

"That's what you were talking to Theodor about in the woods the night before the attack began?!" Anders asked.

Ivan nodded, "That is what Merglan is searching for. It isn't a trinket or an item; it's you."

"What? How? Why?" Anders asked in rapid succession.

"Merglan sensed it in you when you were just a baby. He tried to capture you once before, when you were younger."

"Is that how my parents died?" Anders asked, already knowing the answer.

"Yes," Ivan said with a sigh.

"He was wrong; Merglan got it wrong!" Anders shouted in desperation. He didn't want to accept what Ivan was telling him. "I'm not anything special! I am just a person who wants to get my family back." He jumped to his feet and stormed off away from camp.

"Anders, wait," Ivan said getting up to follow him.

"Let him go," Nadir said, motioning Ivan to sit back down. "He needs time to process this revelation."

Later that night, Max pulled Anders aside and asked, "Hey, are you okay?"

Anders shrugged and glanced to make sure that Ivan and Nadir weren't within earshot. "How can what they said be true? Zahara and I shared the feeling of being separated from our families, but that was it. We didn't form a special bond. The only thing that has changed is now I know why terrible things have happened to my family. It's all because some crazy sorcerer believes I am going to defeat him. I can hardly fight off more than one orc by myself. I am not who they think I am."

"At least you know why bad things have happened to your family," Max said.

"What do you mean?" Anders asked.

"You know how I told you Bo and I were adopted by that family in Brookside?" Anders nodded. "Well, they had to adopt us because my parents were murdered in their sleep."

"That's awful," Anders said, shocked that Max was telling him this.

"Tony always thought I did it to them and hates me. One day when I was out riding with Tony's oldest daughter, nomads from the Bareback Plains attacked us. I hid in a coyote's den after they knocked me off my horse. She didn't make it in time and the nomads killed her. Once they were gone, I brought her body back and Tony nearly beat me to death. No matter how many times I tried to tell him what happened, he remained convinced that I'd killed his daughter. I don't know if that makes you feel any better or worse, but at least you know why Merglan is attacking your family. I don't know why people attacked mine," Max returned to the camp, leaving Anders standing alone.

Anders came back to his spot around the fire, lay down on the ground, closed his eyes, and went to sleep.

Over the next several days, Anders and Max followed Ivan and Nadir through the forest. Ivan and Nadir didn't mention anything more about Anders being the Prophecy. He was actually beginning to think it might have just been a bad dream. It had been a week since they left the Rollo Island warriors to visit the elves. They walked along a lightly used path that wound through the dense forest and across the occasional meadow. Anders wished he could explore the area further, but knew they had to catch up with the warriors.

As they marched through the forest, Anders tried to keep his mind away from the sadness he felt about leaving Zahara behind. He found himself recalling a story his uncle used to read to him and his cousins before bed. Anders remembered it as one of his favorite stories and spoke of an elven hero with bronze skin and dark curly hair. For the first time, it dawned on him that he hadn't seen anyone like the hero described in the story. So he asked the Elf Prince, "Nadir, can I ask you something?"

"Yes you may," the Elf Prince said in a soothing voice.

"One of my favorite stories I remember from my childhood was about an elven hero with bronze skin and dark curly hair. When we were in Cedarbridge I didn't see anyone who matched that description. Are there only fair-skinned elves in the capital?"

Nadir nodded slowly, "I know of which tale you are referring to. Yes the elves you saw at the High Council in Cedarbridge are all of fair skin tone and silver hair, but this is not how all elves appear. Just as you humans have your differing ethnicities, so do we elves. Your time in the capital city was cut short so you did not explore much. If you had, you'd have seen that the city is filled with diversity and many differing elven cultures."

"I guess that gives me another reason to return," Anders said finding his mind returning to Zahara once more. After several minutes of silence, Anders asked the Elf Prince, "What's it like in Eastland? Have you ever been there?"

Nadir smiled and nodded, "I have been, several times. The mountains of Eastland are the oldest in our world. The first inhabitants of the mountains are what we call mountain trolls today. They once thrived in Nagano as one of the first species to inhabit Kartania. Their villages were scattered across the fruitful valleys of Nagano."

"I didn't know trolls were such an ancient species," Anders said. "They lived with the dragons?" he asked.

"You could say that," Nadir said. "It wasn't a very healthy relationship, however. Dragons were the main reason the trolls were forced to move from their villages and up into the mountains," he continued, motioning toward the snowy peaks above them. "Trolls are not very fast creatures and they're very simple-minded. They primarily eat meat, but living on the valley floor for so many years, they adjusted, eating grains and greens, or pretty much anything they could find. When the first dragon eggs appeared and hatched, the dragons needed something to eat as well. Being carnivorous creatures, and growing to great sizes, dragons began to hunt trolls.

"Since trolls are simple-minded, it took them a while to adapt to the changes they were experiencing. Those who survived were the trolls that had enough sense to flee the valleys. Every troll that insisted on staying behind, lacking the understanding that they were easy prey for dragons, was eaten. At this point in history when dragons were new to our world and they had plenty of trolls to prey on, the population of dragons increased rapidly.

"For a while, trolls were able to roam the mountains freely without worry; but once all of the trolls in the valleys had been eaten, the dragons adapted by expanding their hunting grounds. Trolls that had become accustomed to the safety of the mountains were at greater risk of being eaten by dragons than those now hunted in the Eastland Mountains. Those that had enough wits about them to realize they were no longer safe, hid in caves and holes in the ground. Diving deeper into the darkness to flee the dangers above ground, trolls quickly discovered they were not the only ones who occupied these mountains." Nadir said and then suddenly stopped talking.

Standing together, Anders followed Nadir's gaze to see the Rollo Islanders' camp below. He was glad to see that the group was roughly the same size as it had been when they left.

"We'll continue this conversation another time," Nadir told Anders before they walked downslope to meet the warriors.

Upon their arrival, Red, Jorgen and several other leaders welcomed Ivan, Max and Anders, but gave Nadir a hateful stare. Ivan had to quickly calm them down when they saw there was an elf in their company.

"He is here to fight our common enemy," Ivan said to Red, who was drawing his sword in anger. "I have negotiated with their people; they are willing to keep the peace while we combat Merglan and his forces if you are."

Red let his hand drop off his sword and stepped back. He turned to the other leaders. Their quick discussion ended in Red storming off to his tent. Red's father, Jorgen, said to Ivan and Nadir, "We agree to keep the peace and work together to fight our enemy. You are welcome to join our efforts, elf. Please excuse my son; he does not yet understand the gravity of the situation."

"On a better note," Ivan said. "I have the location of Merglan's base. He has been building an army there. The orcs came from this location. Asmond, Nadir's father, had elf spies tracking his location. After the orcs attacked, the elves were able to get an exact location on where they began their campaign."

"This is good news," Red's father said. "Yesterday we caught up with the orc tribe. There were no survivors on their end."

"That will surely irritate Merglan," Nadir said with a brief smile.

"If he doesn't already know of this, he will soon. And with that knowledge, he will send more orcs out to meet us," Ivan said. "We must move south, across the Eastland Mountains. Merglan's fortress is at a place called Black Water Bay."

"I will notify the others," Jorgen said. "We will leave posthaste." He and the other leaders went off to tell the captains of their plan.

Nadir turned to Ivan, "We'll have to be on our toes; we've had reports of mountain trolls and goblins in the Eastland Mountains, not to mention Merglan's orc and kurr armies."

"Sounds like a dangerous path we'll be taking," Max said.

"It's the only way to get to Merglan before he assembles his army and sends them at us," Ivan said.

"We are going to need help from my people sooner than we anticipated," Nadir said.

Ivan nodded, "Send word to them at once. We need to

get a move-on if we are going to have a chance at this." Ivan reached into his pack and gave Nadir the mirror he'd used to communicate with the elves.

Over the next hour, Anders helped the warriors gear up for their departure through the Eastland Mountains. He was worried about the next part of their journey, but also determined to rescue his family. He just hoped Merglan hadn't killed them yet.

FIFTEEN

THROUGH THE MOUNTAIN PASS

Ivan and Nadir led the way, guiding the Rollo forces through the Eastland Mountains. Red and several other captains, including Anders and Max's friend Britt, were sent to get the ships that hadn't burned during the battle with the orcs at Glacial Melt Bay. Several of the warriors had kept the ships at least one day behind the rest of their forces while they pursued the orcs, with the idea that if the orcs had launched another attack, the ships would be safely hidden. The Islanders needed their vessels to carry them home after the campaign. Red was the first to volunteer for the mission to sail the ships around the mountains. Anders knew the reason Red was eager to volunteer for the ship retrieval mission stemmed from his frustration that his father had allowed an elf to join their ranks.

Wondering when the rest of the elves would be joining the march, Anders asked Nadir, "How long will we have to wait for the elf army to join our forces?"

Nadir chuckled at the question, "Elves are much faster than humans," he said. "We can travel great distances much more quickly than you humans can. Our speed is similar to your horses, and we can sustain ourselves at that pace for days without getting tired. If we need to keep pace with a dragon, however, we expend our energy more quickly."

Anders had his doubts about an entire army being able to move with such speed, but he hoped Nadir was right.

Before Red and the other captains left, Ivan showed them a roughly drawn map and where to anchor the ships on the other side of the mountain range. It went without saying that the ships would make better time than those on foot. It would take them several days to journey through the mountain range on foot; with as many people as they had, Red and those who sailed with him would have to wait for them, out of sight from Merglan's fortress.

Leaving Red, Britt and the other captains behind, Ivan and Nadir led the Rollo forces into the mountains. Anders found Nadir and said, "I've been trying to imagine what it would be like if dragons were still hunting trolls in the area."

NADIR TURNED to look at Anders and smirked, "Dragons will sometimes discover a mountain troll in these mountains and devour them on sight. They're a delicacy of sorts to a wild dragon of Nagano." He paused, trying to recall where he'd left off telling Anders about the history of Eastland.

Anders tapped the hilt of his sword, watching the wave of recollection wash over Nadir's face as he picked up where he'd left off, "Dwarves and goblins had been living underground for centuries by the time the trolls sought refuge in the Eastland Mountains. The dwarves of Eastland are notoriously unforgiving of those who attempt to invade their homes. Being masters of mining and precious ores, the dwarves had been protecting their underground cities from the goblins for almost as long as the dragons had hunted trolls."

"Goblins will do anything to get their hands on a precious ore like gold," Max chimed in. He'd been walking behind the two and listening in on their conversation.

"Yes, they will," Nadir said, looking over his shoulder at Max. "The constant battle between the dwarves and goblins didn't help the trolls' efforts to make a home of their own under the mountains. Between being hunted by the dragons and killed by goblins and dwarves, their species faced extinction. We know of several groups that still live in abandoned goblin villages within these mountains."

Amazed at how much the young elf knew about the world, Anders asked him, "How do you know all of this at such a young age?"

Nadir laughed and said, "I may be young to my people and look it to you, but I am almost one hundred years old. I have seen much in my years and read much in the great library in Cedarbridge, but I am not as experienced as many in my culture."

"You're a geezer!" Max exclaimed. "You're older than the oldest man I know, Solomon the wise."

Nadir smiled, "Looks can be deceiving."

"Are you filling these boys' heads with nonsense?" Ivan asked upon his return from scouting out a campsite for their large group.

"Just giving them a little oral history of the Eastland Mountains," Nadir said.

Ivan raised his eyebrows and nodded his head slightly,

"Trying to take their minds off prophecies of old and the fight to come?"

"Just passing the time, old friend," Nadir said.

Ivan coughed seeing the uncomfortable look on Anders' face, "There is a place several miles ahead where we should stop to camp. The sun is about to set and, at these altitudes, the temperature drops rapidly once it's gone."

Once the camp was established, Anders huddled around a warming fire with Max, Nadir and Ivan. It seemed that even though the Rollo people had declared their temporary peace with the elves, they didn't want to be friendly with the Elf Prince. He drew dirty looks from the warriors all day and every once in a while he was called 'elf-grime and other curses Anders didn't like to think about.

"How do you put up with all of the hate they have for you and your people?" Anders asked him as they stood close to the warmth of the flames.

Nadir looked up and sighed, "It's something that comes with experience. I can remember stories of the time when my father was a young man and the warriors first landed on our shores. Our people had always been friendly with the humans, so when I learned of how they betrayed our offering of peace, it made me want to hate all humans. And for a time, I did. I have seen more fights with the Rollo people than any one of them here today.

"I learned during my years of constant fighting with them that the fighting only fuels the fire between us. One attack on their people is followed by sorrow. Then they seek revenge and hurt our people. We grieve and are angered by this, so we retaliate. At a certain point, the reason for the fighting and hatred blinds you and you forget what started it all in the first place. All you know is that you hate them and you want them destroyed.

"One particular instance changed my opinion about hating these humans. It happened after defending one of our villages from an attack. We were tracking Islanders down. They had tried to shake us off their trail by hiding in a well-known goblin cave. It did not, however, fool us and we assumed that if they were able to hide in the cave, the goblins were not a threat. Upon entering the cave, we drew our focus on the men. Weapons at the ready, we stared each other down in the brief moments before engaging in combat. At that moment, like a spider catching its prey in a web, we were blindsided by a large group of goblins. I hadn't noticed until that instant that among the Rollo Islanders were both women and children. In that moment, I realized that they were families, just like ours. The fear on their faces of the overwhelming odds was staggering. During the fight, I watched as a young boy wildly defended an injured woman I could only assume was his mother. He was about to be overtaken by goblins when I stepped in and drove them back. As members of both of our groups fell in the fight, I made a decision that I would get the Islanders out to safety. I cleared a way out for them and they took it. Once out of the cave, they thanked me and ran back to their ships.

"So to answer your question, I deal with the hate because I know if I retaliate it will only make things worse. I must show by example that if we can work together, the benefits outweigh the grudge that has lasted between our people for centuries."

"I never thought about it like that," Anders said. "You see a future that not many are willing to see, at least in this camp."

"Unless that future is crushed like a bug by Merglan," Max said tossing another log onto the fire.

"Oh, come on," Anders said. "Don't be so negative."

"He's right," Nadir said. "We must first focus on the greater evil that is Merglan before our people can settle our disputes. That is the only reason why Jorgen has agreed to the temporary peace."

"While we are on that subject," Ivan said. "Tomorrow night we need to discuss battle strategy before we reach the other side of the mountains."

"Agreed," Nadir said. They remained silent the rest of the night and went to bed shortly after their exchange.

Anders didn't like not being able to sneak off and meet Zahara. He missed her. As he lay looking up at the stars shining brightly in the dark sky, he wondered if their paths would ever cross again.

The next day, Ivan led them along a narrow path. They tried to stick to the lowest points of the mountain passes and stay out of the deep snow that blanketed the mountaintops. The cold mountain air numbed Anders' cheeks as they hiked.

He was impressed at Ivan's and Nadir's ability to find the best passage through the scree fields scattered below the steep rock cliffs that skirted much of the mountain range. They walked along small streams fed by the melting snow, pooling into tiny lakes and ponds downstream. Anders tried to imagine how hard it would be to live here as the trolls from Nadir's story had. There was no good place to farm and very few animals inhabited the area. The valleys below were much richer in these resources. Anders felt some sympathy for the trolls that were forced from their lands. He appreciated how lucky he was to be human. Although, if he was in fact who Merglan, Ivan and the elves thought he was, perhaps he wasn't going to be lucky enough to lead the simple life he cherished from his youth.

That night at camp Ivan, Nadir, and the Rollo warrior leaders talked battle strategy. Once again, Anders and Max were not privy to the conversation, but afterward Ivan and Nadir filled them in around the campfire.

"Red and those with the ships will be waiting for us in a small cove at the base of the mountains. We will come out of the mountains here," Ivan pointed to one side of the mountains he had drawn in the dirt next to the fire. "It's close to where the boats will land, but there is some flat ground between the foothills and the shoreline."

Nadir joined in, "My people will meet us here," pointing to a spot next to their planned exit from the East-land Mountains. "They will be prepared for battle and join our ranks."

"We will hold our position in the foothills while a small party goes to collect Red and the others waiting at the ships," Ivan continued. "Once we have retrieved them safely, our collective armies will march to Merglan's fortress. To stay unnoticed, we will wait to cross the valley under the cover of darkness. If by then he does not know our position, it won't take long once we are out of the mountains for him to sense our presence. It is imperative that we make it across the valley before he sends his forces to meet us."

"And if we don't?" Anders asked.

Ivan took a deep breath and said, "If we can't catch Merglan by surprise, then it is likely that the orc and kurr army he has will greatly outnumber ours and we will be sitting ducks."

For a moment nobody spoke, realizing the seriousness of the situation.

"We must trust that our information is accurate and that he hasn't been paying attention to the happenings of the world around him," Nadir said.

"So our plan hinges on the hope that this evil guy has his head stuck in the sand and doesn't notice a large army of elves and men marching on his gates? And if he is paying attention, he'll destroy us all and we will have come all of this way for nothing?" Max said with a tinge of sarcasm.

"Yes," Ivan said straightly.

"That's mad!" Max exclaimed. "I was in this when I thought it was just a raiding party that captured Anders' family. I'm not even sure that my brother was captured. I don't want to be slaughtered over some lunatic who believes Anders is a powerful sorcerer."

"No one is forcing you to do this," Ivan said.

"Hey," Anders interjected. "Max is here because of me, let me talk to him about it." Anders pulled Max aside and said, "Look, you and I have grown to become close friends, and I appreciate all that you've done for me. You've stuck by my side through the toughest moments of my life. I get it if you don't want to do this, though. This fight was mine from the beginning and apparently from long before we met. You don't owe me anything. Don't throw your life away for my cause. If you want to leave now and search for your brother elsewhere, I won't blame you."

Max looked down at the ground and said, "This is crazy. I grew up hearing all about the battles during The War of the Magicians. I never thought I would be caught in the middle of one."

"My world changed for the worse that day we met, but through our journey I have been proud to have you as a friend and a person I could always rely on when the going got tough. Thank you for everything you've done for me," Anders said putting out his hand as an offering.

Max sighed as he looked around, grabbed Anders hand, pulling him in for a hug and said, "Ah, hell. Who am I kidding? Thargon definitely has Bo. If he didn't, Bo would've been waiting for me in Brookside. I've been involved this long. What are a couple more days?"

Anders pulled away laughing, "You're a good brother and a better friend, Max."

The two returned to the fire and Max reassured Ivan and Nadir he was going to stick it out. After discussing where they would be placed and who their commanding officers would be, the four of them went to bed.

The next day required strenuous hiking over mountain passes, across plateaus and along steep slopes. Anders spent the day talking again with Nadir, whose wealth of knowledge he found fascinating. Nadir distracted Anders by telling him all about the dwarves and their culture. Anders learned Mount Orena was home to the largest colony of dwarves, and had been since the dwarves first came to the Eastland Mountains. Their ancient city, Hardstone, was built near the mine where they extracted the many riches of the earth that made their people so well known in Kartania.

"It sounds like a wonderful place," Anders said when Nadir had finished describing the great halls of Hardstone.

"I'm sure it is," Nadir said.

"You've never been there?" Anders asked surprised. He assumed Nadir had been there after providing such a detailed description of the dwarf kingdom.

"No," he said. "I've never received an invitation to go, which you'd think I would have by now. My father put me in charge of trade negotiations with the dwarves several years ago. I suspect it's because our peoples are mostly at peace with each other and they don't want to foul anything up. For the most part we stay out of each other's politics and as a result our relationship remains healthy. Every once in a while some argument occurs between our political houses and the trading stops. But in the end, we've always come to some kind of agreement to make the commerce work."

"Well, I've never met a dwarf either," Anders said.

"And you wouldn't unless you lived near these mountains and traded with them," Nadir said. "They keep to themselves under that mountain and rarely do they come out. Like I said before, they'll defend their homes fiercely. That's how they've managed to survive in the same place for so long. Well, that and they have a very wealthy mine."

For the rest of the day, Anders tried to keep his mind off the rapidly approaching battle. It was hard, however, because he knew they had only one more day of travel through the mountains before they would be looking down the valley at Merglan's fortress.

Upon establishing their camp that night, the only thing anyone could talk about was the battle they would be fighting the next evening. Anders hoped he would see his two cousins again soon. It seemed like years since he'd last been in their company.

He reflected on how dramatically his life had changed and wondered if he would be able to go home after it was all over. An idea popped into his head that once he and Thomas and Kirsten were reunited, he could take them back to the elf city where they could live with Zahara. It was a fantasy, most likely impossible. He'd never heard of a human living with the elves, other than when they were training for war, as they had with Ivan.

They woke at dawn and spent their last day hiking through the Eastland Mountains. Anders kept his thoughts to himself; it seemed no one wanted to talk. Everyone focused on the battle. They stopped in the early afternoon. Ivan and Nadir went ahead to scout. The army took this time to eat and rest one last time before the march on the fortress. The two were gone for several hours before returning to the group. It was late in the afternoon and the sun was beginning to hang low in the sky.

"Red and the other captains are in position. All we need to do is send a group of men to get them to join our ranks," Ivan said to Nadir and Jorgen. Anders and Max stood nearby, listening to their conversation.

"There is a problem," Nadir said. "I couldn't find the elves who were supposed to be here by now. I've tried to contact my father with the mirror, but it's not working."

"They have forsaken us," Red's father said. "I should have known your people would never help us."

Irritated by this, Nadir said, "My people understand the threat that Merglan poses to them as well as to you. They would not abandon us. Something else has happened to them. There's no other explanation."

"Bah," the leader of the Rollo people said, throwing up his hands and uttering a sling of Rolloan curses under his breath.

"I believe him," Ivan said. "The elves would not let a petty dispute between your people risk the destruction Merglan could bring to their kingdom."

"What do we do?" Jorgen asked.

"We stick to the plan," Ivan said confidently. "We must trust that the elves will be there to assist us when the time comes."

Jorgen made some grumbling noises and agreed he would continue with their plan. "I'm not counting on them," he said as he walked back to inform the others. Ivan turned to Nadir and told him to continue searching for the elves, while he assembled a team to retrieve Red and the other captains.

"With or without them, we will march down the foothills and out across the valley at nightfall," Ivan said to Nadir before he left. Nadir nodded his head and took off at a run to search for the absent elves.

SIXTEEN

CRYSTALS IN THE DARKNESS

Meanwhile, life as a prisoner in Merglan's fortress posed daily challenges. Each evening Thomas ached from the hard day's work in the mines. His crew and others dug deep into the ground in search of metals that could be forged into weapons and armor for the master's army. While digging deeper into the terraced slopes of the pit, Thomas discovered brightly hued crystals embedded in the rock. The first time he'd seen the brilliant blue hue emanating from the scored rock it scared him. The darkened wall of the pitted hillside suddenly began to glow. With each swing of his pickax, the rock chipped away and the blue light grew stronger until it consumed the darkness surrounding him. Each time he uncovered one of these crystals, one of the heavily armed guards would quickly confiscate it, stuffing it away into a locked crate.

One day Thomas found himself working alongside a tradesman from Southland who'd been captured during the attack at the Grandwood Games when they broke through rock together, exposing one of the brightly shining crystals.

The tradesman from Southland had seen many shiny trinkets in his thirty years living in Kartania and told Thomas he'd never seen any stone that could match the beauty of this crystal. The man pried it from the wall and hastily stuffed it into his pocket. Thomas tried to warn him against it, but one of the guards had seen the glow from farther down the shaft. The Southland tradesman attempted to act as if nothing were amiss, but it didn't take the guard long to discover the blue light shining through his pocket. Instead of handing over the crystal and hoping for a lenient whipping as punishment for his crime, the prisoner struggled to keep the crystal. Before Thomas could help him out, the guard had drawn his long knife and stabbed the tradesman in the gut. The guard took the crystal and left the prisoner to bleed out slowly on the mine's cold floor. There was nothing Thomas could do to save him. After witnessing this, Thomas quickly abandoned any notions he had of keeping any crystals he discovered following that day.

Kirsten and Maija continued to clean the rooms of Merglan's highest in command. They were forced to scrub every inch of the stone floors in the chamber rooms, often until their knees were bruised and bloody and their hands raw from the strong soap and water. The head maid, Chantal, had placed guards at the stairwell leading out from the chamber rooms. If they noticed the girls weren't down on their hands and knees scrubbing, one of the guards would pin them down while the other guard whipped them with a bullwhip. Maija struggled less than Kirsten, and her lashings weren't as severe as her cellmate's. Stubborn and strong-willed, Kirsten would struggle to free herself from the guards, but the muscular men overpowered her with each whipping. Soon Kirsten realized it hurt less to have bloodied knees and sprained wrists from scrubbing the floors than to have half-inch-deep lashings across her back, cutting through the fabric of her thinly woven wool prisoner garb.

Despite the guard's watchful eyes, Maija and Kirsten discreetly searched the belongings of all whose rooms they cleaned, but never found anything of interest. Kirsten hoped desperately to find something that would help them escape. Having no luck in the chambers, Kirsten couldn't help but think of Merglan's door just down the hall. She was convinced Merglan had locked something away upstairs in his chambers that could be the key to their escape. The urge to sneak into Merglan's room became overwhelming, but she never allowed herself to fall victim to her curiosity. Kirsten didn't want to find out what the guards would do to her if they found her sneaking about in Merglan's chambers.

They'd whip me to death with that awful bullwhip, she thought. *If only those guards would leave for an hour.*

While Kirsten schemed with Maija on how to break into Merglan's chambers unseen, Thomas discovered more crystals in the mine. As each day passed, the torturous way in which the prisoners were being treated drove many individuals to attempt an escape; yet each one met the same end. Thomas watched several people try to scale the cliff walls. If they reached the top without falling, an invisible force launched them off, sending them high into the air before falling to their deaths.

Kirsten and Maija saw others who attempted to run through the open gates if the opportunity presented itself. These would-be escapees were either killed on sight by the guard's blades or, if they made it past the guards, immediately transported back to where they began their escape attempt.

Most evenings when Maija, Kirsten and Thomas returned to the courtyard, they'd be escorted directly into their cells by several armed guards assigned to their cell-block. On occasion, however, they'd return to the courtyard and find the guards hadn't yet arrived. Whenever this happened, they were glad to find a moment's reprieve from the harshness of prison life. With a watchful eye out for Merglan's guards, they would share whatever had happened since the last time they'd been able to talk. Thomas told them about finding the crystals and having them immediately confiscated each time. After mentioning the crystals, Maija recalled seeing guards carrying heavy crates into Merglan's chambers.

"I thought they were just crates of stone. It seems like each delivery is always followed by muffled knocking sounds, like they're tapping on rocks, or whatever they are, to build something," Maija said.

"I haven't noticed any of that. I wonder what he's doing with them?" Kirsten asked.

"Whatever it is, it must be something important," Thomas said. "The guards are quick to take the crystals from anyone who discovers them."

"Maybe it has something to do with the magic he's woven into this place." Kirsten suggested. "Maija and I have been searching through all of the belongings in the rooms we clean. Nothing so far has revealed itself to be helpful for an escape plan, but maybe Maija is right and these crystals are the clue we've been looking for?"

"Let's say they do have something to do with the magic of this fortress; Merglan would make sure they were heavily guarded, wouldn't he? If he won't let any of us prisoners leave, how heavily protected do you think he'd have something like these precious crystals?" Thomas asked.

"If we're going to escape, we'll need to risk finding that out. I say it's worth the risk," Kirsten said boldly.

Maija nodded, "I think you're right. We should find out where they're taking the crystals and see for ourselves if they have some kind of magical powers keeping us trapped inside these walls. Doing something is better than doing nothing."

"If you insist on snooping around, be careful," Thomas said. "I think something big is about to happen."

"What do you mean?" Kirsten asked.

"I mean like a battle or something. I overheard some guards talking about orcs and kurr gathering by the hundreds outside the walls. We're mining so much metal for their weapons. On top of that, I've noticed enough frantic activity that I'd say they're going to war," Thomas said with his eyebrows raised.

"I hope it's the two that Merglan and Thargon were talking about in secret that have come to fight them and get us out of here," Kirsten said.

"You two try to find out how they're using the crystals and I'll try to get some more information about the army of monsters gathering outside the gates," Thomas said, delegating duties to support their plan.

They agreed and went to their cells for the evening before the guards arrived, sure to give them a lengthy lashing if they caught them consorting.

After a guard locked their cell door and the sound of his footsteps faded into the distance, Maija whispered, "Kirsten."

"Yeah," she whispered back.

"I heard Merglan talking about us today."

"Really? When?"

"It was when we were about to eat lunch. He told Thargon to have the guards keep an eye on us. He said he noticed something strange about us, that he can't read our thoughts the same way he can everyone else's."

"That's weird."

"Yeah, I think that might be why he always stops and looks at us when he leaves his chambers. I'm worried he might be onto us about our plans for escape," Maija said with a concerned twinge in her voice.

"You just said he couldn't read our minds, so how could he know what we're plotting," Kirsten said, trying to comfort her.

"I guess you're right. We might want to be more careful about talking in front of any guards. Also, it might be hard to sneak into Merglan's chambers if we're being watched," she said.

"Then we'll just need to be more careful. I hope the guards become too distracted with their preparations for battle to pay more attention to us," Kirsten said. "We'll have to wait and see what happens, I guess. Goodnight," she rolled onto her side and closed her eyes.

"Goodnight," Maija replied.

Kirsten could hardly sleep thinking about the crystals and the army of orcs and kurr. The next morning when the guards came by slamming sticks on their cell bars to wake them, Kirsten was already up equipped with a plan for the day. She would clean the rooms until just after lunch when Merglan usually left his chambers for several hours. Then she and Maija would make sure no guards were around and sneak into his chambers to look for the crystals.

The morning spent cleaning went as it usually did. Kirsten noticed a guard at the end of the hall watching them as they worked. They scrubbed the floors and carried out the dirty laundry and waste left on the floor by the filthy occupants. Maija and Kirsten stopped cleaning and ate lunch early, hoping to be in the hallway to see Merglan leave his chambers. After a quick bite and a talking to from Chantal about how to properly make the beds, the two went back to work. By mid-afternoon they were running out of things to keep them busy when Merglan left his chambers. He walked down the hallway as he usually did, pausing to stare at them as they scrubbed tirelessly at the same section of spotless stone floor before he continued on down the length of the hall.

"It's so creepy when he does that," Maija said to Kirsten, irritated by his leering look.

"Yeah, he definitely doesn't like not knowing what everyone in his fortress is thinking," Kirsten said. "Is he gone?"

"The door at the far end of the hallway just closed," Maija said tilting her head to listen.

"What about the guards?" she asked.

Maija leaned a little harder toward the entrance to the hallway, "They followed Merglan." The upswing of the last syllable she spoke told Kirsten she was surprised the guards also left.

"It's crazy that you can hear things so well," Kirsten said.

"I know, its weird. It's something that just started happening recently," Maija said. They looked into the hallway, checking both directions.

"All clear," Kirsten said.

"And Chantal left before we went for lunch. She hasn't come back yet," Maija added.

"Perfect," Kirsten said while stepping hesitantly into the hallway. Maija followed and they ran up to the door that led to Merglan's chambers. As Kirsten pushed, the door squeaked on its hinges and swung open. They slowly climbed up the staircase, making sure to be quiet in case others were in Merglan's chambers. At the top of the staircase a second doorway led into a room. Kirsten turned to Maija and put a finger over her lips to let her know to be extra careful as they approached the top of the staircase.

Kirsten watched closely as she neared the top stone step and could see more of the room beyond the doorway. She didn't see anyone as they inched closer. The room was large with extremely high ceilings. She could see tables, chairs, and a desk through the doorway. Checking in both directions, she gave Maija a thumbs-up and motioned to follow her into the room. Enormous bookshelves lined the walls, rising high into the air. Both of them stood in the doorway in awe.

"Wow. It's beautiful," Kirsten said, taking in the magnificence of the chambers.

"Remember, we need to find the crystals before he comes back," Maija said, nudging Kirsten to keep her on track.

The two began searching the room. Not entirely sure what they were looking for, they rifled through the desk, searched throughout the shelves, and even looked under the rugs. They searched everywhere but didn't find anything that resembled a crystal.

Finally Maija called to Kirsten, "Come over here! Check this out."

Maija pulled aside a banner hanging as a decoration on the wall. Behind the banner several lines deeply engraved into the wall resembled a doorway.

"Is that a door?" Kirsten asked.

"I think so," Maija said. "But there's no handle or knob," she said as she searched the area where a handle would normally be installed on a door.

"Look at this," Kirsten said pointing to the ground. On the floor next to the wall was a strange marking, a spiral carved into the stone floor.

"Maybe it's the doorknob?" Maija said.

Kirsten bent down and felt it. She pushed on it. Feeling it release, the spring-loaded spiral carving extended up from the stone floor. She turned it to the right. It twisted and the hidden door in the wall cracked open.

"Wow!" Maija said, amazed at the secret doorway's complexity. Maija pushed the door open. It led into a long narrow passageway. It grew dark in the narrow hallway as the light from the chamber room grew more faint. In the distance at what appeared to be the other end of the passageway, they could see a glow. As they approached, the glowing light seemed to shine a brighter blue. The passageway led to another large room with high ceilings. The only light in the room was a glowing hue of light blue that radiated from the end of the narrow hallway.

"Maija look!" Kirsten said. She pointed across the room to the origin of the blue light. There, neatly stacked into a giant slab rising twice the height of her family farmhouse and running nearly the length of her barn back in Grand-wood were brightly glowing crystals, emanating the unusual light.

Maija tugged on Kirsten's shirtsleeve. She looked at her with a furrowed brow, "What is it?"

Maija's eyes widened as she pointed at the ground in front of them. Kirsten's eyes, at last adjusted to the dim blue light, could now see clearly what she had failed to see before. On the ground in front of them lay an enormous dragon spread in a heap, comfortably-sleeping on the floor. She watched as its dark scales rose and fell with each breath. Kirsten almost shouted in fear, but put her hand over her own mouth to avoid making any noise. She returned Maija's wide-eyed look. Just as they exchanged their fearful gaze the dragon stirred. It's enormous black-scaled body shifted as it rolled onto its side and let out a drowsy growl. Kirsten and Maija didn't wait to see if the dragon's eyes opened. They darted down the narrow passageway and back into the master's chamber. Kirsten closed the hidden door behind them and pushed the spiral nob on the floor back into its locked position. Both of them breathed heavily as they looked at each other.

"A dragon," Kirsten said, shocked. "He has a dragon in there." She pointed to the wall where the banner now covered the secret door.

"Yeah, an enormous one too," Maija gasped. "But hey, at least we know where the crystals are," she said sarcastically.

"Come on, let's get out of here before we get caught," Kirsten said as she rushed across the room toward the door. Before they reached the stairway, though, they heard the door at the bottom of the stairs close. They also heard Chantal calling for them.

"Crap!" Kirsten mouthed. "What do we do know?" she whispered.

Looking around the room, Maija said, "Hold on, I got this." She went over to the desk and grabbed some dirty dishes stacked on the corner and handed some to Kirsten. Then she led them down the stairs and out into the hallway where Chantal stood, obviously looking for them.

When they opened the door leading out of Merglan's chambers, Chantal immediately chastised them, "What in the world were you two doing in there? You're not allowed to be in there, only I and..."

Maija cut her off, "The master asked us before he left if

we would be so kind as to return his dirty lunch dishes to the kitchen." Chantal looked at her with hands on her hips angrily tapping her foot. Maija continued, "We told him that we were explicitly told never to enter his chamber room. He said to forget what we were told and follow his orders. He wanted the place tidy and clean when he returned."

Chantal scoffed and said, "Well that's ridiculous, the master has never complained about his dishes remaining in his room for too long. I clean them up before dinner every day."

Maija handed her the dirty dishes and said, "I was just obeying his direct orders." Kirsten loaded more on top of those Maija had handed her.

"Anyway," Chantal continued. "You're needed to help prepare for tonight's dinner. The master will be entertaining special guests and there is much to do beforehand."

Maija and Kirsten rushed off to the dining hall, leaving Chantal with an armful of dirty dishes.

"That was brilliant," Kirsten said as soon as they were out of earshot.

"Thanks," Maija said, blushing. "I saw those dishes when we entered the room and thought that they'd serve as a good excuse if we got caught leaving."

"It worked beautifully," Kirsten said happily.

They reached the dining hall and began helping the others set up tables and chairs.

"Is there any special reason why the master is having guests tonight?" Kirsten asked one of the kitchen servants.

"I heard something about a battle. It seems the master is hosting a strategic planning meeting with some of his commanders tonight," the servant told her. Kirsten thanked him and kept the news to herself.

She briefly entertained going back to Merglan's chambers while he was busy at the dinner, but Chantal had told Thargon to place two guards at Merglan's chamber room door, which made a second visit impossible.

That night after they had cleaned up the mess the orc, kurr, and men made during the feast, Kirsten and Maija stayed up talking with Thomas about the events of the day. After making sure no guards were spying on them, they told Thomas about finding the crystals in the secret room with the sleeping dragon. They followed up with details about the meeting Merglan had with members of the orc, kurr and human armies at his command.

"I heard about a fight with the Rollo Islanders," he said. "The orcs attacked a group of Rollo Island warriors, taking them by surprise in their sleep, but the warriors fought them off."

"I hope they kill every last orc and kurr in Merglan's army," Kirsten said angrily.

"Me, too," he agreed. "And the crystals, you said they were behind a secret door or something, guarded by a dragon?" he asked.

"Yeah, so they're definitely important," Kirsten said.

"They must be used for magic," Maija said. "It's the only explanation that makes any sense to me."

"So, how do we get to them if they're guarded by a dragon?" Thomas asked. "I didn't even know dragons still existed. Father told us the last dragon left this world after it destroyed the castle at Highborn Bay."

"But Merglan's got one. We saw it," Kirsten said. They perked their heads up as they heard guards coming through the hallway to the courtyard.

"We'll talk more tomorrow," Thomas said and quickly ran to his cell. Kirsten and Maija did the same.

Once the guards were gone, Kirsten said to Maija, "There has to be a way to get the crystals. If they are, in fact, the key to the magic here, then maybe we could use them to escape."

Maija said, "All we have to do is get past that dragon and we are home free."

When Kirsten awoke to the banging on the cell door, she still hadn't come up with an idea on how to get past the dragon guarding the crystals. She spent all morning thinking about it. Every possible scenario she dreamed up ended with either the dragon eating them or Merglan killing them for attempting to steal the crystals. They were cleaning the rooms near Merglan's chambers when Maija stopped mopping the floor and leaned over with her ear. Seeing her do this, Kirsten came to her side.

"What is it?" Kirsten asked.

Maija said, "Merglan is arguing with Thargon." She walked to the edge of the room and leaned her head out the doorway into the hall to get a better angle. "Merglan says he's leaving," Maija said, looking back at Kirsten. "Oh, get back to work; Thargon's coming." They continued to mop and scrub the floors and watched as Thargon left in a rage.

"Did you hear where Merglan was going?" Kirsten asked.

"No, just that he was leaving at once," Maija said.

They kept cleaning the rooms long after they were spotless, but Merglan never left his chambers.

"Shouldn't he be gone by now?" Kirsten asked. "I thought he said he was leaving right away."

"Yeah," Maija agreed. "He should've left by now."

"Should we check to see if he did?" Kirsten asked. "Maybe he's got more than one secret passageway out of his room?"

"Okay, let's do it," Maija said. "But be careful; we can't get caught."

The two silently snuck up the stairs. They examined the room at the top of the staircase, but Merglan wasn't there.

"He's gone," Maija said

"Now is our chance to get the crystals," Kirsten responded.

"I just hope that dragon is gone," Maija added as they rushed over to the secret doorway.

Once open, they nearly ran down the narrow passageway once again, careful not to make too much noise in case the dragon was still in the secret room. Something about the trip down the hallway seemed different; somehow darker than before.

Maybe the door is closed, Kirsten thought, noticing the absence of the blue glow.

They felt along the cold stone walls with their hands, making sure they didn't pass the doorway and stumble into the dragon's keep. When they reached the doorway, the glow was gone, as were the dragon and the crystals.

Kirsten looked around the darkened room confused, "Where did they go?"

"Do you think Merglan took them with him when he left?"

Kirsten shrugged in response and together they left the secret room and followed the dark hallway back to the master's chambers. Once back in the main chamber room, they searched for any other secret doors Merglan could have used, but they didn't find any.

Giving up on their hopes of finding the crystals, the two realized they would have to wait until Merglan returned for them to try again. Now that Merglan was gone, the slaves and prisoners didn't have any preparations to accomplish in the dining hall for his evening feast, so they were sent along with the other chambermaids to work the remainder of the day in the mine.

Like the miners, they took up picks and followed orders. Kirsten and Maija were sent to work a section of terraces on the other end of the mine away from all of the other maids. Arriving at their assigned terraces, they were surprised to see Thomas working there too.

"What are you two doing here?" he asked when he saw them.

"Merglan has left the fortress. We didn't have any work to do in the castle, so we were sent down here to work," Kirsten said.

"Back to work you three," a guard shouted and cracked a whip at them. They did as he ordered, fearing a whipping.

Talking as they worked under the cover of the noise of picks striking rock, Kirsten told Thomas about going back into the secret room to get the crystals.

"They were both gone," she said.

"Do you think he took them with him when he left?" Thomas asked.

"That makes the most sense to me," Kirsten said. "Either that or he found out we were in there and moved them to a new hiding place."

"But if he knew we'd been in there," Maija said, "we wouldn't have been allowed to work; we would've been tortured or killed or something, right?"

Nodding, Kirsten said, "Then he must have taken them when he disappeared today."

"But how? Those crystals filled many crates and weighed more than he could carry."

"Quiet down," the guard yelled and cracked his whip again. Kirsten glanced over her shoulder at him and noticed something familiar about the guard, but she couldn't put her finger on it.

"You know how I told you there was something big happening?" Thomas whispered with his back to the guard so the guard couldn't tell that he was talking.

"Yeah," Kirsten said.

"Well, I think it's going to happen very soon," Thomas said. "All of the guards have been acting weird. Many left the fortress gates earlier dressed in helmets, chestplates, arm guards, and iron-linked long-shirts. I've also seen wagon loads of swords, spears and shields being hauled out of here all day."

"Do you think the Rollo warriors have made it to the fortress?" Kirsten asked, hopeful.

"Could be," Thomas said. "Whatever it is, it has the whole place spooked."

The three continued to work the remainder of the day and into the evening. They stopped when Thomas turned around to see the guard was gone. They walked to the edge of the terrace and gazed out from the pit and across the open courtyard. The whole fortress was strangely quiet.

"Where is everyone?" Thomas asked.

"You tell me," Kirsten said. "I usually only see the inside of the walls. I don't know how many people there are working out here with you all day."

"There's usually a lot more activity than this," he said. "I mean the guards, we're usually overseen by many more."

"Maybe they're off preparing for the battle that's got everyone spooked," Kirsten suggested.

"We could stop working now and go back to the courtyard," Thomas said.

"Or we could go look around Merglan's chambers for

any crystals that might have been left behind or hidden in a new spot," Maija added.

"No way. The guard left all this food behind," Kirsten said walking over to the spot where the guard had been stationed. "There's even a pile of firewood here. Let's stay here until someone makes us leave. I hate the cold floor of that cell."

"Okay," Thomas said. "We've got a nice view of the place from this terrace anyway."

The three of them sat by the fire they'd made and talked late into the night, feasting on the jerked meat, cheese and day-old bread the guard had left behind.

"I guess the rules around here are relaxed once the boss is gone," Kirsten said as she enjoyed a thick slice of jerky.

"I could get used to this," Maija said, warming her hands against fire.

Suddenly she perked her head up in the way she always did when she could hear something interesting happening in the distance.

"What is it?" Kirsten said, recognizing the look.

"I can hear fighting," she said, standing up.

"What?" Thomas said, confused and trying to hear what she was talking about.

"Maija has incredibly good hearing, almost like a super power," Kirsten said.

"Oh," Thomas said, confusion written across his face.

"There's a battle going on beyond the walls," she said.

"I knew it," Thomas said. "Who are they fighting?"

"I can't tell. It's far off in the distance, but there's definitely a battle going on out there," she said confidently.

"Well, I guess all we can do is wait," Thomas said.

"And hope that whoever it is wins and frees us from the evil that lives here," Kirsten said.

The three stayed up all night wondering and waiting for something to happen. It wasn't until the sun rose that they saw the first sign that the battle was nearing an end. Kirsten worried things weren't going well, because guards had returned to the courtyard, forcing prisoners back to work. She heard the voice of a guard returning, shouting orders to those who'd stayed among the terraced slopes of the pit while the battle raged through the night. She'd been eyeing the bullwhip left among the guard's abandoned items and quickly grabbed it, readying herself for his return. As he came into view, Kirsten recalled why the guard looked so familiar to her; he'd been the one she almost struck on their first day in the fortress. Letting the whip uncoil at her side, Kirsten wasn't going to let him boss her around. She didn't care if the battle had been lost; she was going to fight back and now was her chance.

Maija pointed to the sky and gasped. A silhouette of a dragon flew over the fortress walls, and their hearts sank.

Merglan has returned, Kirsten thought.

SEVENTEEN

BATTLE AT THE FORTRESS

Ivan led a small group consisting of two other warrior scouts to retrieve Red and Britt's party who were waiting with the ships. Ivan instructed them to stay out of sight, keeping within the low wrinkles in the hillside. Before they left, Ivan made sure the Rollo leaders knew where to organize their ranks.

"Form your lines just over this hill," Ivan pointed ahead of the mass of men and women, who stood clad in their leather-plated armor awaiting orders and armed to the teeth with freshly sharpened swords, axes, daggers and spears. "A fan of rocks juts up out of the foothills. That is the closest and best concealed place to prepare for the march across the valley."

Jorgen nodded, understanding where he was to bring his people while they waited for Ivan's return. "Come back safely, with my son," he said to Ivan when he had finished delegating responsibilities to his troops.

"I will, you have my word," Ivan responded seriously. Ivan turned to Anders and gave him a nod before leaving with the two scouts.

Anders and Max fell in with the Rollo forces as they began to move over the hill and down to the hiding spot. As they crested the hill, Anders laid eyes on the vast expanse of the Eastland Territories for the first time. The setting sun at their backs created a rainbow of colors across the landscape before them. Yellows, oranges, pinks, purples, and blues mixed in a changing blanket of light that darkened as it shrank, fading into night. His eyes remained transfixed on the towering fortress in the distance.

That's Merglan's stronghold, Anders noted to himself.

The fortress was built seaside along a band of cliffs that extended down to the murky bay below. Smoke billowed from the chimneys scattered throughout the fortress. He could hear the faint sounds of shouts and metal tools banging against rock. Anders wondered what Merglan was doing at this moment. He hoped that whatever it was would be enough of a distraction that he wouldn't notice the army of men, women and, hopefully, elves hidden along the mountainside just across the valley.

"That's some view," Max said, waking Anders from his momentary trance. "Do you think the elves are really going to show up and help us?" he asked Anders.

"I really hope that all elves are of the same mind as Nadir," Anders said. "I honestly don't know what to expect, but it sounds like we're going to need their help."

"The orc attack was overwhelming for us at first. I think an army of orcs and kurr will be even tougher to handle," Max said.

"If this doesn't work and if the elves decide to pull one over on the Rollo warriors, I'm afraid this fight will be over quickly, and not with a good ending," Anders said.

They walked down the face of the mountain. The cliffs blocked their view of the valley as they descended into their designated hiding place. The mass of thickly leather-bound warriors carrying shields, spears, axes and swords gathered into their respective groups. The lead captains were spread out evenly among the ranks. All other captains and their crews formed lines directed by each leader. It took them several minutes before the ranks were sorted out.

Anders and Max joined in with the group previously captained by Britt. Max and Anders had fought with them once before and trusted that crew more than the others. Anders knew he could count on each one of them to watch his back during any fight. They stood near the center of the forces, next to Red's father. Huddled together in the twilight, they anxiously awaited the return of Ivan with Red, Britt and the others.

"Something must be holding up the elves," Anders said to Max in a low whisper so others around him wouldn't hear. "I'm confident they wouldn't betray their word with Ivan. The elf king seems to hold him in a high regard."

"I just hope they make it in time to help us," Max said worriedly.

Darkness surrounded them as they waited behind the cliffs at the base of the mountains. They stood in silence; orders to avoid making excessive noise were given prior to assembling in their formations. Anders heard rustling and whispers from the men and women around him. Ivan had returned with the captains and the two scouts. They pushed their way through the crowd to join in with their respective crews. Anders and Max welcomed Britt with full arm handshakes and beaming smiles.

"Glad to see you both are here to fight alongside us," Britt said proudly.

"Wouldn't miss it for the world," Max said, giving Anders a glance.

The rest of the crew was glad to see Britt back in command. Anders looked over and saw Red standing near him. He gave Anders a glaring look, a certain harshness in his eyes. Anders returned the glare, no less harsh. Ever since the competition at Grandwood, Anders didn't particularly like the brute, but he respected his loyalty to his people and his fighting ability.

When the mass of warriors began to move, Ivan pushed his way through the crowd to Anders.

"Shouldn't you be at the head of the army with Red's father?" Anders asked. He expected Ivan would be leading that march alongside the leaders of the army.

"He knows what to do," Ivan responded. "This is not his first battle and, with any luck, it won't be his last. Besides, I was the one who brought you on this journey. It seems fitting that I should be by your side at the end." Ivan gave him a half-cocked smile and started marching with Anders and the others right behind him.

The cool night breeze swirled around them as they emerged from behind the cliffs. Anders was more nervous than he'd ever been in his life. He didn't know if he'd survive the night. Especially with the absence of the elves, he wasn't sure if any of them would. Still, his focus remained on his two cousins who'd been abducted by Thargon. He would stop at nothing to get them back and away from Merglan's grasp. The normal weight of his leather armor felt lighter than it ever had. Britt's crew had given him and Max the leather body protection; they had some to spare after suffering the losses at the Glacial Melt Bays.

The valley was now blanketed in darkness. The moon had set and clouds covered the stars. Their army marched in silence out onto the grassy fields that sprawled between the mountain's edge and the dimly lit fortress in the distance.

They hadn't traveled more than a mile from the foothills before those in command halted the army. Anders heard gasps from those around him. He turned to Ivan who he saw was looking toward the cove where their ships remained hidden. He cursed as Anders first saw what everyone else was looking at. Bright yellow and orange flames licked the air above the ships' location.

"We've been made," Ivan said loud enough for Red and the other captains around him to hear.

"Somehow they knew we were here. Now we have no escape," Red said.

Anders heard Jorgen shout, "Prepare for battle!"

Anders drew his sword along with everyone else. Those along the army's edges locked their shields together in front of their torsos. Those next in line locked their shields atop the first row, forming a six-foot-tall shield wall around the Rollo forces. Anders looked through the gaps in the shield wall to see what was happening in the dark space beyond. Not seeing anything advancing at them he looked behind him. Several rows of archers stood at the ready, arrows nocked. Behind them more warriors created a wall of shields at the army's rear. He still couldn't see anything coming toward them.

"Hold the wall and continue marching!" Red's father commanded. Making as little noise as possible, they continued forward into the darkness, ready for an attack from any direction. The command for the army to halt came once more. Anders' heart beat so hard he thought it was going to come right out of his chest. Next came a rushing noise through the air, like wind blowing rapidly through the trees.

All of the commanders shouted in unison, "Shields

up!" which cued everyone who was holding a shield to place it up over their heads. A blockade of wooden shields clashed together over their heads, nearly immediately followed by the sound of arrows thudding against them. Those who didn't raise their shields soon enough suffered the consequences; the arrows pierced many of them. Some arrows made it through the gaps near Anders and Max, lodging firmly in the ground alongside their feet. Max looked at Anders wide-eyed and Anders back at him.

Now hundreds of footsteps rumbled the ground in the distance. Anders tried to see where they were coming from, but the night remained too black and he couldn't see a thing.

"Archers!" Anders heard Jorgen command. Well trained, the army re-formed the shield wall once the arrows had stopped raining down on them. The Rollo archers behind Anders stood drawn and at the ready.

"Aim," the command came loud and clear. The archers pointed the arrows up over the heads of their army. Anders waited eagerly for the command to fire. The thundering of footsteps grew louder. At last Anders could see where they were coming from. Orcs and kurr together, blades drawn, ran in an ugly mess toward them. The kurr stood taller than the orcs and resembled Thargon. Anders gulped hard as he heard the command to fire. In unison, the twanging of bowstrings followed. Arrows whizzed across the night sky toward their enemies. He watched as the first row of charging orcs and kurr dropped, riddled with arrows.

"Spears," Red shouted. Those up in the front at the shield wall lowered their spears through the small gaps.

"Brace yourselves!" Ivan and Red shouted together as the wave of orcs and kurr came rushing at them head on.

The clash of flesh and steel on the wooden shields was deafening. Those at the front shouted as bodies came flying into them. Several warriors in the front lines were knocked over as the large kurr charged into them. Wherever the line broke, the warriors next in line quickly filled the gap, trapping whoever broke through into their ranks. Anders watched Red hack the head off a kurr who broke through, killing five of the men behind the wall.

On their captain's command, the shield barriers would open slightly so a host of slashing and stabbing could be delivered at the orcs and kurr pushing against the shield wall. Ivan would command them to open the wall and let in several at a time. He would quickly dispatch them with his skilled swordsmanship. Others saw him doing this and began to follow suit.

Britt shouted at the members in her crew to open the wall and let some through. Anders and Max raised their swords. Five orcs came tumbling through the wall, which quickly closed behind them. Looking startled as they fell into the midst of their enemies, the orcs hesitated for a second. Both Anders and Max saw this and struck out at them. They quickly stabbed two of the orcs. Britt took care of another. The two remaining fought back. Anders blocked the wild swings of the orc. Ivan came down on him hard with his blade. Max and Britt together slew the fifth.

This strategy carried on for what seemed like nearly an hour. They pushed forward stepping over the dead bodies from both sides. Anders thought the battle was going well for them when he heard a thunderous voice calling the enemy to back away from the shield wall.

The warriors held their ground as the enemy stepped back almost in unison from the shield wall, leaving several yards of open space between them. Anders noticed Thargon, who rode his giant hound, the fairnheir. He waited for Ivan, Red or Jorgen to command them to charge, but none came. Instead they held their position.

Thargon ordered the orcs and kurr to surround them. It wasn't until the enemy's front lines backed off and began to circle them, that Anders saw the full scale of their opposition's army. A sea of orc and kurr heads extended back into the darkness, their torches glowing as far as he could see. Anders felt sick at the overwhelming odds. There was no way they would be able to defeat such a force. Even if they had been able to keep up their shield wall strategy, pulling them in a handful at a time, there were just too many.

Red's father barked orders for the archers to fire at will. They did as they were commanded and were able to knock down some of the enemy that surrounded them, but more just replaced them. Anders watched as the arrows shot toward Thargon. Any arrow that came close shattered to pieces and deflected away from him.

He has powerful magic, Anders thought. *If only the elves were here; they could improve the odds greatly.* He looked out to the darkened mountains behind them, but couldn't see any elves.

Ivan turned to Red and shouted, "If we are to have any chance, we must break the wall and charge them head on. Cut the head off the snake and they will break. If we remain like sitting ducks any longer, they will squeeze us in on top of one another until we trample each other to death."

Red looked around and saw his father give him a nod of approval; then he shouted so all could hear, "Shields down!" Those who made up the wall separated back into marching formation. "Draw your swords!" They drew their swords in unison. "CHARGE!" Red shouted, sounding half crazed.

Anders looked at Max and said, "Good luck," then screamed and rushed forward.

He didn't care for his own safety; he just knew that if he fought as hard as he could, perhaps they would make it out of this alive. He rushed alongside Ivan, Red, Max and Britt. They crashed into the awaiting arms of their enemy. Anders blocked blows and struck out at every orc and kurr to appear before him. He focused only on his blade and where it was going. Ivan stayed close to him and together they fought into the thick army ahead of them. Using the limited magic he could muster, Ivan was able to kill more of the orc and kurr than the other warriors. For now, it was working. Red, Max and Britt got pushed together and retaliated as best they could. Over the heads of orcs and kurr, Anders could see Thargon commanding his forces.

Anders slew an orc, yelling at the top of his lungs as he did so. He became so enraged when he saw Thargon that he began to push farther into the mass of orcs and kurr ahead of everyone else.

Ivan saw Anders making a push for Thargon and shouted to anyone who could hear him, "With me!"

Red and Jorgen were quick on Ivan's heels and rushed toward Thargon. They sliced their way through the group of orcs and kurr that separated them and caught up to Anders. Being held up by a particularly difficult group of kurr, Ivan called to Thargon who was now no more than twenty yards away.

"Thargon!" he bellowed, making his voice heard over the clash of battle. This got Thargon's attention and he turned to look at Ivan and the others who dispatched the remaining kurr they were fighting.

"Ivan," Thargon replied, spitting on the ground at the sight of him. "I should have known you would be here." He led his hound toward them and bound through his forces, not caring if they got out from under his fairnheir. The giant hound he rode toppled over orcs and kurr as he charged at Ivan.

Ivan muttered something under his breath as Thargon drew near. As the phrase left his lips, Ivan quickly pulled a dagger from his belt and threw it at Thargon. The blade flew straight as an arrow, glancing off Thargon's invisible barrier, and striking his hound squarely in the head, and digging the blade hilt-deep into the fairnheir's skull.

Thargon leapt off the beast as it crashed to the ground and landed at a dead sprint, seemingly unfazed by the death of his hound. He barreled into Ivan, tackling him to the ground. Having no time to react, Ivan was sent flying across the ground wrapped tightly in Thargon's grasp. Anders ran to them and brought his sword down as hard as he could on Thargon's body. Just before digging into Thargon's back, the blade glanced off to the side striking the ground with great force. Anders was frustrated; how could he deliver a deathly blow if every time he tried to attack, Thargon's magic succeeded in protecting him?

Thargon felt the attack and while keeping an arm firmly gripped on Ivan, dealt Anders a hard backhand blow that crashed into his ribs and sent him falling backward. Thargon rose to his feet, towering above Ivan, who lay unconscious. He turned to Anders and sniffed the air.

"You!" Thargon said in a dark and powerful voice. "It's you. I can smell it." He rushed at Anders, his axe held high above his head.

Just as he brought it down, Jorgen rammed into the giant kurr, knocking him to the ground. Anders clambered to his feet to see Thargon take Jorgen by the head and snap his neck violently. Red's father, the respected leader of the Rollo people, fell lifeless to the ground. Anders heard Red's cries from behind him. He'd gotten separated from them and was fighting a large group of orcs on his own.

Anders gripped his sword tightly as he faced the beastly Thargon head on. "You killed my uncle," Anders said through his gritted teeth.

"I greatly enjoyed killing that puny, pathetic, shrimp of a human," Thargon said coldly. An orc charged from behind Anders, attempting to kill him while his back was turned. Thargon stuck out his arm and swept it to the side, sending the orc flying in the other direction. Then he shouted to all those around them and pointed at Anders, "No one kills this one. He is mine." Thargon bent down and picked up the axe he'd dropped when Jorgen tackled him.

Anders took the opportunity to charge the large kurr. Thargon blocked Anders' sword and kicked him hard in the chest sending him flying backward again.

"My master wants me to keep you alive and bring you to him," he said as he approached Anders. "I don't see why he thinks you're so special. You are pathetic and weak, just like your uncle. After I kill you I'll tell my master you were slain by an orc and you were not the warrior he claims you to be." With that Thargon raised his axe and swung it at Anders. Anders met the falling axe with his blade, knocking it to the side. The deflection saved him from being hacked in two, but the blow was delivered with so much force it shattered Anders' sword in half.

Thargon raised his axe again. Anders reached for his

dagger and threw it quickly and accurately at Thargon as he rolled away from the kurr's attack. Just as he expected, however, the dagger was blocked by Thargon's barrier and Anders was left with just his knife. Drawing it from the holster at the small of his back, Anders stood alone clutching the knife tightly in his hand. Thargon laughed and attacked Anders. He was able to dodge a few of Thargon's swings, but the kurr swept his leg under Anders' knocking him flat on his back. Anders watched helplessly as the axe came barreling down on him. He thought surely this was the end.

Suddenly, the axe stopped just before it split Anders' chest in two. He looked at it frozen in mid-air, and then looked at the expression on Thargon's face. Confused, he tried harder to force the axe down on Anders.

A deafening roar caught everyone's attention. Anders saw a large pair of wings sail right over the top of him as a dragon landed on the ground next to them. Zahara.

Anders watched her thrash her body, clearing out all the orcs and kurr surrounding them. She whipped her deadly tail and gnashed her teeth, killing many orcs and kurr with ease. Thargon's axe remained frozen near Anders' face. He could see Thargon was struggling to move the axe or let go of it, but some invisible force kept him locked in the same place. Anders rolled out from under the axe and rushed to Zahara's side. As he ran to her shouting her name in surprise and joy, she engulfed him with her expansive wings. Anders wrapped his arms around her neck feeling her warm embrace. Within the heavy cloak of Zahara's wings, Anders found himself separated from the chaos around them. He was encapsulated within the safety of her grasp. As Zahara again lowered her wings, Anders could see the horde of the enemy army attempting to attack them and he became fearful once again. To his surprise, however, they were unable to strike. He and Zahara seemed to be held in a protective bubble where no harm could befall them.

Anders let go of Zahara's neck and tried to pull away but something drew him back, forcing him to remain near the dragon. Without thinking he instinctively leaned his head toward hers. Placing his forehead against the large flat surface of Zahara's brow he felt a calming sensation wash over him. Somehow, he knew they belonged with one another.

Anders closed his eyes and felt a surge of energy pass between them. An electric flow of energy more powerful than any of the other times he'd been with Zahara; it was unlike anything he'd ever felt in his life. For a moment the surge of energy scared him, but once it took hold of him, he put forth no resistance giving himself fully to the force consuming his body and mind. The exchange of energy flooded into him like a tidal wave and he felt Zahara's spirit binding with his. Syncing their bond, their consciousness melded together as the raw energy of the magical force that bound all living things together coursed through their bodies. In that moment, Anders' bond with Zahara heightened every sense to a new threshold. Their separate heartbeats syncing as one, every breath warm with the dragon's fire; Anders knew his life was forever changed. Zahara's gift was his to cherish for a lifetime.

With a blinding white flash, their foreheads pulled apart from each other and a shock wave rippled out from between them knocking over everyone around them.

"Did you just," Anders asked her as he peered into her eyes. She nodded in response and he knew what had happened. Zahara had chosen him to be her bond, her other half, and by doing so gifted him with magic.

The shock wave broke the curse that had caused Thargon to be held motionless and Anders saw him charge at them out of the corner of his eye. Anders turned and called upon his new powers. A trembling energy within him began to boil upward, flowing through his body. He held out his arm, releasing the building energy inside him at the charging kurr. He watched as a jet of energy exploded out from his arm and sent Thargon spinning across the battle-field in the opposite direction.

Anders stepped forward and picked up the axe Thargon had wielded in attempt to kill him and ran, bounding after the kurr. Just as Thargon was rising to his feet, Anders pushed off his left foot, leaping through the air while raising the axe high above his head. As he descended, Anders brought the axe down hard on Thargon's body. This time the axe passed right through Thargon's invisible barrier, separating his head from the rest of his body. He watched as the lifeless kurr dropped to the ground in a limp pile.

Realizing that he'd managed to cut through Thargon's magical barrier, Anders could not believe it; Thargon was finally dead. He turned to see Zahara chasing a large group of orcs and kurr. The orc and kurr army fell into disarray after watching their leader fall in battle. Anders heard the rallying cries of the men and women near him as they began to fight harder, driving the enemy forces back. Anders returned to the spot where Ivan had fallen and was surprised to see him standing. Knowing that Ivan was back on his feet again, Anders rushed back to Zahara who was now waiting for him.

"How did you do that?" he exclaimed.

She smiled, *It just happened. I knew the moment you left that we were intended to be bonded.* Anders couldn't believe what had just happened. *Climb on,* she said, lowering her shoulder so he could scramble on top of her.

"Are you sure?" he asked. He never thought he'd have the opportunity to ride on the back of a dragon. He wasn't sure if there was a formality to it or some kind of sacred dragon ceremony he must complete before he could climb atop her scaled back.

Anders, trust me. You and I are one now, and hurry up before an orc tries to shoot you with one of their arrows.

Slightly surprised by her informal approach in dealing with the situation, Anders did as she told him.

Anders placed his left hand on Zahara's wing where it attached to her body and used his right hand to grip a hard scale on the leeward side of her back. He hoisted himself up onto her spine and positioned himself between her shoulder blades. He hooked his legs snuggly into the pits of her wings.

The moment he was situated, Zahara said, *Hold on tightly.*

Before Anders knew what had happened, she'd bent her knees and pushed up off the ground, flapping her powerful wings and climbing into the sky.

The force of taking off so suddenly pulled his upper body down hard and Anders would have fallen off, toppling forward had Zahara's thick neck not stopped him. With his face pressed firmly against her tough scales, Anders could just see around her neck the masses of orcs and kurr below. Anders placed his hands on Zahara's neck and pushed himself up, to a seated position. He'd ridden many horses and several ox, but nothing could have prepared him for this. Anders became aware that he could feel her wings beating against the early morning air as if he were working them. He looked to his shoulders to make sure his arms hadn't turned into wings like hers. A sigh of relief came to him as he saw the familiar bulk leading down to his hands. Yet he couldn't understand how he felt her body as if it were his. He could feel her tail swaying to balance herself in the air. Experiencing their bonded connection for the first time, it surpassed anything he'd ever thought possible.

Zahara, I can feel your body as if I were the one flying, Anders said as they flew over the battle.

It's our bond. You can now feel what I'm experiencing and thinking.

Whoa, that's amazing! Anders exclaimed.

We're connected in a way no other animals can experience; we are bonded.

Anders clung to Zahara as they soared through the air. The morning sun was just beginning to emerge in the east as they leveled out high over the valley. Anders could see the entirety of the battlefield now. Dismembered and mangled bodies lay thickly scattered along the grass, leaving a trail of blood and horror from the battle's starting point. The orc and kurr army had outnumbered their band of Rollo Island warriors and stragglers by three to one. Anders gawked at the size of the enemy's forces. He watched as the Rollo warriors advanced further into the enemy's ranks.

Zahara, the orcs are retreating! Anders exclaimed through their connected minds. *And look,* Anders pointed. *The Elves have arrived! Nadir found them!*

The mass of the elf army swept in from the northern reaches of the valley forcing the orc and kurr forces to retreat.

I came with the elves from Cedarbridge, Zahara told him. *When Nadir sent for the elf army, I knew I must to come to your side.*

Why did it take you all so long to get here? Nadir said the elves would meet us before we marched.

Merglan headed us off before we reached the mountains. He somehow knew we were coming and attacked us on his dragon, she said.

How did you escape him?

Two other dragons and their riders accompanied us. They knew I needed to reach you, so they distracted him while I escaped.

I can see the elves made it past him, but I don't see the dragons, Anders said.

They might have led him away from here in their attempts to distract him.

Why would Merglan let himself be led away so easily?

I'm not sure. All I know for sure is that the riders were with us when I escaped and now the elves have made it past him. I would bet they somehow convinced Merglan to follow them.

Anders noticed Zahara had begun to fly south, away from the battle and toward Merglan's fortress. *Shouldn't we go back and help them win the battle? Ivan, Red, Max and Britt might need our help.*

Now that the elves have arrived, we'll have no trouble winning the battle. There is something else we need to do, that I must do for you, she said while flying toward the fortress.

Anders tightened the grip of his legs around her as she surged faster. All he could do was trust that Zahara knew what she was doing.

Approaching the fortress, Anders could begin to see over the massive walls that loomed over the dark fortress. Somehow the tall towers climbing toward the sky seemed hollow and empty. He sensed an absence from the stone buildings and at the same time a familiar warmth that he hadn't experienced since he left Grandwood.

Zahara flew over the walls of the fortress and they could see groups of people huddled together.

The prisoners taken from Grandwood, Anders thought.

Your family is here, Zahara said. Through the heightened connection of their bond, she felt his hopes of finding his cousins alive. *I must repay you the favor you did for me, but first we need to rid this place of the evil people who've kept these innocent people enslaved here.*

Anders understood her exactly. They dove down together at the few armed guards who'd stayed behind to keep the prisoners in line. Zahara streamed into the fortress coming down on the prison guards with hell's fury on her wingtips. She loosed a deafening roar as she chased the fleeing guards. Protracting her large talons she skewered Merglan's men as she turned back toward the sky.

Anders hesitated for a moment, just trying to hold onto Zahara as she darted through the fortress. Realizing he too could be useful from her back, Anders called on the new magic running within him. Focusing on one guard at a time, Anders targeted them, snapping their necks and bringing them to a swift death. It didn't take long before the prisoners within the fortress joined in the fighting. The prisoners now outnumbered the guards. Seeing that they had help, the prisoners began a full-scale uprising within a matter of minutes.

Anders watched as unarmed men and women rushed armor-plated guards with swords in their hands. Their bravery was devoid of reason as they bombarded the armed men. Several men and women sacrificed themselves so others could overtake the guards.

Zahara landed lightly in the middle of the courtyard.

Climbing off, Anders began searching through those who rushed past him. He shouted his cousins' names but was met with the blank stares of people he didn't recognize. Panic began to set in. Had Kirsten and Thomas been killed on the journey to the fortress? At least a month had passed since he'd seen them and he had no way of knowing if they'd made it there alive.

Finally, he saw a familiar face, Bo. Max's younger brother waved him down. Anders forced his way past a host of prisoners rushing past him toward the fortress gates.

"Bo! You're okay!" Anders exclaimed. "Where are my cousins, Thomas and Kirsten?"

"As of yesterday they'd were assigned to mining duty," Bo pointed a grimy finger toward the pit that lay just beyond the courtyard.

"Are they there now?" he asked.

Bo shrugged, "Could be anywhere. Once everyone realized you weren't Merglan returning, all hell's broken loose. Anders, where's Max? Did he make it home to Brookside?"

Anders realized Bo had no knowledge of what had happened to his brother since the attack on Grandwood. "Yeah. He's with the Rollo warriors now. We marched on the fortress and, with the help of the elves, pushed Merglan's forces back."

Bo smiled from ear to ear, "I knew Max would come for me."

"Yes, he has. And now I must find my family." Anders nodded his thanks to Bo and called for Zahara.

He climbed onto Zahara's back once more and they swooped over to the far side of the pit. Anders strained his eyes as he scanned the terraced slopes. Each terrace had dark shafts that tunneled down, deep into the slope. Anders heart leapt when he spotted them.

Kirsten cracked a bullwhip as she chased down a guard. Anders grinned at the tenacity of his younger cousin. Thomas and Maija had just finished running off another guard, kicking him in the rear as he stumbled away. Anders steered Zahara and they flew in low over their heads. Kirsten cracked one more whip of the bullwhip on the guard's behind before seeing Anders on the back of a dragon. She halted her pursuit and dropped the whip.

Zahara banked around, coming to land lightly along the terraced slope. Anders could see the bulging eyes and dropped jaws of Maija and his cousins as he dismounted Zahara. He realized she would be a shock to them, but he was beginning to think they might be dreadfully intimidated by her presence. He held the wide grin on his face and after several moments, Anders saw the joy of their long-awaited reunion grow on their faces.

Kirsten shrieked with glee and led the charge as Thomas and Maija followed her in a run to greet him. Anders met them with open arms, beaming as he held them tightly in a group hug. Tears of joy streaming down all of their faces, even Zahara became emotional and Anders could sense her happiness toward them.

Wiping away the tears with the back of her grimy hand, Kirsten sniffled, "I knew you'd come for us, I knew it."

"We've missed you terribly," Maija's glossy brown eyes fluttered at seeing Anders again.

"I have so many questions, too many to comprehend right now," Thomas added with a nervous laugh, one of relief after so many tribulations.

Anders sniffled and gave them a broad smile. "I'll explain it all later." He wiped his nose with the sleeve of his leather cuff and attempted to straighten his face into a more serious expression, "Well, lets get you out of this place."

"Anders, wait. There's powerful magic imbued into the walls of this fortress. Even the gates are enchanted," Kirsten warned him.

Anders grinned, "Don't worry; Zahara and I can get you out of here."

"You'd better hurry. Merglan left a while ago and could return any minute," Kirsten said.

Nodding, Anders returned to Zahara's side and climbed onto her back. She leapt off the flat step and opened her wings to their full expanse. She soared effortlessly out over the people gathering in the courtyard, gliding toward the fortress' main gate.

Kirsten, Thomas and Maija stood still, jaws hanging open while gazing at the sight of someone they knew sitting atop a real dragon. After a moment of bewilderment, they began to make their way to the courtyard.

Once at the main gate, Anders and Zahara worked to break the spell that held Anders' cousins within the fortress walls. They drew on the force of energy that flowed within them and tried to focus it on breaking down the tall iron gates. Anders couldn't quite hold his grip on the amount of energy they were producing. Each time he attempted to channel it on the gate's hinges or lock, he'd become over-whelmed by the power surging through them. When he tried to lessen the force of magic he drew on, the spell Merglan placed on the gates remained too strong for them to break.

The *magic on these gates is too strong for us to break alone,* Anders said. *We need help if we're going to bring them down.*

We'd better hurry in case Merglan returns, Zahara agreed.

Before leaving again, Anders found Kirsten, Thomas and Maija amidst the crowd gathering near the gate.

"This magic is too powerful for us to undo alone. Zahara and I are going to get help from Ivan, he's an old rider who might be able to help us." Anders looked sorrowfully at them and continued, "I'm sorry. I wish we were stronger, but our powers are new and I'm not trained in how to use them properly. We'll be right back, okay?"

Thomas, Kirsten and Maija nodded understandingly.

"Hurry back," Kirsten called to him as he bid them farewell and saddled Zahara's neck.

"I will, I promise," he called back as Zahara took flight once more exiting over the fortress walls.

By the time Anders and Zahara returned to the battlefield, it was over. The elves and Rollo warriors had made sure the enemy's armies were no longer a threat by forcing their retreat. Anders could see the last of the orcs and kurr running away across the valley as they flew in for a landing. The host of the Rollo warriors cheered victoriously when Anders and Zahara returned to them.

"Ivan, Nadir," Anders said as he ran to them and hugged them tightly; happy to see they were alive. "We need your help. My cousins and many others are locked in the fortress. The magic binding the gates is too powerful for us on our own."

Ivan understood the haste required by the situation. Combining his dwindling magical abilities with their untrained energy, they might be able to break down the gates to free the trapped prisoners inside.

"Zahara, can you carry us both?" Anders asked out loud so Ivan could hear.

Of course I can. I'm not a weakling, she replied.

"Okay, I just wanted to make sure," Anders said. *I'm*

new to this and didn't know if you'd be offended by letting Ivan ride you as well, he said to her with his mind again.

I appreciate you asking, but in this time of urgency I don't need to toil on proper customs and all that nonsense.

Anders led as he and Ivan hoisted themselves onto Zahara and she returned to the sky. Within short order, Zahara was landing just outside the main gates to the fortress.

"You and Zahara try to focus your energy as best you can. Summon all you are able and I'll help you to control it," Ivan told them once in front of the gate.

Anders and Zahara drew on their powers and the well of magical energy within them bubbled to the surface before they let the full store of magic loose. Anders couldn't control it, it came from his mind in wild flashes, but suddenly, he could feel Ivan's presence. Like standing in the eye of a hurricane, Anders suddenly felt the calming sense of control he'd been lacking. Ivan allowed them the control they needed to focus on bringing down the gates. The three of them pried open the lock that held the two iron gates in the center. With a slow creak they began to open. The crack turned into a gap, and then a wide space. Then suddenly the spell holding them broke and the gates rocked open, slamming into the dark stone walls of the fortress.

By the time the gates fell, both human and elf armies had gathered outside the fortress. The newly freed prisoners rushed out as soon as the gates opened. Anders watched as Rolloan families began to reunite all around them.

Anders scanned the faces of the freed prisoners as they flooded out from the fortress. Anders' eye caught a familiar face and watched as Bo saw his older brother for the first time since being taken captive. His gangly, dark-haired friend ran to Bo and hugged him tightly. It gave Anders great satisfaction to witness the two brothers reunite after the long struggle to free those taken captive from Grandwoods shores.

Pulling himself away from his brother's grip and holding him at arm's length, Anders overheard Max say through tears of joy, "You smell like crap. Have you been locked in a prison cell for the last month or something?"

Anders burst out laughing at the insensitive joke he'd grown to expect from his dark-haired friend. At that moment, he felt an overwhelming sense of pride.

As he chuckled off Max's insensitive joke, Anders saw Kirsten and Thomas come running out through the gates with the crowd. He shouted their names and ran to meet them. With their second reunion, Anders composed himself. He laughed and hugged his cousins again.

"I can't believe this is happening," he said, as he looked them over.

"We've been waiting for this moment for so long, I thought it would never come," Thomas said.

Getting a second look at them, Anders became more aware of Kirsten and Thomas' ragged appearance. Their clothes were haggard and worn. Their skin bruised and scabbed from weeks of rough treatment.

Kirsten must have noticed Anders' stare at their wounds and asked, "How did you manage to find us?"

"If it weren't for Ivan's help, I wouldn't have had a chance of finding you," Anders motioned to Ivan who stood near Zahara's side.

"I'll need to thank him for helping you," Kirsten said.

"And Zahara," Anders added.

"That's your dragon?" Thomas asked.

Anders nodded and looked over to Zahara, "She's a lot more than just a dragon. She's family." He knew Thomas and Kirsten wouldn't understand what he meant by it, but soon he'd explain everything. Before he could, though, there was another person who he'd been longing to see and talk to. Anders had noticed that Maija was standing awkwardly behind them, unsure if she should interrupt their family moment. He excused himself from his cousins and jogged the short way to where she stood. Coming near, Anders wrapped his arms around her and she gladly held his embrace.

After a long moment of holding each other tightly, Maija said, "Well Anders, it would seem that I am, once again, in your debt."

He smiled, "That may be, but I think there is still one more thing I must repay you with."

"Really. And what might that be?" Maija asked playfully.

"This..." Anders leaned in close to Maija. Her full lips locked with his and for a moment, he forgot all about the war, the magic, and the hardships he'd endured to get there. It was just the two of them, kissing beneath the morning sun.

A combined group of cheers and whistles brought them back to reality. He turned to see Thomas, Kirsten, Max, Bo, and Ivan all shouting for them. Even Zahara was roaring loudly to join in the cheering. He felt his cheeks burn and saw Maija was blushing too. The two held each other close; one arm wrapped around one another as they joined in with the group of friends and family.

Anders watched as everyone around them hugged and smiled, happy to be reunited with one another. As he looked at the familiar faces surrounding him, he knew everyone in the world who he cared about was right in front of him, and he was happy. Though the threat of Merglan's return still loomed over their heads, Anders didn't allow it to bother him for the moment. He looked to see Ivan place a gentle hand on Zahara's neck and give a meaningful nod to Nadir, the elf prince. The look he gave Nadir told him that Anders and Zahara had fulfilled the prophecy Merglan had been attempting to prevent; at least for now.

CONTINUE READING
TO THE NEXT BOOK

Bond of a Dragon: Secrets of the Sapphire Soul

A dragon and her rider put to the test. Betrayal among allies. With Kartania's fate in the balance, who will take control?

Anders knows the war to stop Merglan from reclaiming his grip on the world is just beginning. With no certainty about where or when Merglan will attack next, Anders and his companions must take action to stay one step ahead of the cruel sorcerer and his evil dragon.

As he searches for ways to stop Merglan's domination of their world, Anders discovers more than he expected. With several nations of Kartania on the brink of collapse, he must make a difficult decision. Is the young rider ready to deal with the consequences he's facing? Can Anders overcome the odds and unravel the secrets of the sapphire soul?

Bond of a Dragon: Secrets of the Sapphire Soul is the second novel in an adventure fantasy series.

If you like gripping suspense, bold dragonriders, and page-turning action, then you'll love A J Walker's latest installment in the *Bond of a Dragon* series.

Discover *Secrets of the Sapphire Soul* by picking up a copy today!

GET YOUR FREE BOOK

NEWSLETTER SIGN UP

Sign up for my newsletter and you'll never miss another A J Walker book launch. You'll receive my prequel novellas, ebook promotions, monthly writing updates and more.

Building a relationship with my readers is the best part about being an independent author. I send out a bi-monthly newsletter with details on new releases, special offers, and other updates concerning my writing progress.

When you sign up for my newsletter, you'll get an exclusive book:

Dragon Wars: War of the Magicians
Free Download Link -
https://www.subscribepage.com/w9t1m7

REVIEW

CONSIDER POSTING YOUR REVIEW.

Leaving a book review is a very powerful tool when it comes to getting attention for my books. As an independently published author, I don't have the connections or financial muscle of a New York publisher. Getting my books to the front of the bookstore or in full-page ads in the newspaper is something I'm not able to take advantage of, not yet anyway.

But I do have the advantage of speaking directly to you, the reader. Spreading news about my books by leaving a review not only proves my story's worth to others who might enjoy it, but word-of-mouth and social prof can be more powerful than anything New York publishers can offer.

Honest reviews of my books help attract other readers. If you've enjoyed this book, I would be very grateful if you would spend just five minutes leaving a review — it can be as short as you like.

Thank you so much.
  Happy reading,
  A J Walker

ALSO BY AJ WALKER

In Rulers of Tarmigan Series (an epic fantasy)

Emperor's Fate

Upcoming in Series

Shepherds of Fire

Shattered Dragons

In the Bond of a Dragon Series (a young adult epic fantasy)

Zahara's Gift

Secrets of the Sapphire Soul

Fall of the Kings

Rise of the Dragonriders

Bond of a Dragon Prequel

Dragon Wars: The War of the Magicians

(Available through newsletter sign up.)

Bonnie Glock Mystery Series (an urban fantasy)

Into the Mixed

Finding Justice

Exiled and Forgotten

Dark Fae Rising

Soul Harvest

ABOUT THE AUTHOR

A J Walker grew up in Bozeman, Montana. In his youth, writing fiction and becoming an author was a distant dream, something a young dyslexic didn't think was achievable. A J was diagnosed with dyslexia at a young age. He struggled through most of his education with an elementary school reading comprehension level. When he was sixteen, A J found neurofeedback therapy. With the help of this new technology, he quickly learned how to read and write to the level of his high school peers. Before striving to become an author, A J's love for whitewater kayaking and the outdoors led him to study at the University of Montana. In his university years, A J worked as a wildland firefighter and graduated with a bachelor's degree in the Science of Forestry. Currently, A J lives along the Yellowstone River near Columbus, Montana, with his wife and their dogs.

A J Walker loves hearing from readers, so please feel free to contact him on social media or by sending an email to ajwalker@ajwalkerauthor.com.

Thank you for reading. :-)